Death of a Toy Soldier

Bridal Bouquet Shop Mysteries
(Writing as Beverly Allen)

Floral Depravity

For Whom the Bluebell Tolls

Bloom and Doom

Death of a Toy Soldier

A Vintage Toyshop Mystery

Barbara Early

CROOKED
LANE

NEW YORK

Copyright © 2016 by Barbara Early.

Published in the United States by Crooked Lane Books, an imprint of The Quick Brown Fox & Company LLC.

Crooked Lane Books and its logo are trademarks of The Quick Brown Fox & Company LLC.

Library of Congress Catalog-in-Publication data available upon request.

ISBN (hardcover): 978-1-62953-838-9
ISBN (ePub): 978-1-62953-839-6
ISBN (Kindle): 978-1-62953-840-2
ISBN (ePDF): 978-1-62953-841-9

Cover design by Louis Malcangi.
Cover illustration by Hiro Kimura.
Book design by Jennifer Canzone.

Printed in the United States.

www.crookedlanebooks.com

Crooked Lane Books
34 West 27th St., 10th Floor
New York, NY 10001

First Edition: October 2016

10 9 8 7 6 5 4 3 2 1

Dedicated to all those who reached adulthood
without forgetting how to play.

Chapter 1

Cathy slammed the receiver down, and the phone's eyes wiggled. Yes, our telephone has eyes. These things happen when you work in a vintage toyshop and your phone was custom painted—and mounted on wheels—to resemble an iconic pull toy.

I winced. "Please tell me that wasn't a customer."

"Not a customer, Liz." Cathy tucked a strand of her now mostly black hair behind her ear. A pink tendril still dangled between her eyes, so she went back for it. "Just another Julia Roberts wannabe thinking we're offering acting classes."

I shook my head. "Next time maybe just explain we're not a drama club."

The phone rang again and Cathy answered. "Thank you for calling Well Played." She smiled sweetly at me before adding, "We're not a drama club."

While she fielded the phone call, I made a solemn vow never to hire another relative, then inspected our most recent estate-sale acquisition: a *Bionic Woman* lunchbox, complete with thermos. A gentle, thorough cleaning had revealed only one minor nick in the finish, but otherwise, it could have perched on a store shelf back in the seventies. I found it a prominent place on our display wall and returned to the front of the shop by the time Cathy was hanging up—this time not so forcibly.

"I vote again for changing our name," she said. "What's wrong with Good Ol' Toys?" She gestured dramatically, allowing me a good view of her spiky, pink-and-black leopard-print fingernails. Cathy considers herself an artiste—yes, with an *e*—and claims people expect her to show it in her appearance.

When I didn't respond, she continued. "Toy Meets World? Toy Wonder?"

"If I had to pick, my favorite was Backstreet Toys. But you know Dad once he's decided something."

"You always take his side."

The bell over the door interrupted our argument. Not that this discussion was heated or that Cathy and I bickered often. I doubted my sister-in-law could focus on a single topic long enough. She wasn't flighty, exactly, just smart and so enthusiastic about a million things that her mind tended to wander.

Cathy swept back to the doll room, and I spun to face our newest customer. He deposited an old cardboard box on the floor and took his time stomping the snow and salt from his boots. He removed a pair of glasses that were fogging up and wiped the condensation from the lenses.

But I doubted this man was a customer. People who came in with boxes often wanted to sell or consign old toys. He lingered in the doorway way too long, appearing nervous. Or perhaps he was just being a little OCD about clearing the snow from his boots. His skin was pockmarked but tanned—odd in itself for Western New York in the winter—and he wore scrubs under a heavy parka. I hadn't laid eyes on him before, so he wasn't one of our local collectors. He finally hoisted his box and headed my way.

"May I help you?" I asked.

"Uh, I have an appointment with Hank McCall." The man shoved his glasses back onto his nose and began rubbernecking the shop.

There's a lot to tempt the eyes in a vintage toyshop. Colorful classic toys of every decade lined the shelves, the most expensive in glass cases. Toy cap guns were displayed in a glass cabinet we'd obtained from an old gun shop. If we left them out, the place would fill with young boys staging shootouts, twenty-four seven. Action figures, play sets, and miniature vehicles jammed several aisles. About a foot below the ceiling, all around the perimeter of the shop, ran Dad's prized toy train tracks. Not that we operated the trains much these days, since Othello, our black-and-white tuxedo cat, had commandeered the tracks as his personal catwalk and often snoozed in the tunnels.

"Cathy?" I didn't have to raise my voice. She was still hanging in the doorway to the doll room. "Could you tell Dad he has a guest in the shop?"

"Will do." Cathy headed to the back room and the roped-off stairway to the second-floor apartment where my father, Hank McCall, and I lived. At thirty-something, I took little pride in admitting that I lived with my father. In fairness to myself, I suppose I should add that I moved in mainly to cut costs until the business turned a regular profit.

While Cathy's footsteps echoed up the stairs, I turned back to the customer. "I'm Liz McCall." I didn't offer to shake hands, mainly because his were full. "My father should be here in a moment. He's the expert, but I'm fairly good at evaluating toys myself." And if I didn't know something, that's why they printed value guides. I reached for the box. "Shall we take a gander at what you brought?"

The man shrugged and shifted the box onto the counter, almost reluctantly. Why was I under the impression that he was terrified to be here?

"Are these items you're looking to sell?" I asked.

"For now, I just want to know what they're worth."

Toy collectors tend to obsess over toys from their own childhood. We call it the nostalgia factor. This man was probably in his forties, so his collection would likely hearken from the late seventies or early eighties. Early Ninja Turtles? Star Wars action figures, maybe? I was eager to get my hands on some more Masters of the Universe.

The cardboard box smelled musty and felt brittle, like it had been in storage for a long time. I held my breath to avoid inhaling the swirling dust as I lifted the flaps.

These were no Ninja Turtles. "Oh! These have some age." The box contained tin mechanical toys, the kind that you wind up, and they whir and move. "Antiques." I wasn't about to remove them from the box. I'd leave that to more expert hands. No harm in looking, though.

A tin elephant occupied one corner. I suppose it drew my attention first because of the bright colors. The red and gold paint on its elaborate blanket still shone bright, with only a few minor chips and dents. Based on the joints, I suspected it could pick up a coin in its mouth and swallow it.

Next to it, two tin boxers squared off, staged on one pitted platform. The condition seemed excellent, although the colors were more muted. The figures were mounted on wheels. I wasn't sure if you pulled the toy or if there might be a winding key underneath.

Next to them, an overweight tin mother pushed a child in a wheelbarrow. The child was missing a hand but otherwise seemed in good shape. A winding key jutted from the mother's white apron.

Suddenly it made me ill that these toys were jostling and bumping against each other in a cardboard box.

"They all, uh, work," the man said. "I can show you."

I quickly flipped the lid of the box shut, letting the dust fly. "These are liable to be fragile. I think you're right in asking my father to look at them. He has a lot of respect for antique toys." Respect? I think he worshiped them. Lionel trains. Toy guns. Even old dollhouses. Running the toyshop was his life-long dream. Too bad it had to wait for his retirement, and under difficult circumstances.

Cathy hurried down the stairs, making even more noise than she had going up. "Liz, I'm afraid your dad . . . *stepped out*," she said in a voice that sounded calm. Her wide eyes told me that was a lie. "His, uh, stuff is gone."

Instantly my heart began to race. "How much of his stuff?" I asked with a forced smile, mimicking Cathy's fake good humor.

"Quite a bit of it, actually. *You know.*"

I kept my smile, but only by gritting my teeth. "Stuff" served as our code word for the accoutrements of my dad's former profession.

Now, many retirees dabble in their former occupations. They become consultants. Advisors. But most of those aren't cops. And they certainly aren't chiefs of police who had sustained a near-fatal gunshot wound in the line of duty.

After that came retirement and fulfilling his lifelong dream of opening Well Played. Most of the time he appeared happy in his new line of work. But on a bad day—and I had a feeling this was a very bad day—he'd seem to forget all about his grand retirement party and hefty settlement and would gather his "stuff," including handcuffs and his legal firearm, and head back out to maintain law and order on the not-so-mean village streets. Last time, he arrested five people. Citizen's arrest, of course.

I forced a grin at the customer, realizing I still hadn't caught his name. "It seems my father is tied up at the moment." I only hoped he wasn't *locked* up. The new police chief didn't seem too fond of Dad's "little sprees," as he called them, and had threatened to nail him with an obstruction of justice charge. "It's probably going to take some research to find good numbers on these anyway. Could you leave them for a day or two?" I put my hand on the box. I didn't want these babies to go anywhere. If this man let us handle the sale of these toys, the commission could pay our burgeoning heating bills until February.

His mouth opened but nothing came out. For a moment, I feared he would whisk the box right away from us and take his chances on eBay. Instead, he said, "Sure. That'd be okay. I'll check back in a couple of days."

He'd made it halfway to the door when I called after him. "Do you have a card or contact information in case we need to reach you?"

"Uh . . ." He dug into his coat pocket and pulled out a business card, looked at it, and held it out to me. Then he walked back out into the cold.

As soon as he'd cleared the threshold, I kicked off my flats and shoved my feet into my boots, which I kept near a heating vent behind the counter. Cathy ran out of the back room with my blue wool pea coat. I slipped it on and whisked my gloves out of the pockets. "Mind the shop!" I said as I pushed open the door. I raised my collar against the chill and did a spin, taking in the 360-degree panoramic view of the village's idyllic Main Street. Banks of snow lined the brick thoroughfare and slush covered the sidewalks. Folks who'd braved the cold hurried to get where they were heading. Other times of the year, the walkways would be teeming with strolling visitors who came for various festivals in the spring and summer and later to see the leaves change, or maybe just to visit the historic and delightfully corny five-and-dime store that anchors the street of small shops and eateries. Still, the months prior to Christmas might be when the town put on its best show, with twinkling lights, red bows, and evergreen swags gracing almost every surface, as well as the old-time animatronics, rescued from failing department stores, doing their thing in various shop windows.

If I were a lucky person, Dad would be standing in front of one of the storefronts, watching the old mannequins carry out their jerky motions. I've never been that lucky.

Dad, where are you?

Chapter 2

I glanced at the clock in front of the five-and-dime. Just after noon. Maybe Dad wasn't off arresting people. Maybe he was hungry.

I made a slow pass by the cupcake shop—no sign of him, but the owner waved, so I waved back. Then I started the short hike toward Wallace's, Dad's favorite eatery. Although the sign designated the place as a tavern where customers could order their favorite beers and spirits, Jack Wallace clearly focused on food, evident by the vinegary tang that pervaded the air the moment I opened the door and walked in.

My eyes took a few seconds to adjust from the bright snow outside to the darker interior of the restaurant, but I didn't need twenty-twenty to see that Jack's place buzzed with locals and visiting shoppers, their bags sitting in the booths next to them. Servers wearing elf ears, reindeer antlers, or festive Santa hats whizzed by, carrying oversized pizzas on gleaming steel stands and wings overflowing their platters alongside celery and bleu cheese dressing. A busboy wiped off a nearby table to the cadence of "Winter Wonderland," which blared from the overhead speakers.

When the hostess rushed up with a menu, I waved her off. "Just looking for someone today. Thanks." Although, full disclosure, my stomach rumbled at the appetizing smells. If I found Dad in a back booth, safely nibbling on wings, I wasn't going to leave without my share.

Since the booths sported tall backs that obscured the identities of the patrons dining in them, I had to casually stroll past every single one, stealing a glance at the occupants while trying not to look like a jealous wife out to catch her husband lunching with another woman.

Finally, at the last booth before the restrooms, I spotted a pair of handcuffs dangling from the bench into the aisle.

"Aha!" I said, rounding the corner.

But the uniformed man hovering over a plate of chicken wings wasn't my father. The current chief of police, Chief Young, winced when he saw me.

I slid into the seat opposite him. "Houston, we have a problem."

"*We* have a problem?" The chief set down his knife and fork, then rubbed his fingers with a paper napkin. A knife and fork? Eating an order of wings with a knife and fork would take hours. "And don't call me Houston."

His eyes twinkled a bit, which only made me angry. He wasn't taking me seriously.

"You don't understand," I said. "I'm worried my dad might be—"

"Up to his old tricks?" Chief Young picked up a celery stick and aimed it straight for the bleu cheese. "I know right where your father is. He's down at the station filling out arrest forms."

"Tell me you didn't arrest him."

"Miss McCall . . ."

"Liz."

"Liz, don't worry. I didn't arrest him. His rank and file would run me out of town."

I settled into the plush booth opposite the chief. The youngest man to hold the office in years, he was just a little older than me, with dark hair and eyes that squinted just a little too suspiciously. And although he joked about not being named Houston or being from Houston, he spoke with a distinct twang. North Carolina, my dad had told me.

"Dad has a lot of friends here," I said. "More than thirty years on the job, and then injured in the line of duty . . ."

"Believe me, I don't need his résumé. He left some mighty big shoes to fill. I'm sure that's one reason my immediate predecessor didn't last long."

"That and the embezzling." Dad's replacement had stunned the village when he'd morphed from a decorated officer into a megalomaniac who treated the department funds as though they were his own. After he left in a cloud of scandal and an internal investigation that enveloped the whole department, warranted or not, the mayor had broadened his search for a new chief well outside the village borders, an unprecedented action.

I glanced down. His wings looked awfully good.

"Why don't you join me? I have more than enough. I can order you a Coke." He raised his hand to signal the waitress, then grimaced. "I mean *pop*." I could have sworn he shuddered. "Still getting used to the lingo. As for embezzling, this village has nothing to fear from me. The powers that be practically wrote 'Keep my hands out of the cookie jar' into my oath of office. I have to fill out three forms now to get a bullet. Not to mention a reporter from the local rag follows me almost everywhere. Sometimes I have to duck into the men's room to find some peace."

"So sorry for you, Chief. But about my father . . ."

"Since you and I are likely to encounter each other in a semiprofessional capacity again—at least until someone circles the definition of 'retirement' in your father's dictionary—why don't you call me Ken."

"Ken." I paused. Same as the doll. And yes, the man's brown hair was a little too perfect and his teeth were just a little too white. I'd never get the comparison out of my head.

Ken shuffled a wing onto his plate with his fork. "Your dad made a pretty good bust. Took in a shoplifter. Had she picked a different store to rob this morning, she might have gotten away with it."

The waitress approached the table, and I placed my order, asking for a takeout box.

Ken could barely sit still. There was more to this story.

"I'll bite. Where'd Dad catch her?"

"The chocolate store." Ken's eyes twinkled. "She had several bags of sponge candy stuffed in her . . . uh . . . brassiere." His ears colored slightly at the word. "And

would you believe three pounds of boxed assorted choco-
lates under her skirt?"

"How'd she manage that?" Did I really want to know?

"Similar method as used by a thief in Scandinavia a few
years back. That woman got away with a forty-two-inch television. Walked out of the store with it between her legs."

"Hardy people, those Scandinavians."

"But in this case, the stolen items were chocolate, which
added a new wrinkle to the situation. Your father simply
engaged the suspect in a friendly but lengthy conversation."
Ken's voice was filled with something akin to pride. He was
warming up to Dad.

"He's good at that," I said. "But how did . . . ?"

"It's amazing what ninety-eight point six degrees of body
heat will do to the properties of chocolate. Eventually, it
became quite clear what the thief was up to."

"Ouch." I couldn't help laughing at the picture. "They're
not going to want that merchandise back."

"Yep, your dad has hawk eyes and good instincts. I'm
almost glad I deputized him."

"You *deputized* my father?"

Ken frowned. "It's not like he has no experience. Why not
capitalize on it?"

I could feel my back stiffen. "He's supposed to be retired,
for one reason. It's dangerous. The man walks with a cane.
What would he do if someone put up a struggle?"

"Clobber him with the cane, would be my guess."

I folded my arms in front of me. "I can't believe you're
encouraging this behavior."

Ken let his silverware fall to his plate with a clatter. "Liz, I'm not encouraging anything. He's a grown man who can make his own decisions. As for deputizing him, I did it to protect the department. Since he's now official, more or less, it'll help today's charges stick."

"I suppose he'll have to testify and all that."

"We also have the evidence from the suspect's purse and pockets—and I think we're going to get some nice corroborating video footage when we go through the security cameras. He did good work today, Liz. You should be proud."

I felt my eyes tearing up, and not from the hot sauce, but I bit back a hasty reply. My anger wasn't directed at Ken—or at anyone, really. I closed my eyes, which was a mistake, because then the memories came flooding back.

I'd been living in New Jersey when I received word that my father had been shot in the line of duty. My brother, Parker, had tried to explain exactly what had happened. Dad was a hero and alive, I remember him saying. But the only thought my brain could process was that my father had been shot. I somehow managed to drive to the airport and hopped on the next plane from Newark to Buffalo. I was at his bedside in the hospital that night.

It was touch and go for too long. He'd lost a lot of blood. Various specialists argued about how best to treat him—if he regained consciousness. One neurologist scared me by mentioning the possibility that the extended time without oxygen could have led to some degree of brain impairment. Even if he escaped that, he'd need multiple reconstructive surgeries to correct his other injuries.

I was by Dad's side when his eyelids fluttered open. He looked up, silent and seemingly helpless, smaller than I'd ever recalled seeing him. Then he started pushing back the covers and tried to climb out of his hospital bed. It took both the nurse and me to hold him down until he got his bearings. I was terrified of what it might mean. But then he cupped a gentle hand on my cheek and said, "Sorry, Betsy. I guess you could say I was resisting a rest." With one pun, I knew he was going to be all right, that Dad was still in there. I didn't even remind him not to call me Betsy.

Ken slid his hand over mine. "I'll make sure he gets home okay."

I brushed away an unwelcome tear and looked up. "Thanks."

# # #

"Any word?" Parker and Cathy spoke almost in unison when I entered the shop, swinging my takeout bag.

Othello made his required four jumps down from his catwalk—the first onto the top shelf of board games, the next to the toy gun case, then to a shorter display table of Lincoln Logs, and finally to the black-and-white tiled floor. He rushed up, tail at attention, to sniff my bag.

"Liz . . ." Parker looked disappointed. "Stopping for lunch . . ."

"I found Dad before I got lunch," I said, setting my bag on the counter. Othello contented himself with circling my ankles. "The chief was unusually reasonable this time."

"You could have texted," Cathy said.

"Have you checked your phones?"

Parker guiltily fished his cell out of the pocket of his khakis. He wasn't much of a khaki person, but his pants and the burgundy polo with the insignia of the wildlife center where he worked were part of his uniform.

"No charges?" Cathy asked.

"Not against him. Apparently he collared an expert shoplifter and might end up getting a commendation from the Chamber of Commerce."

"And?" Parker pushed aside a pile of Scrabble games that Cathy had set out for the evening's board game tournament. He hoisted himself onto the table. "How do you account for the chief's change of heart?"

Othello deserted me for my brother. Parker stroked him behind the ears, and the cat responded with a loud purr.

"Not sure I'd exactly call it a change of heart," I said. "Seemed more like a strategic move to please the constituency. Friendlier than last time, at any rate. Told me to call him Ken."

By the spark that flashed across Cathy's face, I knew I'd made a mistake to mention this.

"Oh, *Ken*, is it?" she teased. "I thought so. He likes you, and if he has to put up with Dad's shenanigans to win the daughter . . ."

I rolled my eyes. "Don't go putting a down payment on the Malibu Dreamhouse just yet. Ken knows Dad has a lot of friends in this town. If he's going to establish a long career here, he can't make waves among the locals."

Cathy folded her arms. "He *so* likes you."

"He does not," I said automatically.

"Well, I sure hope he does." Parker pulled Othello from his lap and set him on the table. "It might come in handy having a friend leading the department. Besides, you know what you don't want to become, right?" He reached to a nearby shelf and picked up a deck of vintage Old Maid cards.

I snatched them from his hand and smacked him in the shoulder. I doubted he felt anything under his heavy coat, but he had the good graces to stagger backward and rub his arm as if he'd been mortally wounded.

"Get back to work, mister." I pushed him toward the door while Cathy giggled.

Chapter 3

An hour or so later, Dad walked in, leaning heavily on his cane and escorted by the new chief. Dad was always a big man, not only tall, but ample in all directions. Since retiring, his coat refused to zip over his stomach, and his wavy, salt-and-pepper hair, no longer cut to any regulation, touched his collar. Since Mom's no longer with us, I suppose it fell to me to remind him to get to the barbershop. She had never liked his hair long, but sometimes I let him slide a few weeks longer between haircuts. It covered the scars from where his head had scraped the pavement.

I ran to hug him. "You had me worried!" I rested my head against his shoulder and just hung on.

"Sorry, Lizzie," he murmured into my ear.

When I pulled back, I studied his face. His cheeks flushed and his eyes danced with renewed energy. In short, he didn't look the least bit sorry.

I went over to Ken and shook his hand. "Thanks for bringing him home."

Ken nodded. Then Cathy cleared her throat, and I realized that our hands were still clasped. I recoiled like he was wearing one of those novelty hand buzzers, the type that delivers a small electrical shock. Maybe not the kindest toy ever invented.

Dad must have seen it too. He redirected his scrutiny to the wall of lunchboxes, his shoulders shaking with quiet laughter.

Ken took this as his cue to leave, which it was. When he'd cleared the threshold, I turned to have a word with Dad, but he was already poring over the boxes the UPS man had delivered that afternoon.

"It's here!" He slit open the tape on one of the boxes with his keys. "I was worried we wouldn't see this baby until after Christmas." He pulled out a hunk of brightly colored plastic and headed to the supply closet.

"What is it?"

"A key part of our Christmas display."

I put my hands on my hips and glanced around the shop. Santa hats sat on almost every doll. Glittery crystal snowflakes dangled from the ceiling, and scratchy artificial snow dripped from the panes of our windows. Thanks to Othello, it could also be found in every corner of the shop. Lights blinked everywhere, and our speakers blared only the jolliest music.

"Where could you possibly put one more thing?"

"Ah, but that's the joy of it. He'll also function as our official greeter."

"'He'll'?" The rest of my questions were drowned out by the clatter of the electric pump we keep on hand to fill inflatables. Soon, a full-sized toy soldier rose from the wad of plastic.

"Exactly how much did it cost?" But despite my stress at the damage his purchase would inflict on our bottom line, I found it hard to stay angry when staring into the blank eyes and smiling face of a six-foot-tall toy soldier, replete with bright-red coat and gold epaulets.

"Don't worry. He'll pay for himself." Dad sealed the plug and set the cheery gentleman near the front door, where he'd be the first thing customers saw.

I walked a complete circle around the soldier.

"What are you looking for?" Dad said.

"His pockets. If he's going to pay for himself."

Before Dad could answer, the door swung open. A young couple walked in, and they *ooh*ed and *aah*ed over the soldier. There was another argument I had no chance of winning, no matter how many financial reports I shoved in front of Dad's face. Fine. He could have his soldier. But if he thought his missed appointment and his morning excursion would be ignored, he was wrong. I could choose my battles.

When the shop door rang again, Cathy leaned toward my ear. "I can handle customers for a little while, if you'd like to get Dad upstairs. In case there's anything you need to talk about."

"Chicken," I whispered, and while nobody was looking, she flapped imaginary wings twice.

I grabbed Dad's arm. "A word?"

He didn't answer but followed me upstairs with the same posture a small boy might have on the way to the principal's office.

When the door closed behind him, he leaned against it. "I suppose we're going to have that talk again."

I crossed my arms. "Only because it hasn't sunk into that hard head of yours."

"Well, I do like to be *ahead* of the game. Hey, did you hear about the guy who got hit in the head with a can of pop? He was lucky it was only a *soft* drink."

"If you think you can distract me with more of those silly puns . . ."

"Betsy, I only stepped out to get a haircut . . ."

I squinted at him. "Is that all?"

"Well, I considered maybe tinting a shade lighter. I figured it would be the *highlight* of my day. But then I decided I'd better *mullet* over."

I practiced my best glare. "I know you took your handcuffs. Your gun."

"Perfectly legal."

"Would you like to reconsider your 'I only went out for a haircut' defense? Why would you take your handcuffs?"

"Well, there is a new stylist who's been catching my eye, and my private life is my own."

If he'd meant to mollify my anger, his flippant response had the opposite effect. I marched over until I was in his face. "You promised me." I jabbed an accusing finger into his chest. "You stood right here and promised me."

"I know what I said, and I had every intention . . . Look, it's not like I pinky swore or anything."

"It's all a joke to you." I raked my hair with my hands and spun away from him. "I spent months. Months of my life taking care of you, dealing with your insurance company, helping with your therapy, getting your mobility back . . ."

He came up behind me and put his hands on my shoulders. "I appreciate all the sacrifices you made."

I faced him. "Apparently that life doesn't mean much to you, but it does to me." My voice had started to quaver, so I clenched my fists and stopped talking.

"It was only one little shoplifter. Not very dangerous." He tried to reach in for a hug.

I pushed him away. "It's like Oreos and My Little Ponies. You can't stop at one. And sneaking out? One day I'm going to get a call that something happened, and I won't even know you left the house."

He set his jaw. "A cop is what I've always been."

"A toyshop owner is what you are now."

"A *part* of what I am now."

"Apparently not a very important part. You do realize you missed an appointment today . . ."

"Was that today?" Now he did look contrite. "You may not believe this, but I never intended to go out. I'd seen that woman walk by any number of times, and I always suspected something was off. Today I noticed something odd about her gait." He smiled. "Let me tell you what we found. It's one for the books."

"I've heard the story." The adrenaline ride must have taken a lot out of me. Suddenly I felt exhausted. I collapsed into a kitchen chair and rested my arms on the table.

Dad came up behind me and started massaging my shoulders. "I guess I need to try harder. Please know that I do appreciate everything you've done, moving back home to help a foolish old man."

I patted his hand and then held it. "Not old." I stopped there. He could draw his own conclusions.

"What's this?" Dad headed toward the cardboard box of toys that Cathy must have moved upstairs.

"Toys that came in today." I rose to put the teakettle on. "Your missed appointment. The man who brought them hasn't decided if he wants to sell them. He'd like to know their value." I picked out my father's favorite herbal tea, a combination of orange and spices, while I went for an Earl Grey.

"Did he leave his name?"

"I have his card somewhere. Don't tell me you've forgotten his name." I fanned my face with the empty teabag wrappers. "I have it on the best authority that you have a *photographic* memory."

He paused and tilted his head, then a full smile erupted. "But what if it fails to *develop*? I'm not even sure he gave me his name. He just called and asked to meet over some confidential matter."

"This about toys or something else?" I glared at him.

Dad raised his hands in a show of innocence. "Hey, he called me and said he didn't want to go into any details over the phone." He gestured to the box. "Apparently it was about toys. But if these are stolen and he's looking to fence them, he's come to the wrong place."

"In which case you'll call the police?"

Dad let out a disappointed breath. "Pinky swear."

# # #

I went back to making the tea while Dad continued to make more photography puns, ending with a chorus of "Someday my prints will come."

By the time I turned around with our steaming mugs, he'd donned his gloves and unloaded a number of toys onto the table, gently lifting one and holding it up to the light. He whistled.

"Some good stuff?" I started to set his cup on the table.

"Why don't you keep the tea over there, Lizzie. I wouldn't want to risk damaging these toys."

I took a quick sip of my tea before setting both mugs down on the counter. Most likely they would still be there, full and cold, hours from now.

"What've we got?" I asked.

"German, I think. Prewar, mostly. These would go for a pretty price. Definitely need to keep the punks away from these."

"Punks" were what my father called the aficionados of steampunk. Nice people, from all my encounters. I'd tried to explain the genre, with its mash-up of Victorian society, science fiction, and anachronistic steam-based technology, to Dad once. The closest I got was "If Florence Nightingale and Inspector Gadget had a love child . . ." But Dad flipped when he discovered that they were disassembling old toys to salvage the gears for their costumes and jewelry. To hear him talk, they were right up there with skinheads and terrorists.

He gently lifted the toy boxers. "There's a dealer in Michigan who might know more. I don't recall his name. Is Miles here?"

I couldn't help but smile. Miles was the college student whom Dad had hired to build a website for the shop. The guy didn't talk much when he first came, and Dad volunteered little about how they'd met. The website turned out fabulous, however, and Miles then suggested he could place some of our inventory for sale online. The venture proved so successful that he now handles all our Internet sales and auctions and occasionally rolls up his sleeves and works in the shop during busy holiday periods.

Using my cell phone, I took a picture of the toy boxers from several different angles, including the winding mechanisms, and e-mailed them to Miles, asking if he knew anyone who could provide an estimate.

By the time I needed to head down to relieve Cathy, a stack of pricing guides was piled on the table. Dad's reading glasses were perched on his head as he examined the elephant bank with a gigantic Sherlock Holmes–style magnifying lens. I made him a sandwich, which I left sitting next to his cold tea, and sneaked downstairs. In a flash of either pure genius, or possibly postadolescent defiance, I stopped to change the alarm code on the back door. No way Dad was going to pull a Houdini tonight.

Cathy had set up four tables with eight Scrabble boards between them, and tiles and racks awaited our guests for the evening.

"Quiet this afternoon." Cathy slipped on her coat. "I wish I could stay to help tonight, but I've got a poetry slam over at the community center. I think the snow is going to keep a few people away, so I've got a pretty good shot at taking a prize." Cathy adopted a dreamlike visage and gazed into an imaginary distance. If she had focused, she'd be looking at Toss Across, a croquet set, and the lawn darts—strictly for display—we kept locked in a glass case.

"'Sweet smiling village, loveliest of the lawn . . .'"

"Hey, that's pretty good," I said. "I like that one."

"*That* was Oliver Goldsmith." She cleared her throat. "The trees are claws, scratching the evening sky, as I gaze at blue-gray span with blue-gray eye." She paused and waited.

I nodded.

"Get it? It's personification. Trees don't scratch. And a nice metaphor, I thought."

I nodded again.

"Everyone's a critic." She rolled her eyes and bustled out the door.

I put on a fresh pot of coffee for our guests. By the time the evening got rolling, our regular gamers filled all but one of our tables, and a stack of bills and coins was growing on the counter where the players left payment for the nostalgic candies that they selected from our display. I broke away from my own game twice (yes, I'm an avid board gamer) to ring up a Snoopy music box and a vintage Spock action figure, complete with tricorder, communicator, phaser, and belt.

After this last transaction, I felt a rush of satisfaction as I took my seat. This bump in impulse sales was precisely what had inspired me to suggest regular game nights—that, and a chance to play some of my favorite games. The nostalgic candy was also my idea. It seemed the perfect complement, tempting customers with the tastes of their childhood, especially varieties that were harder to come by today: Necco Wafers, Turkish Taffy, and a full assortment of Pez.

Tonight I played opposite the mayor's wife, whom I trailed by twenty points. Lori Briggs hovered over her rack of tiles. With the candy cigarette hanging out of the corner of her mouth, she looked a bit like a hustler. She was one of those petite fortysomethings, all eyelashes and dimples, who could pass for twenty. And prettier now than I had ever been. Not that I was a cow or anything. But I had gotten "big" genes from my Dad, not fat exactly, but tall and built solid as a Buick.

Usually I could take Lori in Scrabble with my eyes closed, but I was off my game. Every noise seemed to distract me, especially the *clickety clack* of knitting needles. Peggy Trent, a mousy older woman sitting kitty-corner from me at the same table, had brought her knitting to occupy her hands between turns. At least I wasn't playing opposite her tonight. Jack Wallace had that honor. The restaurateur was seated next to me, smelling heavily—and heavenly—of hot sauce.

"I heard your father is back on the job," Lori said, rearranging her letters. "Are you sure he's up for it? You know we're all so concerned . . ."

I gritted my teeth. By "we're" Lori meant the whole town, of which she'd appointed herself spokesperson.

"Hmpf," Peggy said, more through her nose than her mouth.

"We're *not* concerned?" Lori turned to her, raising one incredibly sculptured eyebrow.

"I didn't say anything." Peggy clicked away. "Of course the whole town is concerned. Go on."

"He's not back on the force," I said. "This was an isolated incident."

"You mean he's not a deputy?" Lori asked.

"Technically he is, but—"

"Took a lot of guts for that nice new police chief to offer him a place," Lori said. "I do hope you plan on thanking him. He didn't have to do that, you know. Especially after so many . . . isolated incidents."

"That *nice* new police chief?" Peggy said. "Apparently he hasn't towed your Volvo yet. I've noticed you've taken to parking in the tow-away zone in front of city hall again."

Lori flipped her hair back. "Perhaps Chief Young thinks the family of the mayor should be granted some special consideration."

"Or maybe it's all that flirting at the last Chamber of Commerce social," Peggy said, with an innocent air I suspected was feigned.

"I don't know what you're talking about," Lori said with that same nonchalant tone. "I'm a happily married woman." She set her tiles on the board, spelling out *viper*. Fitting. The *i* sat below an empty triple letter space. Hmm.

"I love small towns," Jack muttered under his breath.

"Ken had only the nicest things to say about Dad." *Today, that is.* I shifted my letters, then rubbed my temples, trying to think. I'd been holding onto the *x* for several turns now.

"Ken?" Jack said, and then quickly glanced down and studied his letters. "I didn't know you knew him that well."

"I, for one, am happy you two are getting better acquainted," Lori said. "You're single. He's single." She directed a smile toward Peggy, as if this proved she hadn't flirted with the new chief. "It would be nice to give that man some roots in the community. Now that he's gained more experience here, we wouldn't want to lose him back to the South the next time he gets a hankering for grits."

Jack blew out a forceful sigh and continued to shuffle his letters. Either he was stuck with a rack of vowels or he found this conversation as uncomfortable as I did.

"Thanks, Lori," I said, "but dating is not a priority right now. I have my father's business to focus on." Especially since his own focus tended to wander.

The clicking stopped. "Speaking of your father," Peggy said, "maybe I should run up and check on Hank. Do you think he's up for a visit?"

Oh, boy. Peggy had started hovering around my father at Mom's wake, sending not one but *three* casseroles and her signature apple fritters to the house. After allowing him a brief mourning period, she somehow finagled my father into asking her out. Once. Despite their common interest in toys—Peggy curated a small toy museum—they just didn't hit it off. Well, not according to Dad, at least. Still, Peggy continued to hover, harder to shake, as Dad would say, than a Yahtzee with only four dice.

"That's so kind of you, Peggy," I struggled to say with a straight face. "But Dad is resting tonight. Some other time, maybe."

Actually, Dad was probably still poring over his toy guides, but for him, that was restful. Peggy might be able to help identify the toy he had difficulty with, but that would be the opposite of restful, so I didn't mention it.

"Well, look who's flirting now," Lori said, but before Peggy could respond, she turned back to me. "You are too young to be cooped up in this shop all day and night. You should be getting out more. Seeing people. I'm sure there are places that would take your father."

"Places?" I could feel my cheeks coloring while I repeated the mantra *The customer's always right.*

"That new senior complex just outside of town, for example. Everything on ground level. I heard it's very nice."

"That, and her brother owns the place." Peggy peeked up from her knitting. "Well, it's a fact." She gestured with her knitting needles. She could poke an eye out with those things, if she were so inclined. And if she were so inclined, it would probably be in defense of my father.

Out of the corner of my eye, I caught Jack looking down quickly in a failed attempt to hide his smirk.

"Just keep an open mind," Lori added, still shuffling her tiles. "They have regular apartments, assisted living, and a nursing home. You could even start him in the day program. Crafts and such. Always good to keep busy. Once he's in their system, it's easier to get into the nursing facility."

"Who said he needs a nursing home?" I asked, perhaps a little too loudly.

"Well, one must plan for the future."

"He's barely sixty," Peggy said, shoving her knitting back into her PBS tote bag. "And pretty virile if you ask me, even if he doesn't play to everyone's demographic."

"I didn't mean . . ." Lori looked up and finally saw half the eyes of the room on her.

Jack put his hand over mine but shifted to face Lori. "Hank McCall is a hero and an asset to this community." He leaned closer to me. "I mean it." He squeezed my hand.

I swallowed hard, then let out a cleansing breath. "Thanks."

While he returned to his game, I blinked to clear the tears forming in my eyes—not over Lori's comment, which I'd already put behind me, but because I was touched by Jack's sentiment. We didn't talk about it, ever, but if anyone had a right to hold a grudge against Dad, Jack did. Dad had arrested Jack's brother, who had never returned to the village after serving his time. So Jack's support meant a lot.

I focused on my letters, then played *xu*, above the *ip* in *viper*, putting the *x* on the triple word score. I scored a cool fifty-eight points for *xu*, *xi*, and *up*. Then I sent a warm, if not completely heartfelt, grin to Lori.

# # #

Crisp, clear days allowed the sidewalks to dry to bare pavement, and the blue skies and rare sunlight lured happy streams of shoppers to Main Street. Internet sales were also up, and customers called to check if we had some sought-after items in our inventory.

Dad, good as his word, was visibly present in the shop during the busy hours. In the lulls, he went upstairs to try to figure out the value of the antique toys left for evaluation.

When I laid my head on the pillow after a few exhausting days of robust pre-Christmas sales, no sugar plums but rather visions of black ink and a balanced spreadsheet danced in my head.

The crash woke me up out of a sound sleep. At first I thought that Othello had gotten down into the shop and knocked over one of our displays. He'd done it before, once sending a vintage Charlie Brown lunchbox crashing to the ground and denting it. I remembered waiting for my dad to yell at the cat. Instead, all he said was "Good grief!" Dad must be mellowing in his old age. If Parker or I had done the same thing growing up, we would have been grounded for a week.

I sat bolt still, listening in the dark. Well, not really the dark. Between the moon and the streetlights and their reflections on the snow—even through the slats of my blinds—that whole luster-of-midday line from "A Visit from St. Nicholas" was true in that respect.

No sound at all. I began to think I'd dreamed the crash. Othello was certainly not to be blamed, as he was still on my bed. But he was listening too, on high alert, his ears perked to catch any sound. Moments later, he bolted into the closet. The phrase "scaredy cat" comes from somewhere.

I tugged on my robe and stuck my feet into my slippers. I hoped Dad wasn't mucking about in the shop in the middle of the night. Or worse, trying to sneak out. As I passed his room, I listened for the reassuring sound of his snores but was met with nothing but silence. I pushed open his door. His covers were thrown back and his bed empty. Now I hoped it *was* him in the shop. Better that than carding the customers at Jack's place—again.

Or perhaps he'd beaten me down the stairs to investigate the crash. I paused at the top of the steps, straining to listen for more noises. Maybe a minute passed, but I heard nothing more.

I crept silently down the steps, skipping the squeaky ones. I reached the bottom before I heard another noise, more of a sliding sound.

"Dad?" I called.

No one answered. Suddenly my adrenaline started pumping. If Dad made the noise, why were the lights off and why didn't he answer? The burglar alarm hadn't gone off, so if someone else had visited the shop in the middle of the night, they must have the code. Someone like Parker or Cathy. But they would have answered me. Unless Parker was playing one of his practical jokes again.

Something seemed off. I flipped the switch to turn on the shop lights. Nothing. Maybe a breaker had blown in the middle of the night and Dad went down to check on it.

A chill ran up my spine, and although I couldn't see them, I suspected goose bumps were erupting all over my arms and legs. The only light in the shop came through the storefront window, but as soon as I rounded the corner, I noticed that the front door was ajar. Next to it, the toy soldier shifted in the breeze, then leaned, and finally bent at the middle. It was collapsing quickly, with that frozen smile still on its face.

More scuffling sounds followed. This time, they came from one of the aisles.

"Dad?" I called again.

The noise stopped.

I froze in place and listened, wishing I had supersonic hearing. My eyes were now fully adjusted to the dimness, but the crazy reflected light from the snow bounced through the shop, highlighting every white surface.

A maniacal tin toy rabbit crouched in one cabinet. A suspicious windup skier tried to look innocent. Meanwhile, a Marx Pinocchio lithograph openly leered at me, daring me to move forward. But the tin robot—I swore it blinked.

I willed myself not to even glance in the direction of the windup stuffed monkey with the cymbals, the toy consistently voted number one in the category of most likely to be possessed by a horde of demons. This was why I didn't work in the doll room.

After I ran the gauntlet of staring toys, I paused, listening for any sound that could be heard above my heart pounding. Fiddlesticks. I was a cop's daughter; I should have more sense than to put myself in a vulnerable position. I should have called the police from upstairs. Like most people, I have twenty-twenty hindsight, but that couldn't help me now. Nor could I stay frozen to this spot for the rest of my life.

I was, however, standing in front of the toy gun case. I hit the catch—we don't tell the kids this, but we only pretend it locks—and armed myself with the most realistic toy gun in the collection, a Marx target pistol. I made sure it didn't have a suction cup dart sticking out of it. That would spoil the effect I was going for. Then I straightened up and put on my best female cop voice, more *Cagney & Lacey* than *Charlie's Angels*. "Who's there? I'm armed and the police are on their way." Okay, maybe I went too deep. I sounded more like Papa Bear when the librarian read *Goldilocks* to the preschoolers. I brandished the gun in front of me anyhow.

"Betsy?" Dad came around the corner, hunched over. His arm trailed the shelf, knocking over several Fisher-Price pull toys, which fell to the floor and started playing music. Then he collapsed to his knees.

I rushed over to him. "Dad, are you okay?"

"I think we have a problem."

I rubbed my hand against his face and felt blood. "Dad, you're bleeding. What happened? Did you fall?"

He shook his head and pointed to the aisle from where he had just come. I picked up the gun and headed in that direction. If anyone had messed with my father, he was going to have to deal with me.

When I turned down the aisle, however, there was no menacing figure. I focused on the parka first, lying there in the aisle next to a shimmer of broken glass. But it wasn't empty. Below it was a pair of legs. I inched closer and recognized the man who had visited the shop earlier in the week with a box of toys. Only difference was, then he didn't have a lawn dart jutting from his chest.

And he'd been alive.

Chapter 4

I squirmed in the folding chair the police had set up for me in the little back room behind the shop. Perhaps calling it a room overstated its status. It was merely the landing for the stairway, with a few cubby spaces where we'd stashed our coffeepot and a minifridge that was always on the fritz. Somehow, our contractor had shoehorned in a bathroom. While the sign said the restroom was reserved for staff and paying customers, we weren't all that strict about it, and more than one tourist had left much relieved and singing our praises.

I couldn't distinguish the muffled voices coming from the apartment upstairs where Chief Young was interrogating my father. The chief had been demoted from first-name basis as soon as he arrived, all official, and started barking questions at my father. Dad was bleeding, and he really needed to see a doctor but had refused. Nor was he very forthcoming, to either me or the police, about how the pockmarked man ended up dead on our shop floor. Now I felt betrayed, isolated, and worried beyond belief. A crash came from the shop—something knocked over by one of the crime scene investigators—and I nearly startled from my chair.

I got up, paced to the coffee maker, and lifted the carafe, but the thought of coffee made my stomach churn more acid. I scrounged in the cabinet underneath and scored a can of ginger ale and a half-stale box of Wheat Thins but abandoned both after a few sips of the ginger ale.

What were the chief and my father talking about for so long?

I pushed open the back door to let some air in. The alarm chirped, letting me know I had maybe thirty seconds or so to disarm it. Or what? The monitoring company would call the police? Too late for that. The place was swarming with them. Still, after I used my chair to prop the door open, I dutifully entered the code.

The alarm. That thought niggled in my mind and wouldn't stop niggling, like some alien parasite. My mind had been on spin cycle, powered by pure adrenaline, ever since I discovered a dead body in the aisle of the shop. Why hadn't the alarm sounded when the intruder entered?

I rubbed my temples, trying to play the scene in my head. The intruder had broken in. Maybe he had only come to the shop earlier in the week to "case the joint," as they say in old movies. Only, in his attempt to steal from us, he made some noise and woke my father. Dad must have confronted him. They struggled, and Dad grabbed the lawn dart and struck in self-defense?

Stop. Rewind. If the intruder had broken in, the alarm would have gone off. I recalled the light switch not working, and I glanced up at the alarm panel. When the power is cut to the alarm, the alarm company calls. If nobody responds, they notify the police.

I fished my cell phone out of my pocket—I'd put it there when Chief Young reluctantly let me leave the scene to change out of my Tweety Bird pajamas—and dialed the number on the decal attached to the alarm panel. After being shuffled to about half a dozen different people and holding during the slowest and dreariest rendition of "Away in the Manger" I've ever heard, someone on the other end of the line confirmed that the power-loss signal had been registered during the night and that a call was attempted.

"I never talked to anyone," I said. "We had a break-in during the outage."

"We have a record that the call was made and answered," said the woman. "Please hold and I'll confirm."

I held for what seemed like forever. Police officers wandered about the shop and voices hummed from upstairs. My stomach gave another lurch.

"I listened to the conversation myself," she said. "The responder didn't remember the alarm code but did correctly answer both security questions."

"You have the call recorded? Can you play it for me?"

Soon I heard my father's voice try the old alarm code, and when that didn't work, he answered both security questions, calmly adding that there had been a power outage on the street but that everything was fine.

That blew my first theory. No intruder had disabled the alarm.

I closed my eyes and reset the mental images. No intruder awakened Dad. He was already awake. Maybe he had been in the shop when the power went out. He'd assumed it was an outage and answered the call when it came in. That made sense. Then he'd encountered the intruder. They fought . . .

Before I could get too relieved, I recalled that police had restored electricity by popping the breaker. So unless the victim was a ninja, or one of those *Mission Impossible*–style intruders with a backpack of thin cable, lasers, and assorted high-tech whatchamacallits and doodads, the breaker was pulled from inside the shop, and the alarm company appeased before the victim entered.

Dad had pulled the breaker. Why? My mind fished for other explanations. I gave up when I got to "the intruder climbed in through a secret tunnel dating back to the Underground Railroad." While the Underground Railroad did convey a number of escaped slaves through Western New York on their way to Canada, it was too Scooby-Doo to be truly plausible.

There was no intruder. The only explanation that fit was that Dad had pulled the breaker and then fielded a call from the alarm company, all while I slept.

I allowed my gaze to trail up the stairs to the closed door. *Dad, what were you up to?*

# # #

Eventually the apartment door opened. To my relief, my father wasn't being led away in handcuffs.

While Dad walked down the stairs, Chief Young called to me. "I can take your statement now."

Dad put his hand on my upper arm. "Just a formality, Lizzie. Tell him the truth, and you'll be fine."

My feet were lead when I climbed the steps. Chief Young waited at the top, stifling a yawn.

"Are we boring you?" I wasn't sure if I was trying to be funny or sarcastic. I hadn't had enough sleep to make the distinction.

He let his shoulders droop. "Middle-of-the-night call." Then he gestured over to our kitchen table. Dad's guides were still stacked in several piles, one propped open with his magnifying glass holding his place. The old toys, however, were nowhere in sight.

I sat, then Chief Young sat. Then I sat up a little straighter, as did he. He shuffled through several papers, then looked up at me. "How about we start by you telling me exactly what happened, in your own words."

I almost said, "Who else's words would I use?" Instead, I recounted everything that had happened from the moment I awoke back to how I'd met the man in the shop earlier in the week.

"Did you know the man's name?" he asked.

"Don't you know it?" I spared a moment to push my glasses up. In my brief opportunity to dress, I hadn't taken the time to put my contacts in.

Ken shook his head. I'd cooled down a little bit, so his name reverted to Ken in my mind. "He had no ID on him, and your father claims not to remember his name."

"No, I . . . Wait! He handed me his business card."

"Where is this card?"

I reached into my pocket. "I put it in the pocket. Of my other sweater."

He nodded, and I ran to my bedroom to retrieve my black cardigan. After a brief search, I found it on a chair, topped off by a sleeping cat. I gave Othello a brief scratch behind the ears before settling him on the bed. He squeaked in protest but soon began circling my pillow. While he curled up to continue his snooze, I brushed a little fur off the sweater. That's the bad thing about tuxedo cats. If the black fur blends in, the white fur shows, and vice versa. Meaning I was covered in enough animal fur at any given moment that I was in danger of being targeted by PETA.

I fished the business card out of the pocket. I knew Ken would take the card, so I handled it only by the edges in case he wanted to check for prints. I'm not sure what sparked the idea, but before I left the bedroom, I took a picture of the card with my cell phone.

He took the card without caring about fingerprints and slipped it into the clipboard portion of his notebook.

My jaw must have dropped.

"If you're wondering about prints, I'm sure yours are already on it," he offered by way of explanation.

I scooted my chair to the table and held my tongue. I suspected that most of the ire I felt had to do with the lack of sleep and Ken taking up court at our kitchen table. A fleeting thought made me wish I had loaded the dishwasher before I'd gone to bed. That was replaced by the cool voice of reason, which reminded me that Ken had to be there. Someone had died in our shop, and we needed to cooperate fully with the authorities. I attempted a cooperative smile. Then that cool voice of reason was drowned out by the voices that wanted to panic. I'm sure that smile grew scary. "Would you like some tea?" I asked.

Ken was looking down at his notes, which he'd perched against the table's edge. "I bet you mean hot tea, don't you? No, but if you'd like some, go right ahead."

I got up to put the kettle on. "I could run some over ice if you'd like. A little lemon?"

"That sounds amazing," he said. "Whenever it's on the menu here, it's either hot or that prebottled stuff." Ken flipped through a few pages and then eyed me with an almost pained expression. "Can I be candid with you?"

"I wish you would. I want to help." I put the kettle on to heat. "My father always instilled in me the need to be open and honest with the police."

"Your father's statement. It's a little confused."

"He *was* hit on the head."

"The EMT checked him out. Said it was a superficial injury. Frankly, I'm wondering if he's deliberately withholding information."

"Oh, come on! Do you seriously believe he murdered that man?"

"I didn't say I believed he murdered him." Ken kept his tone calm. "I'm not accusing him of anything at this point. I just don't think he's telling me everything he knows. Liz, this is difficult because he's your father. Maybe you could explain some of the discrepancies."

At this point? "I don't know how I can help. I was asleep until I heard a noise in the shop."

"Did your father know the victim? Enough to let him in the shop in the middle of the night?"

"Not that I'm aware of," I said. "I'd never seen him before this week. Dad claims he didn't even know the man's name."

"But your father did have an appointment with the victim."

"That's what the man claimed. I didn't know anything about it until he showed up."

"Does your father keep an appointment book?"

"Scraps of paper. Scrawls on the calendar. Post-it notes." I pointed my head in the direction of the bulletin board, then got up to answer the teakettle. When I glanced back, Ken was studying the bulletin board mounted on the wall near the phone.

He tapped the calendar. "There's a time circled here. No name, no description."

I squinted. "That's when he came by the shop. Dad must have made the appointment and forgot."

"But he didn't write down the man's name or the reason for the appointment. Is he in the habit of doing that?"

"All his life," I said.

"Hard to imagine how he managed a whole police department."

"He had a remarkable secretary, if you must know," I said, then occupied myself by retrieving a lemon from the fridge. I'd been after Dad for months to write down all appointment information fully.

"And you said he didn't tell you about the appointment?"

I shook my head and made a clean slice through the lemon. I realized at that moment that I clearly hadn't merited a spot on Ken's suspect list if he allowed me to handle a sharp knife during our discussion.

"Do you think he might have been shielding it from you in some way?" he asked.

I set down the knife and whirled to face him. "You mean *hiding* it from me, don't you?"

He didn't answer, confirming that's exactly what he'd meant.

I paused to think. I'd intended to cooperate fully, but the direction his questions were taking challenged that resolve. "Look," I said, "Dad didn't include me in every aspect of the business."

"So this wasn't unusual?"

"It was atypical, but not unheard of." I struggled to keep focus on the tea preparation. Only my hands must have been shaking, because several cubes missed the Mason jar and ended up skittering across the linoleum. I bent down to retrieve them. "Evaluating old toys is something he's had more experience with. Especially toys as old as these."

"But he wasn't here when the man showed for the appointment."

I set Ken's tea in front of him and retook my seat at the table. "Exactly what are you getting at?"

"Has your father always been open and honest with you?"

"You're a cop. Are you always open and honest with your family?"

"I don't have much of a family."

I shrugged. "Dad didn't often bring his work home with him. Not that he was secretive. When he was home, he liked to focus on being at home, being a father."

"But now that you're an adult . . ."

"I think he's developed the habit of being guarded in what he says. Not that he'd lie to me. If he said he didn't know the . . . victim, then he didn't."

Ken pulled out the card. "The name Carson Suffern doesn't mean anything to you?"

I took a sip of my tea to stall. "It sounds familiar. I don't ever recall Dad mentioning him, but I've heard that name before. I don't recall in what context."

"If it comes to you, you'll let me know?"

I nodded, then blew on my tea to cool it, steaming my eyeglasses in the process. I removed them and set them on the table.

"You're thinking about something," he said.

When I glanced up, I realized that he'd been studying my face. "I have some concerns about the . . . chronology of events," I said. "The alarm system. The power outage. How exactly that man . . . Carson Suffern . . . got in."

"It's pretty evident, isn't it?" He kept up that piercing eye contact. "Your father let him in."

Chapter 5

I set Othello's carrier down. "Okay to let him loose?" I asked Cathy. "And thanks for letting us stay. Hopefully it will only be a day or two."

Ken had declared our home and shop a crime scene. We'd been asked if we could vacate until they finished collecting evidence and the crime scene cleaners had come through.

Cathy, now decked out in faux leopard print, walked across her living room and gave me a hug. "You guys can stay as long as you need. And Othello can come out. Parker decided Clyde was ready to release."

"Clyde?" Dad said.

"A possum," Cathy explained. "He was limping pretty badly, so we had him in for a few days. Just a sprain, we think. He was doing better when he didn't have to forage for food."

"An animal from the center?" I asked.

"Oh, no," Cathy said. "Just from the neighborhood."

Parker came in the door juggling more luggage. It looked like Dad and I were moving in for a month. Strange, the things you want to take with you when you don't know when you're going to see home again.

When the door was closed, I knelt down and opened the carrier. Othello didn't budge. Even the brightly blinking Christmas tree in the corner wasn't enough to lure him out. I had a feeling in an hour or two, I'd be peeling him off the branches.

"No, we're not at the vet," I said.

He sniffed, as if he were checking out the place, then took a few cautious steps forward.

"Don't rush him," Cathy said.

I sat with my back against the coffee table and waited him out. "Thanks again for letting us crash here."

"Oh, you know me," Parker said. "Always glad to help the strays and the refugees."

"Hear that, Othello?" I asked. "He's calling you a stray."

Othello peeked out of the carrier when I mentioned his name. He put one paw on the carpet and stopped before scanning the faces in the room. Then his nose went to sniffing madly.

"I'll bet he smells Clyde," Parker said. "He's gone."

Othello stared up at Parker as if he understood him, then took another cautious step out of the carrier. Convinced that no deadly danger was near, he started sniffing around the room, rubbing his cheek against the corners of the coffee table. He didn't venture far before looking back to make sure I was there.

"He'll be fine." Dad sank down into an overstuffed recliner. He let his head fall back against the pillowed chair and closed his eyes. "I could sleep a week."

"You didn't get much last night, Dad," I said.

I hoped that would start him talking. He blew out a long breath, then opened his eyes. "Sorry, Lizzie."

"For what?" I tried to sound nonchalant.

"For worrying you."

"For worrying me?" I could feel my volume and pitch rise but checked myself. When he was stressed, he'd clam up. Maybe it was a cop thing. Interrogations only worked with him when he was the interrogator. If he was going to volunteer any info, it would be when he was calm and relaxed and in familiar surroundings, which was one more reason I hoped we could regain our home and open the shop soon. That, and I'd grown fond of being able to pay my bills, having a roof to keep the snow off, and eating.

"I'm fine, Dad," I said in my most reassuring tone, despite the knot in my belly. "But I would like to know a little more about what happened. Did that man come back for his toys?"

"The toys?" he asked.

"Yeah, I noticed they weren't in the apartment."

A vague expression crossed his face, as if he struggled to focus. "I suppose the police could have taken them into evidence."

"You don't know?"

"I don't . . ." The vague look disappeared and he set his jaw. "Do we have to do this right now?"

I put a calming hand on his and squeezed. "Only when you're ready. In the meantime, everything's okay. We're safe and together." I patted his hand, then looked up at Parker, who hid his own worried look behind a reassuring smile.

"I should bring in the rest of the luggage," he said, then vanished out to the car.

# # #

I woke up early the next morning, aware of another presence in the living room. Yes, Othello was sleeping on my chest, but then I heard someone clearing his throat.

"Parker?" I pushed myself up, trying to ignore the achy feeling in my back from sleeping awkwardly on the couch.

"Shhh." Parker already wore his work uniform and sat in the overstuffed chair drinking his coffee. He was quite blurry since I didn't have my glasses on. "Everyone else is still asleep," he whispered.

I picked my glasses off the coffee table and managed to get them on my face. I pointed to his coffee cup. "Any more where that came from?"

"Whole pot. Do you still like it insanely sweet?" he asked.

"I cut back to two sugars," I said, "and some milk."

While he headed back to the kitchen, I sat up and ran my fingers through my hair, which in the morning tended to stick out at odd angles, similar to Bozo the Clown's. When Parker came back with a full snowman mug, I was sitting cross-legged on the sofa rubbing the sleep from my eyes. For several minutes, we sipped our coffees in silence.

At all the big junctures in life, it seemed Parker and I shared a quiet cup of coffee. When Mom went to rehab. Before Dad's major surgery. On the day after I came back after breaking up with my former fiancé. The morning he married Cathy. We'd start by each draining a cup of coffee in silence, then we'd talk things through during the second cup. Today, I dreaded finishing the first one.

When I had, I rummaged through my suitcase, dug out my slippers, and padded out to the kitchen to pour more for both of us. When I spun around holding two steaming cups of coffee, I spotted eyes peering in at me from the patio door. I jumped, sending scalding coffee spilling over my fingers and onto the tile floor. Only then did I realize the eyes were not of the human variety.

I breathed in through my teeth, set the cups down on the counter, and dried my hands on my sweatpants before steeling myself for a closer inspection of the critter. A possum, its pink nose twitching at the end of its long snout, was balanced on the gas grill outside, craning to look into the house.

Othello had followed me into the kitchen, probably wondering if it was time for him to eat yet. The possum caught his attention, too. The cat was in full stalker mode, advancing an inch or two at a time toward the door, then freezing, but never keeping his eyes off the possum.

"What's wrong?" Parker said, coming up behind me.

"I think I met Clyde," I said.

"Sis, you and I need to have that talk again. That there is Bonnie."

Since rolling your eyes at your brother doesn't count when it's before dawn and he can't see you, I punched him in the arm, and then we carried our coffees to the kitchen table.

"How much trouble is Dad in?" Parker asked.

"I wish I knew." Although that wasn't entirely true. I actually wished I could crawl back into my own bed, fall asleep, and wake up discovering everything that had happened was a dream. But that wasn't an option. "Chief Young seems like he's pretty good, but something's off with Dad. That's going to hamper the investigation. You know as well as I do that these early hours are so important."

Parker stared down into his cup. It went without saying that whenever something big happened in East Aurora when Dad had been the chief of police, days often passed before we saw him. That's usually when Mom took to the bottle. Somehow, Parker managed the laundry, I learned how to cook, and he and I became best friends.

I rubbed the sleep out of my eye. "Dad says he didn't know the dead guy, but I'm sure I've heard the name before."

"The police haven't released the name. Who was he?"

"Carson Suffern." I sipped my cooling coffee. "Why does that name sound so familiar?"

"Carson . . ." Parker started to shake in silent laughter.

"I fail to see what's so funny."

"You. Carson Suffern? As in, 'Don't suffer with stopped-up drains. Call Carson Suffern!' and 'Sticky septic issues? Don't suffer; call Suffern!'"

"Oooohhh. The self-anointed kingpin of plumbing." All those corny radio commercials came back, with the same announcer screaming at the top of his lungs. I caught myself smiling, but then the corners of my mouth drooped. "What was the kingpin of plumbing doing dead in our shop?"

\# \# \#

The next great tragedy in our lives came when Cathy insisted on making egg salad for lunch. She overcooked the eggs, leading Dad on a merry chase through every Seussian and green-egg pun he could think of. When Cathy got tired of hearing that Sam-I-Am wouldn't eat them extra large or on a barge or from a moat or in a coat or in a lump or while taking a . . . she turned on the radio.

Cathy pranced around the kitchen to the end of "Jingle Bell Rock." When the news came on, she reached to switch the station, but Dad stopped her.

The report was vague. "An unidentified man was found dead in an East Aurora shop after hours. Police are investigating and will release a statement later."

After a weather report (cold with a chance of snow—big surprise there), the station aired, ironically, an ad for Suffern Plumbing.

I winced but immediately glanced at Dad. If he knew Carson Suffern, his face sure didn't betray that fact.

"Dad, have you ever met Carson Suffern?"

"Who?"

"The commercial that was just on. The kingpin of plumbing?"

"No, I don't think so."

"Hmm . . ." I repeated my personal mantra. *Dad would never lie to me*.

We barely had time to dispose of our lunch when Cathy answered a tap at the door and ushered Ken back into the kitchen.

"Would you like some egg salad?" Cathy asked.

I wasn't sure if he caught a glimpse of the bowl or if he just wasn't hungry. "No thanks." He took a seat at the table opposite Dad.

Dad half rose and shook Ken's hand. "I see you're still not releasing the name of the deceased," he said. "I take it you haven't been able to notify the family."

"Well, we started to," Ken said, also waving off a cup of coffee. "Only when we got there, the man we thought was in the morgue was actually sitting at his kitchen table. Whomever we found in the shop is clearly not Carson Suffern."

Dad cast me a quick glance, and I could feel my face begin to blush. He'd caught me fishing for information.

"I suppose those dreadful commercials will continue then." Cathy sighed as she pulled up the remaining chair at the table. "It's a pity."

"I wonder why he gave me Carson Suffern's card," I said.

"Maybe he mistakenly handed you the wrong one," Cathy said.

I shook my head. "Nope. He looked right at it before he handed it to me. Do you think he was deliberately hiding his identity?"

"Sounds like it." Ken leaned his elbows onto the table. Already he had dark circles under his eyes and a scruffy bit of beard started on his chin. The perils of being a small-town police chief in the middle of a murder investigation.

"So I'm assuming you ran his prints in the FBI database," Dad said.

Ken rubbed the stubble on his chin. "Well, funny thing about that . . ."

"No record?" Dad asked.

"Actually, no prints."

Dad's eyebrows shot up. "The victim had no fingerprints?"

"That's odd," I said. "Do you think he tampered with his own prints like some of those old-time gangsters?" Who was this victim, and what was he up to that he'd go to such extremes to conceal his identity?

Ken shrugged. "That's one theory. Although the good folks at the FBI suggested other possibilities. Apparently certain occupations can damage the fingerprints over time. Bricklaying, for one, or handling paper or cash money regularly. Even industrial accidents with fire or acid have been known to strip prints. So I came over here to see if either of you recalled anything more about the man."

Dad closed his eyes. His face was unreadable.

"Scrubs," I said. "He was wearing scrubs the first time I saw him. And he was very tan. Bricklayers would be tan."

"But they wouldn't wear scrubs," Ken said.

"So he could be a medical worker who frequents tanning salons or a bricklayer who finds scrubs comfortable. Or maybe the scrubs were a ruse to make us think he was a health care worker."

Ken squinted at me.

"If he'd gone to such lengths as to conceal his name and obliterate his fingerprints, why not wear a disguise?" When I said it out loud, it sounded more outlandish.

Ken jostled his head from side to side as if contemplating my logic. "I guess it can't hurt to check with the local unions. See if anyone recognizes him. Anything else?"

I thought for a moment. "I honestly have nothing. But I did want to ask if you'd removed any toys from the shop. As evidence, I mean."

"Miss McCall, we wouldn't take any of your toys."

"No, these were very old toys that the victim had brought to us to be evaluated. The last I saw them they were on the kitchen table upstairs, but they weren't there when you and I . . . talked."

"So you're saying you think someone broke in and took them?" His voice bore a hint of skepticism.

I chose my next few words carefully. "I'm saying I don't know where they are."

"I guess I can keep my eyes open for them," Ken said. "Is there a list or something so I know what I'm looking for?"

"On the kitchen table in the apartment. Just make me a copy," Dad said, then his eyes widened. "Carson Suffern."

Ken sat up in his chair. "What about him?"

"The vic had Carson Suffern's card in his pocket?"

"That's right," I said.

"Then he had to get the card somehow. Maybe Carson Suffern can identify him. Take a picture over there and see if he can cough up the name of our John Doe." Dad was back in chief mode.

If Ken resented this, he didn't show it. He practically saluted on his way out. I kept an eye on Dad all that afternoon. His suggestion to Ken had sounded like an order, and the last thing we needed was Dad inserting himself into an investigation in which he was also a suspect.

Fortunately, a nice board game marathon brought him back to his kindly toy store persona, even if he did almost kick my butt in Catan. Just before Dad scored enough points to win, however, Othello darted across the table, sending hexagons and playing pieces skittering in all directions. I took to my hands and knees to salvage the ones that had fallen to the floor—all except the one my cat happily batted under the refrigerator. He'd been lying on his side, poking with his paws, trying to retrieve his prize. Before long, I was doing a reasonable impersonation, trying to sweep the missing piece out with a butter knife. I finally connected and sent it spinning toward me, amid a collection of cheerios, apparent possum fur, and a dust bunny the size of Texas. Othello started sniffing the possum fur, making that disgusted face cats make when they focus on a new smell.

Othello had been the inspiration for another pet project of mine: missing game pieces. He loved disrupting games and chasing stray pieces so much I realized that other households with pets or small children must have the same problem. So during the summer, when I typically scavenged area garage sales for old toys and games, I bought board games regardless of their condition. Incomplete games could be combined to form one complete set and the rest sold for parts. Missing Scrabble tiles from almost all editions, assorted playing pieces, get-out-of-jail-free cards, and yes, the original marbles from Hungry Hungry Hippos were all available at the shop. Cataloging was a bit of a nightmare, but the venture had shown some profit. That is, if we ever got back into the shop.

Before I was off the floor, I heard a familiar voice, and Miles was heading toward the kitchen table, carrying his own coffee in an insulated Spot Coffee mug.

I stood up, then dislodged another dust bunny from my hair before putting the last game piece safely in the box.

"No classes?" Dad asked.

Miles slid his glasses lower down his nose and stared at Dad over the frames. I wasn't sure if Miles was a full-out hipster or not, but he looked the part: chunky glasses, casual unkempt hair that he occasionally ran his fingers through to keep out of his face, and clothing choices that looked like he wore the first thing that came to hand when he crawled out of bed. His attempt at a beard was a little pitiful, but perhaps that gave him extra hipster points.

He removed his latest device from his bag and fired it up. "I updated the website to let people know we're closed, and I can run a twenty percent discount coupon to all our e-mail subscribers as soon as we open again." He paused and looked up. "If that's all right?"

"Twenty?" Dad scratched his chin.

"Any less than twenty and I'm not sure you'll draw them in."

Dad turned to me. "Will we lose any money on twenty percent off?"

I shrugged. "Maybe on some things."

Miles smirked. "Then mark those up before you reopen. Twenty gets the customers back in the store. Some will come anyway. The gawkers. But that doesn't mean they buy."

"Exclude candy and new toys on the coupon?" I said.

Miles's hands flew across his keyboard. "Done. Meanwhile, a couple of auctions have ended, and I'll need to get in the shop so I can ship the merchandise. We don't want to lose our customer rating."

I threw up my hands. "Talk to Chief Young."

"I was rather hoping you could do it." Miles sent a cheesy grin in Dad's direction.

Miles and Dad had a long history, apparently, and not one that I was privy to. Miles had grown up on the Cattaraugus Reservation, affectionately known as the res. His mother moved to East Aurora when he was fourteen. He didn't take the move well, getting into some trouble, I gather, while running with the wrong crowd in high school. Both Dad and Miles were pretty hush-hush about it. Now Miles was in college and doing quite well, even if he was taking too many classes and working too many jobs.

Dad tapped the table. "I might not be his favorite person right now." He looked at me.

"Why am I his favorite all of a sudden?"

Dad started to open his mouth, but before he could make a sound, I said, "Fine, I'll ask him."

"Good," Miles said. "Next order of business . . ." He clicked over to the picture of the toy I'd e-mailed him.

"Have you found anything out?" Dad asked.

"Not yet," Miles said. "I didn't know if I should keep trying. It's rare, but that's all I know for sure. Everyone I've approached has a different idea. Might be a prototype. Might even be a fake. Then they give me the name of someone they think might know. I didn't know how much energy I should invest in the hunt. After all, if the guy who wanted to know the value is dead, is there a reason to keep pushing?"

"There's a reason," Dad said. "A man has died because of those toys."

Every head at the table pivoted toward Dad so quickly, we might have been able to qualify for a group discount on a whiplash case from a friendly personal injury attorney.

"You think the toys had something to do with why that man is dead?" I asked. Was he admitting something or just making his own inferences?

"Think like a cop, Liz. A man goes into a toyshop carrying a box of toys. Days later, he dies in the same toyshop, and the toys are missing. I can't prove it, but yes, I think his death has something to do with the toys."

Miles saluted. "I'll keep looking, Chief."

Chapter 6

A couple of days after he'd been hit on the head, I'd managed to coax Dad to the doctor.

He held the door open for me as we exited the medical complex. "That was a waste of time."

"How could you call it a waste of time?" Multiple tests and hundreds of dollars in copays later, the verdict was a concussion, which could have triggered the memory loss—which Dad had finally come clean and admitted.

"Well, it's not like they did anything about it, right? Just said take it easy, no driving, and avoid stress, and my memories might come back in time."

"Why didn't you tell me you had amnesia?"

"It's hardly amnesia. It's not like I've forgotten my name or how to dress myself or anything important. The hours around the accident are . . . just a little bit hazy, that's all."

"Not an accident. You were attacked!"

"I didn't want to worry you. With everything going on, the last thing you needed to bother about was me."

"You could have told Chief Young. Right now he must think you're being uncooperative. It makes you look guilty."

"And what? Claiming I can't remember what happened makes me look more innocent?"

I brushed a thin coating of dusty snow from the windshield while Dad used his jacket sleeve to clear the passenger side. Suddenly I didn't care that I was in the doghouse for nagging him to see the doctor. I was just glad that Dad was okay, reassured by every puff of breath that fogged in the cold air that he was warm and alive.

When we climbed in, his hand went right to the radio. "I want to see if there's any news." He tuned in the news station, but they were detailing an arson fire in Buffalo. The report finished without mentioning the murder.

I backed out of my parking spot. "If you were still chief, I'd bet you'd have identified the victim by now. I mean, even without fingerprints, I don't understand what's taking so long. Can't he use DNA or dental records?"

Dad shook his head. "Not so easy sometimes, Lizzie. The problem with DNA and dental records is that you have to have something to match it to. I'm sure they're canvassing the area with his picture. But if nobody has reported him missing . . ."

"How could anyone not miss a whole person?"

"Maybe they didn't. Maybe he's not from around here. Or doesn't keep in touch with family. Maybe he has no family. Neighbors or landlords don't always notice someone is missing, at least not right away. An employer might assume he quit without notice. They get ticked when someone doesn't show up for a shift, but they don't often think to call police or report him missing."

"That's kind of sad."

"The only things we have to go on are what he looked like, what he was wearing, and that box of toys. And that business card. But if Carson Suffern recognized the dead guy, I think the news would be reporting his identity by now."

"Another dead end," I said. Then I realized Dad was craning his neck to scope out the toy museum as we passed.

"What are you looking for?"

"That woman's car."

"Peggy Trent? Dad, are you sure this is the right time to kindle a romance?" I was teasing him, of course. His feelings toward "that woman," as he usually referred to her, were as clear as Wonder Woman's invisible jet.

"I don't think she's there," he said. "Car's not, anyway." Peggy Trent drove a boxy Kia that my dad considered the ugliest car in the world.

"So you don't want to stop," I said.

"No, I *do* want to stop. As long as you still have the picture of that toy on your cell phone."

"That I do, but I'm not sure where you're going with this. Are you suggesting I now chauffeur you around while you put yourself in danger carrying out your own investigation? Why can't you be satisfied being a toy store owner?"

"Well, Lizzie." I could feel his eyes on me. "Seems to me that in the past few days, it's not been much safer in the toy store, has it?"

That man's logic was infuriating. "And I'm supposed to wait in the car and hope for the best?"

"Actually, I was hoping you could come in with me. In fact, if that assistant curator is there, you could do the talking. I think I scare her."

I circled the block while I debated the matter. Should I humor him and help him with his investigation? Or take him back to Parker and Cathy's house, in which case he'd likely sneak out on his own at the first opportunity. At least this way, I could keep an eye on him. I found a spot on the street. I'm not the best parallel parker, but after a few embarrassing attempts, I managed to wedge the Civic between two cars and the curb.

Moments later, we walked into the small storefront that served as the town's toy museum.

I loved the old place, once a tailor's shop. Instead of tile floor like our shop had, all the layers of flooring had been removed until the original plank subfloor was revealed. Stained and full of holes, it screamed, "I'm historic!" The museum was jammed from front to back with display cases, all bought secondhand so none of them matched. In each of these were old toys, many manufactured in the area. Dad and I had an annual membership, so we didn't have to pay an admission fee. And Dad was like a kid in a, well, toyshop.

He stopped to examine a tin Lone Ranger figure. The masked crime fighter was mounted on a rearing Silver, and his lasso was complete and in the air. "This is nice," Dad said, practically on top of the display case.

"Isn't it?"

I jumped at the unexpected voice but fortunately didn't knock anything over in the process. I whirled around to face the assistant curator, my heart thumping. Not that she was in any way scary. Jillian Hatley was one of the least scary people around. She had straight blonde hair, a meek expression, and a voice that couldn't be heard above the average toaster. Seriously, when she did a tour, you needed to be right next to her in order to hear. I'm convinced people in the back just nodded and then went to their doctors for a hearing test.

I tapped Jillian's forearm. "You scared me."

"I didn't mean to." A few seconds later, she smiled. Jillian didn't lack a sense of humor, but she was the one at the movie theater laughing five minutes after the joke. "Have you come in to see the newest items in our collection? I'm afraid there are only a few recent additions." She cast a nervous glance over at my father.

Maybe there was some truth in Dad's impression that he scared her. He walked farther back into the museum.

"I hope you might help me with something." I pulled out my cell phone. "Did you hear about the man who died in our shop?"

A few seconds passed. "Was that your shop? The radio said one of the shops on Main. I thought maybe it was that new tattoo parlor." She wrinkled her nose. Whether it was over the death or the thought of tattoos was anyone's guess. "Dreadful. Was it somebody you knew?"

"No. I'd met him earlier in the week, but he gave me a fake name. He wanted an appraisal on some toys. I took a picture of one of them. It seems it's rare, and Dad couldn't find it in any of the books."

"Perhaps Peggy . . ." she began.

"Well, maybe," I said. "Is she here today?" I felt a pang of guilt for asking a question I was pretty sure I already knew the answer to. And if Jillian couldn't give us any leads on the toy, perhaps we'd have to try Peggy. Or *I* would have to try Peggy. I think Dad was considering a restraining order.

"Oh, I'm sorry." Jillian looked overly penitent. "It's her day off."

I flipped through my pictures—I had taken a couple of new pictures of Othello and a cute one of him staring at Bonnie and Clyde through the glass patio door—until I got to the one of the toy.

She leaned in to study it. "I have seen this before. I'm pretty sure."

"Are you positive?" Which was a lame question, because she'd already said she was pretty sure. Conversations with Jillian tended to go this way.

She nodded. "It's part of a collection bequeathed to the museum."

"You mean it belongs here? Was it stolen?"

She shook her head. "The owner was planning to leave it to the museum in his will." She shrugged her petite shoulders. "But he hasn't died yet. Which is a good thing."

"Have you seen this man?"

She nodded again. "Once. Since he's technically a donor, he can visit the museum for free, but I gather he didn't get out much." Her eyes fell to the floor. "Do you think he might be the man who died in your shop?"

"Was he very tan with a pockmarked face?"

Jillian must have thought about this question for a full minute. I wouldn't call her stupid, just slow to respond. As if the whole world had high-speed Internet, and she still had dial-up and was waiting for the modem to connect. I half expected the next words out of her mouth to be, "You've got mail." She tilted her head and gave it a brief shake. "I don't think so. But I do have the donor's name and address on file, if that helps."

Moments later Dad and I headed to the address Jillian had printed out from her files, after apologizing when she had to reload the paper and then the toner on the printer.

"Quit apologizing," Dad had insisted.

"Sorry," she'd said.

But we'd gotten what we had come for, and without running into Peggy Trent once.

When we drove past Well Played, with the yellow crime scene tape barring the door, Dad merely cleared his throat and I forced my eyes back on the road.

The name Jillian had given us was Syril DuPont, and the address was in a once tony part of town, where grand, old painted-lady Victorians, in various states of disrepair and restoration, were draped with snow, looking like so many gingerbread houses made by a baker a little too generous with the butter cream.

Dad studied the printout as we neared our destination, at least according to the GPS. He tapped the page. "There's something familiar about this address."

When I parked in front of the building, he whistled. "I was right. Betsy, I've been here before."

"Been here before *recently*?"

He shook his head. "It's been a while, but I answered a bunch of calls to this address. Nuisance stuff, mainly."

"What kind of nuisance stuff?"

Dad scratched his bristly cheek. "I can't remember."

I momentarily stopped breathing. The doctor hadn't said anything about problems with Dad's long-term memory.

"Don't panic, Lizzie." He grabbed my hand and laughed. "I don't think I forgot anything. I just don't think that the calls ever amounted to anything that my brain thought important enough to remember. Like calls saying they heard someone prowling about the place, but there was no evidence. Fresh snow and no footprints, that sort of thing. Just some guy with an overactive imagination living in an old house that made odd noises."

I stared up at the house and understood how someone's imagination might run away from him. Against the bleak, gray winter sky, the house did look foreboding, almost Hitchcockian. Cue the *Psycho* soundtrack.

While I sat there pondering the house, a car pulled up behind me and parked. The passengers didn't linger in the vehicle; they hopped right out, slammed car doors, and headed to the house carrying casserole dishes and trays of food.

"Someone's having a party." Dad smirked.

"Should we come back later?" I asked, noticing another packed car working its way into one of only a few empty spaces left on the block.

Dad gave me an impish wink. "Nah, I think we ought to crash it."

Before I could say another word, he was out of the car and hobbling to the front door behind the group of new arrivals. I hustled to get out of the car but then had to jump a pile of slush that had accumulated at the head of the driveway. By the time I made it to the door, Dad had already followed the others inside. I stood, staring at the doorknob. Dad was a lot bolder than I was, but I couldn't leave him in this stranger's house alone. I took a deep breath and tried to open the door. Only the knob wouldn't budge.

"Here, let me get that," said a familiar, masculine voice from behind me. Jack Wallace handed me a covered tray of cookies. He gave the knob a forceful turn while pushing on the door. "It sticks sometimes." Then whoosh, it opened, and he held the door so I could enter.

The house smelled like old people. I wasn't quite sure how else to describe it. There was a mix of that cloying fragrance they add to chemical ointments along with the chemical odors too strong to mask, stale cooking odors, a touch of mildew, and a pinch of urine. I hoped a pet was involved in the equation.

Earlier arrivals had kicked off their boots in the cramped entryway, and I did the same, stepping over the puddles left by melting snow. I missed avoiding one and felt the cold bite through my sock. Jack took my coat and whisked it away. I turned to face the gathering crowd.

I didn't know a blessed person in the room, save for Jack's mother. If she had a first name, I'd never been privy to it. She was always just Mrs. Wallace. Any more familiarity would have been met with an icy stare.

I'd gotten on Mrs. Wallace's no-fly list way back in high school, when I'd supposedly dumped her son. Jack always claimed he filled her in on the true story, but she'd taken his side anyway. Despite the fact that Jack had stood me up for the prom—yes, the prom, leaving me with credit card charges for a manicure, a pedicure, hair and makeup, an unreturnable altered dress, and shoes dyed to match—I came out the villain, at least in her eyes. Not that I was bitter or anything. Even now I sensed my jaw tightening in her presence.

I scanned the rest of the room. Dark woodwork with cracked varnish and dated green wallpaper that puckered at the seams made the overstuffed room feel gloomy and neglected. Water stains dotted the ceiling and ran down one wall. The rug was stained and bare in spots, as was the furniture. The place was cluttered with piles of newspaper, boxes stacked upon boxes, and curio shelves crammed with dusty relics.

People milled around, some in closed-off groups, sharing hushed conversation. Others filled disposable plates from the platters of food laid out on the dining room table. Two elderly women sat primly on what could only be described as a settee.

If we'd walked in on a holiday party, it might be one of the worst ever.

Dad was busy talking to a man I didn't recognize. I was about to join them when Jack returned.

"I didn't know you were acquainted with Uncle Sy," he said.

"Oh, this is your uncle's house?" I wondered which of the men present might be his uncle. Then I realized the others were all wearing suits and most of the women were in dresses or nice pantsuits—if there is such a thing as a nice pantsuit. I felt a little underdressed in my jeans. At least I'd coupled that with a dressier top, a glittery red number with a draped neckline. Cathy had raved about how it flattered my figure and complexion.

Then I noticed something my eyes hadn't caught the first time I'd scanned the room. The official guests were all dressed in somber colors: blacks, charcoal grays, and muted purples.

"Your Uncle Sy . . ." I began.

A nearby man raised a bottle of Michelob in a toast. "To Sy!"

More beverages were raised in his honor, while a number of those in attendance did the sign of the cross.

"May he rest in peace," another said.

I sent a panicked look toward Dad. We'd crashed a wake.

Chapter 7

Dad seemed quick to catch on to the real reason for the gathering. Soon, he was buzzing from one mourner to another like a bee collecting pollen, offering sympathy with a pat on the hand and a consoling expression.

"I'm sorry about your Uncle Sy," I said to Jack.

"My great uncle, actually," Jack explained. "My mother's uncle. I'm surprised you knew him at all. He was a bit of a hermit. I think his picture was in the dictionary under 'curmudgeon.'" Jack leaned an elbow against the top of an upright piano wedged just inside the living room. If he'd worn a suit coat, he ditched it at the same time as his overcoat. But he'd kept the teal-and-gray tie, which looked kind of snazzy, as Dad would say, against his freshly pressed dress shirt. He'd even shaved his ordinarily scruffy face. With his olive skin, intense brown eyes, and hair freshly combed, Jack had only gotten better looking with age. In high school, a lot of girls weren't interested in smart, gangly, geeky Jack. Their loss. Although he'd also picked up a bit of a paunch, probably from sampling a little too much of his own food, it didn't take away from his appeal. The man was just reaching his prime.

And he was waiting for a response. From me. What were we talking about? Oh, yes, Uncle Sy. "I didn't know him," I admitted.

When Jack raised a jaunty eyebrow, I added, "I'm here for Dad, mainly."

"Huh," Jack said. "I didn't know they were acquainted either. Small town, I guess."

"I gather he'd met your Uncle Sy on more than one occasion. Was he sick long?"

"Only all his life. Here." He grabbed my hand. "Come see the shrine." He led me to the fireplace mantel, not that there was a fireplace, at least not anymore. The opening had been sealed and wallpapered over, an apparent victim to central heating, but at least they'd kept the wood mantel. Several framed pictures there showed Uncle Sy. He was alone in all but one of them, a grumpy expression on his face and his arms crossed in front of him. The lone exception was a black-and-white photo of a group of men, dressed in military uniforms, standing stiffly. I caught that signature grumpy look on a man in the back row.

Jack tapped the photo. "Korea. Uncle Sy fought at the Battle of Triangle Hill. If you want to know any more about it, ask anyone in the room. I'm sure we all know it by heart." He leaned toward my ear. "But be warned. Uncle Sy never had a kind word for anyone. Everyone here today is here either because they're expected to be or to stake their claim on their share of the estate."

"And you are . . . ?"

"Expected to be here, although Mother asked me specifically to bring the truck." He winked. Moments later, however, his smile dimmed. I followed his line of vision to where his mother sat, also with her arms crossed, with that same icy stare. Maybe it never had anything to do with me. It seemed to be hereditary. The Wallace glare. I bet it had its own chromosome. She gestured for her son to join her.

"Sorry. Gotta go." He squeezed my arm. "Try the deviled eggs. They're my special recipe."

I found the punchbowl perched on a corner of the dining room table. The recommended deviled eggs were nearby, so I snagged one and nibbled on it. While it tasted amazing, I hoped Dad would be ready to leave soon.

One nice thing about the punch bowl was the absence of company. One of the Wallaces' relatives—my guess, since she had that same glare—was hovering over the desserts. She was fully engaged in that activity, so I didn't have to carry out any coherent conversations or answer any sticky questions, such as how I knew Sy or what I was doing there.

I stopped to inspect a curio cabinet; every shelf was jammed full of knickknacks and figurines. No toys among them, though. I thought I recognized an old Hummel amid a bunch of tacky thrift-store fodder.

When I turned around, the woman eyed me suspiciously.

"Sy was quite a collector," I managed.

She continued to eye me as she chewed.

The bad thing about my location by the punch bowl was that it left me vulnerable to attack from the rear. Mrs. Wallace came up to the table, effectively trapping me. She dipped her chin and greeted the woman standing by me. "Meredith." Friendly group.

She then focused that familiar glare on me. "Hello, Elizabeth." She straightened the napkins and used one to sop up several stray drops of punch. I'm sure she assumed I'd been the one who dribbled. After she'd done a thorough job, she said, "The table is an antique, of course. Has been in the family for a number of years. I've always admired it."

"Mother has, too," Meredith said, then paused to swallow, "and the matching hutch, which I believe Uncle Sy had promised to her."

Mrs. Wallace blinked, as if she couldn't believe what she was hearing. "Well, it would be a shame to separate them. I'm sure it's all in Sy's will."

"If he had a will," Meredith said.

I was in no-man's-land in the family squabble for Uncle Sy's worldly goods.

"I was just remarking that Sy was quite a collector," I said.

"Is that why you're here, Elizabeth?" Mrs. Wallace said. "I'll make sure you're notified when we have the estate sale."

"That's not what I meant," I said.

"She was admiring the Hummel," Meredith said.

"The Hummel will have to be appraised," Mrs. Wallace said.

"I don't collect Hummel, and I'm not here for an advance peek at the estate sale." Although if the toys I'd seen were from Uncle Sy's collection, I'd keep an eye on the notices. I figured this might be the best time to scout for information. "I did hear that your Uncle Sy collected toys."

"Probably," Meredith said. "He seemed to have collected everything else."

"Who told you that?" Mrs. Wallace asked me. She glanced at her son, and then used her X-ray vision to render my skull invisible and probe my very thoughts. Or maybe it only felt that way. "Valuable toys?"

"I don't know the value." That much was true. "And I'm not looking to buy. I heard he was leaving a toy collection to the museum." I left out the part about having seen the collection, carried into our shop by a man now dead.

"I don't know if I've ever seen any toys here," Mrs. Wallace said. "Are you sure about this? Who did you hear it from?"

"I . . ." No way I was going to put Jillian on the hook for spilling the beans. "A man came into the shop." I proceeded to describe the dead man, from his scrubs to his parka to his tanned, pockmarked face. "I didn't catch his name. I gather he was acquainted with Sy."

"I don't know who that could be," Mrs. Wallace said.

"Maybe Tonya's boy, Peter?" Meredith suggested.

Mrs. Wallace vigorously shook her head. "Not a single pockmark on him. Peter's father was a dermatologist. I think they tied Peter's hands to the bedposts when he had the chicken pox so he wouldn't scratch. And he certainly wouldn't be tan."

"One thing you can say about this family," Meredith said, "we have excellent collagen."

"I suppose that if we do come across any toys, we might be able to make a deal," Mrs. Wallace said.

A better businesswoman would have handed her a card. I merely shrugged.

"Sy was a bit of a hoarder," Mrs. Wallace said. "It's going to take a lot of work to clear all this stuff out."

"I suppose that will have to wait until an executor is named," Meredith said. "Of course, that could take even longer if no will is found and it has to go through probate. It, uh, might be in our best interest to work together."

Mrs. Wallace narrowed her eyes.

Meredith blathered on. "I'm sure there are things that you are partial to, and I know there are a few small things Mother and I have always admired. Amid all the junk, of course."

"You think your mother is going to be executor, don't you?" Mrs. Wallace asked.

I took a step backward, but there wasn't enough room. It put me right up against the curio cabinet, which rattled.

"Careful!" both of them said simultaneously.

They moved just enough that I was able to excise myself from the tight space and leave them alone to divvy up the booty.

I glanced over at Dad, but he was fully engaged in conversation. My gaze swept the room and found an unoccupied folding chair opposite the two older ladies on the settee. They looked harmless enough.

I claimed the chair just before a man approached from the opposite direction. I went to set my punch cup on a nearby table.

"Ah ah ah," one of the women warned. "I wouldn't do that if I were you." She poked the other lady in the ribs. "The family thinks it's a Duncan Phyfe."

The ladies shared a brief giggle, then resumed their more somber, funereal expressions.

I cradled my cup in my hands instead and regarded the two women. "Are you family?" While they resembled each other, they didn't share many of the Wallace characteristics. These two had more playful, impish features.

"Heavens no," one of them said, waving a wrinkled, arthritic hand in protest.

"We mustn't sound too excited about that, dear," the other said.

The first turned to me. "We're neighbors." She pointed toward the side window. If I recalled correctly, there was an equally intimidating Victorian in that general direction.

"How long have you been neighbors with Sy?" I asked. "I'm Elizabeth McCall, by the way." I nodded in lieu of a handshake. No way was I going to risk losing this chair by standing up.

"Always," the first one said, her eyes dancing. "And I'm Irene Dedrick. This is my sister, Lenora."

"Sisters," I said. And then Irene's other comment caught up with me. "Always?"

They grinned and nodded, all overly bright lipstick and dentures. "Both houses have been in the families for simply years. *I* was born in the house," Irene boasted.

Lenora sighed. "Because I was born in a hospital, I'm a second-class citizen." But the twinkle in her eye proved her irritation false.

"So you two must have known Sy pretty well," I said.

"Oh, good heavens, yes." Lenora leaned closer to me. "The man was a total—"

Irene interrupted with a loud throat clearing. "Watch your language among the young people," she said.

"I'm not that young," I said.

"How'd you know what I was going to say?" Lenora protested.

Irene smiled coyly. "We both know what Sy was. Can't change it now, and it doesn't make any sense to try to hide it." She gestured at the room. "Not a person here who didn't know it."

"I'm afraid I didn't know him at all. I'm here with my dad." I pointed to where Dad was standing, still working the room.

Lenora shook a bony finger in his direction. "Your dad was the sheriff, right?"

"Chief of police, actually," I said. "Now retired."

"Thought I'd seen that face around," Irene said. "He's gotten older, but then, who hasn't?"

"He interrogated us once," Lenora explained. "He was very nice about it, as I recall."

I could feel my eyebrows hit the ceiling. "My dad . . . ?" There was something a little enchanting about these elderly women in their polyester skirt suits and orthopedic shoes. Maybe it was the pixie-like mischievous grins. I liked them immediately. "Were you ladies being naughty?" I teased.

They looked guiltily at each other. "Maybe a little," Irene admitted. "But if you live next door to someone for more than eighty years, do you really think you'll get along all the time?"

"For a number of years there, we had a right good feud going," Lenora added.

"With Sy DuPont?" I asked.

Irene winced. "Took a nasty turn in the seventies. All those wild parties over here." She folded her arms and leaned back. "Leisure suits and disco music blaring at all hours. And we weren't invited to any of them!"

"Sy had wild parties?" I said. It didn't fit with the antisocial-looking man in the pictures.

Lenora waved off the question. "That phase didn't last long. Confidentially . . ." She scanned the area to see who might be nearby, then said a little too loudly, in almost a stage whisper, "I think he was just trying to get laid."

Several smirks and titters from nearby betrayed the fact that she'd been overheard, and I suspected that's what she'd intended all along.

"Oh, look at her blush." Irene pointed at me. "Been a long time since either one of us blushed like that."

"I wasn't sure young people blushed anymore," Lenora said. "Don't let my sister annoy you. We can talk about something else."

I reached into my purse for my phone. "Perhaps there is something you can help me with." I pulled up the picture of the toy. "If you knew Sy for such a long time, have you ever seen this toy before?"

Irene took the phone first and squinted at it, moving it farther away from herself. "I'm afraid I didn't bring my glasses." She passed it to Lenora.

Lenora rummaged through her gigantic mauve handbag and fished out a pair of reading glasses. "Well, will you look at that!" she said, scrutinizing the picture of the two boxers. "It's Fred and Ginger."

"I think they're actually boxers," I said, hoping that Lenora no longer operated a moving vehicle.

Lenora responded with a throaty laugh. "Oh, I know they're boxers. You must think I'm blind as a bat. But when you wound it up with the little key on the bottom, they moved more like dancers than fighters. So we used to call them Fred and Ginger, and it made Squiggy so mad."

"Squiggy?"

By this time Irene was laughing and trying to focus on the picture of the toy. Lenora continued. "Our father had taken us all to the pictures. Of course, children were mainly taken to cartoons, but our father said all that stuff was fluff and nonsense, so he took us to see Fred Astaire and Ginger Rogers. Oh my, the dancing." She clasped her hands together, cherishing the memories. "The costumes and the dresses that swished and swirled. And such high heels!" She brought her hands to her lips. "Fred and Ginger were the bee's knees."

"But Squiggy . . . uh, Sy didn't think so?" I asked.

"He was a sourpuss even back then." Irene handed me back the phone. "Sy had this toy, you say?"

"I understand he intended to donate it to the toy museum," I said.

"Well, that explains what happened to it." Lenora's brows furrowed. "Where is it now?"

I was taken aback by her question, which came out a little like a demand. Well, more than a little. Irene and Lenora were forces to be reckoned with. "I . . ." Then it hit me. I still didn't know what had become of the toys. "I don't know," I finally said.

But they weren't going to let that pass unexplained. They stared at me expectantly.

"A man brought it and some others into our shop to get an estimate of their value," I finally said.

"Sy?" Lenora asked.

Irene shook her head. "Sy never went anywhere at the end. People came to him."

"The man I met was much younger," I said.

"How young?" Irene asked.

"Forties maybe?" I said, then informed them about the suntan, pockmarks, and scrubs. When I got to the scrubs, Lenora got animated.

"The aide dude!" she shouted.

"Aide *dude*?" I asked, a little more quietly. Our conversation was garnering a few disapproving scowls. I leaned closer, but I wasn't sure these two had a mute button.

"The last fellow Sy fired," Lenora said. "At least I think he was fired. Some of Sy's health care aides got fired and some of them quit, but none of them lasted long, not with his sunny disposition." She stopped, looking like she'd just remembered where she was. She did a brief sign of the cross before continuing. "I heard Sy yelling one day last week. Then that fellow stopped coming and that young woman took over. Real ditz. My, was she bossy! Moved right in, for all the good it did. Sy died a couple days later."

"You must have seen a lot of Sy. When did he tell you all of this?"

Irene waved off my question as if it were absurd. "Oh, we never *talked* to Sy."

"Not since the seventies," Lenora said. "I think that's what the nice policeman suggested." She pointed back toward my father.

"Then how did you know what was happening?" I asked.

"Well," Lenora said, "you might say that neighbors watch out for each other." She leaned back primly in the settee, then allowed her gaze to rest on her sister.

"You watch the house?" I asked.

"No more than Sy used to watch us," Irene said, although she squirmed a little when admitting it.

"So you think the man I met, the man with the toy, was Sy's health aide?" That explained the scrubs. I couldn't recall if he was still wearing them when he was lying dead in the store. I tried to replay the image, but Dad had warned me that human memory didn't work like a video recorder. If a witness didn't remember something the first time he was asked, he wasn't likely to remember it later. In fact, Dad insisted, witnesses would manufacture information at that later point, their subconscious mind supplying details the investigators wanted to hear.

I snapped to attention. I found it weird to think of myself as a witness. When I cast a glance in Dad's direction, he was staring at me, as if he were a part of my conversation as well. *Keep going*, I could almost hear him say.

"Did you know his name?" I asked the sisters. "The aide, I mean."

"Well, we never actually talked to him either, you see," Lenora said.

"Oh, I did," Irene said.

"Know his name?" I asked. I hated to admit it, but beating Dad to a clue was getting fun, like making a good move in a strategy game and seeing things fall into place. I tried to dampen my own excitement. This wasn't a game. We were talking about a man who had died in our shop.

"Oh, no. I didn't know his name," Irene said. "But I did talk to him. Once. He returned our recycling box. They'd gotten mixed up at the curb or something. He was very nice about it." Her countenance fell when she said that last part. "Too nice."

"Here we go again," Lenora said, rolling her eyes. "You'll see, it's a great conspiracy."

"I never said it was a conspiracy," Irene said. "Just an observation." She silenced her sister with a dismissive wave and redirected the conversation toward me. "As you get older you'll notice. Some people have no patience at all with old folks. We're just a time drain and a burden. But not everyone's like that." She waved her finger at me. "But those who do bother with old folks, that doesn't mean they're naturally nice either."

I nodded. "Con men, for instance."

"Right," Irene said. "Like the guy who wanted us to pay him three thousand dollars for a thousand-dollar roof repair. We get them all the time, and they always act like they're there to help us, to keep our house from falling down around us. As if they're doing us a favor when they take our money. Then there are the do-gooders."

"The do-gooders?" I asked. "What do they do?"

Lenora rolled her eyes. "Good. They do *good*. I've never understood the problem."

Irene wagged a finger again. "It's *why* they do good. Some of them, they'll shovel your walk or rake your leaves if you take their pamphlet. Fine. I get them. Then there's the kind that act all bubbly and interested, as if they've just met the Queen of England. But a little patronizing. Almost like talking to children."

I nodded again. Somehow I felt a little less guilty for letting my attention wander when an older patron came into the store and told a long story. "So the man . . ."

"Seemed overly enthusiastic about working with old people," Irene said. "I figured working with Sy would beat that right out of him."

"You never saw him with Sy's toy?" I said.

Irene wagged her finger at me again, and Lenora sat up agitatedly.

"Oh, no," Irene said, "we never saw him with the toy. If we had, there'd have been a lot more feuding going on."

"Why's that?" I asked.

"Because," Lenora said. "Sy didn't have any right to donate it to the museum or give it to that young man. The toy didn't belong to Sy. He must have taken it, that scoundrel."

Irene dipped her chin in agreement. "Fred and Ginger belong to us."

Chapter 8

Irene's claim added a whole new wrinkle to the situation. Clearly she and Lenora had motive—that is, if *Sy* were the victim. I glanced up to see Mrs. Wallace discretely shoving the family silver into her pocket. The heirs apparent were falling over themselves in their attempts to acquire their share of Sy's possessions. They, too, might have had a motive to speed dear Uncle Sy's departure, but what reason might they have had to off their uncle's health care aide?

There was a tapping at the door, and before anyone could answer it, Ken Young pushed his way in. He was in casual uniform, a brief layer of snow clinging to the fur lining his coat and dusting the tops of his boots. He didn't bother to remove them or stamp off the snow. He put his hands on his hips and scanned the room. "Who's in charge here?"

Mrs. Wallace ran to the door to meet him, as did Meredith and a couple of other contenders. This was going to be an epic battle.

But Ken wasn't going to referee it. He looked from face to face, and then addressed them as a group, loudly, so everybody could hear. "I wanted to let you know," he said, "that I chased away a gang of young hoodlums casing the place this morning while y'all were at the funeral. I scared them off before they managed to break in, but let me know if you notice anything missing or out of the ordinary."

"Imagine that," Irene said, "happening under our very noses."

"But we were at the funeral," Lenora added.

"Oh, that's right," Irene said. "I don't like what's happening to the neighborhood."

By this time Ken had spotted my father and made his way over to him. Several family members watched as the chief's snow-covered boots also made the trip. Eventually a few of the relatives compromised enough to locate paper towels and clean up the puddles.

Ken took off his hat and shook my father's hand. "Well, well. We seem to be running into each other quite a bit. Did you know Sy well?"

"Been called to the house before." Dad folded his arms across his chest. "I imagine you've been here before as well," he said coyly.

I excused myself from the two sisters and went to join Dad. "How's the investigation coming?" I asked Ken.

"Which one?" Ken replied. "The investigation into the attempted break-in is pretty cut and dried. I've got a good idea who might be up to their old tricks."

"The other one," Dad said. "Have you been able to identify the murder victim yet?"

Ken shook his head.

"I might have something," I said.

"Remember something new?" Ken asked. "Because if you would like to amend your statement, we can meet at the station."

"It's not something I forgot," I said, not liking his officious tone. "It's something I learned here."

Dad took my elbow. "Liz, are you sure we should bring this up?"

I didn't know what Dad was concerned about, but this was information Ken needed to know. "I think the victim worked in this house. As Sy's health aide."

Ken cursed under his breath. "Do you have any idea what this means?"

"It means I might have helped you figure out who the victim was. I would think you'd be grateful."

Dad let out a sigh. Apparently I was missing something that these two experienced lawmen had already figured out.

Dad leaned closer. "You see, Lizzie, this creates another problem. By tying the dead man to this house, it also puts into question how Sy died."

Mrs. Wallace shuffled over. Despite our muted tones, apparently the family had been listening. "But Uncle Sy died of a heart attack."

"Probably," Ken said.

"Probably?" Mrs. Wallace repeated, and a titter of comments buzzed through the room.

Ken hung his head. "If there's any question that his death might be part of another investigation, we really ought to have the medical examiner reopen the file."

Mrs. Wallace looked fit to be tied, and it might've been safer for Ken if she had been—and gagged as well. Her lips quivered, but no sound came out, until finally she said, "But we just got that blasted man buried!"

When the family rushed him in protest, Ken put his hands up. "I'm not saying we're going to dig him up. And I'm not saying his death is suspicious." He glared at me. "What I am saying is that now Sy's death might be connected to another open investigation. We will keep the family informed."

I tugged on my dad's sleeve. "Is he saying that Sy might've been murdered?"

"He's saying he has to consider it. Which means the body most likely will be exhumed and more closely examined for cause of death. Tox screens and all that."

Mrs. Wallace stamped her foot. "You've got another think coming if you expect any of us to pay to put him back in the ground."

Ken looked like he'd be gladly willing to sink into the ground and take Sy's place. "Listen, if we have to exhume Sy's body, we will make sure he is . . . replaced. At the village's expense."

While the relatives continued to pepper him with questions, Dad pulled me aside. "I'm afraid this doesn't bode well for us, Lizzie." I started to protest, but he went on. "I shouldn't have dragged us here. Think about it. What does the man's death in the shop have in common with Sy's death?"

I struggled to figure out what he was implying. Both deaths had taken place in Ken's jurisdiction of East Aurora. Within a week of each other. And, of course, both men had apparently been in possession of the same toy, now fondly renamed Fred and Ginger. I still wasn't sure what Dad was hinting at.

"You and me," he said. "Specifically, me. If a second autopsy suggests that some kind of foul play led to Sy's death, I've now been placed at both scenes."

"You told me you haven't been here for years."

"That's true. But you gotta figure the good chief's alarm bells started ringing on overload the second he walked into the room and saw me here."

After about fifteen minutes of questioning Chief Young about what would happen next, the mourners at Sy's wake started to settle down, much to the chagrin of Irene and Lenora, who seemed to be enjoying the show immensely. Family members covered leftovers with plastic wrap and aluminum foil, and one by one, the lights in the house were switched on, not because the sun had set, but because the gray snow clouds obscured what little light came in through the wavy glass windows.

I scored one more clue for the evening when I flipped on the lamp above a small secretary desk. On the top of a pile of mail was a bill from a local health care service, the same one Parker and I had used to help us take care of Dad for those first few weeks after he was released from the hospital.

Dad had sunk into a chair and was rubbing his knee. It was time to get him home, or at least back to Cathy and Parker's, where he could elevate and ice it. I had gained Jack's attention and asked for our coats when the door flung open and a young woman walked in. She was in her late teens or early twenties at most, maybe even a student based on the bulging backpack slung over one shoulder. She wore yoga pants and a heavy sweatshirt but was still woefully underdressed for the weather. She stopped in the entryway, her jaw agape as she stared from face to face.

Irene elbowed Lenora. "It's the ditz!" she said.

Mrs. Wallace walked over to greet the latecomer. Ken watched with interest, as did my father, as if they expected trouble to materialize. I tried to recall what the two sisters had said about a ditz coming to replace the aide who had died. Was this young woman Sy's last health care aide? Had the old man died under her care?

And did she have motive to kill either of the men? I supposed she could have killed the aide to replace him. Although as a motive, it seemed sketchy. Home health care jobs always seemed to be in abundance and didn't sound all that appealing. Sponge baths and bedpans and such. I wasn't sure if they paid enough to overcome the indignities of the job, much less to make them enticing enough to kill for. But what if the former aide had to be eliminated to allow this woman access to kill Sy? Along with the rest of the guests, I couldn't peel my eyes away from the girl.

"I think I saw you at the funeral," Mrs. Wallace said, "but we're about to close up here." She started guiding the newcomer to the door.

The young woman planted her feet, put her hands on her hips, and stood her ground. "I'm not going anywhere. I'll thank you all to clear out, and take your mess with you."

Mrs. Wallace grew nearly apoplectic. Her face paled to white, then her cheeks flamed red. Her fists tensed, and she vibrated in place. She resembled one of those rockets in Florida, when the engines have fired up, moments before they leave the ground. "Excuse me?" she said. "And who exactly do you think you are?"

A rumble of conversation went up among the relatives. I was glad Ken and Dad were there, because the Wallace tribe was getting worked up. Lenora and Irene craned their necks for a better view of what was transpiring.

The young woman didn't seem alarmed. She lowered her backpack to the floor, unzipped it, and rummaged through the notebooks and papers inside. Finally, she tugged out a sheet of paper and held it in her teeth while she rezipped her pack. She smoothed a few wrinkles from it by rubbing it across her thigh. Then she held up what appeared to be some kind of official document.

"My name is Kimmie Kaminski. Well, Kimmie Kaminski DuPont. And as of five days ago, Sy's wife."

For five solid seconds, time stood still.

Then everyone started talking at once. Some rushed forward, others stepped back in shock, and almost all the residents of the room collided with one another, jostling like bumper cars.

Ken pushed forward to examine the document. Once he did, he whistled for silence.

"That can't be genuine," Mrs. Wallace said. Her complexion had cycled back to ashen.

"I'll check it out with the courthouse and make sure it's been filed properly," Ken said, "but it looks real to me."

Kimmie Kaminski DuPont stood straighter, strutting all five feet four inches of herself over to the coat rack, where she removed an armload of coats and started slinging them randomly to the crowd. "Now, Chief, if you could ask everyone to leave. I'm tired, and I didn't invite any of these trespassers inside *my* house."

Chapter 9

The mourners slowly made their way to their cars. They had to. If they'd moved any faster, all the silver, china, and bric-a-brac they'd shoved into their pockets—when they thought no one was looking—would have clanked and clattered. Dad had volunteered himself and me to escort Lenora and Irene down to the sidewalk and then back up the parallel walk one house over. From next door, they would indeed have a pretty good view of all the goings-on at Sy's house but wouldn't be able to hear anything, which is probably how they'd mistaken the old gentleman's new twentysomething wife for a health care worker.

"Sy, you old devil," I said under my breath. This was going to put a new twist on the Wallaces' family reunions.

Before I could corral Dad to the car, he'd taken up the trail of some footprints around the old man's—or rather, *Kimmie's*—house. A fresh layer of snow had fallen on top, but it couldn't obscure where a group of people had trudged around the house, from door to window to window, apparently searching for a way in. Soon, Ken joined us.

"These from the fellows you took in earlier?" Dad asked.

"Well, uh," Ken said. "I didn't actually take them in."

Dad squatted to get a closer look at the tracks in the snow, then peered off at more footprints cutting through the yard. His face quirked into a smug half smile. "They got away from you, didn't they?"

"It was harder running through the snow than I thought it would be," Ken said. "I got a good look at them, though."

"Anybody I know?" Dad used his cane to pull himself back up.

Ken exhaled, sending up a puff of white breath that momentarily obscured his face. "I'll let you know when I catch them."

"Any idea who?" Dad asked.

"Kids." Ken pulled up his collar against the chill. "If they were over eighteen, they were just barely. It's a small town. I only have to catch one and ask around to figure out who he runs with. Bring 'em all in. One of them will talk or someone will take a plea. You know how these things work."

Dad was silent as he continued to stare at the snow-covered tracks. "Think it's a coincidence that they targeted this house on this particular day?"

I winced. Dad used the *c*-word on purpose. One thing I learned as a cop's daughter, the police hate coincidences.

Ken wouldn't be baited. He merely shrugged.

Dad took off his glove and used a knuckle to rub the corner of his mouth. "Lots of coincidences. The man who died at the shop, working for a man who also died this week and whose house was broken into."

"And occupied by a woman none of the family knows," Ken added. "Yeah, I know."

Dad started laughing and kept laughing as he walked toward the car. I had to run to keep up with him. When he got there, he opened the door and spun back toward Ken. "Good luck, Chief. I just gotta tell you, I'm glad this isn't my case." He saluted with his cane and climbed into the car, leaving Ken standing in the front yard of Sy's house in the swirling snow.

# # #

The laughter died out pretty quickly as we pulled away from the curb.

"Can we go back to the shop?" Dad asked.

I shook my head. "Still a crime scene. The chief said he'd let us know when it was safe to go back."

"I think he's keeping us out of our own place on purpose. I suspect he doesn't like me very much."

"Why would he dislike you?" Perhaps the taunting I'd just witnessed was a clue.

"Young fellow trying to make his way in a new job. He doesn't want an old geezer around all the time, showing him how it's done."

"Are you a show-off, Dad?"

"Well, not really. I meant *he* might think that."

I signaled to turn down the street that would take us to Parker and Cathy's house.

Dad cleared his throat. "I'm not ready to go back yet. I'm not ready to sit back in a recliner, locked out of my house and out of my shop, and wait to see where the evidence falls and how much of it piles up against me. I want to do something." Dad turned and gave me his father-knows-best expression.

I pulled into an available parking space, shifted the car into park, and twisted in my seat to face him. "You're retired, Dad. You're not part of the force anymore."

"Technically, I've been deputized."

I glared at him.

"You could be my partner," he said. "You've always been observant and insightful."

"I already am your partner. We sell old toys now, remember?"

"Not when our shop is cordoned off with crime scene tape, we don't. I'm not saying we take over the investigation. But there are a lot of angles to cover, and that young man can't be everywhere at once. Maybe we just help out a little and check on a few things." He flashed me a smile, his eyes twinkling. "What do you say?"

I could feel myself being swept into one of Dad's schemes. That's the thing about folks who are sincerely out to save the world: they make excellent recruiters. "What exactly did you have in mind?"

Moments later, we were back on the road, on our way to the health care agency the victim had worked for. I knew a lot about the place already. They were small but had five-star ratings just about everywhere, which, considering what they did, was impressive. The two different women who'd come to the house were personable and professional and flirted just enough with Dad to get him to do their bidding, which was basically following the doctor's orders.

A police car was leaving as we arrived. Dad craned his neck to see who was driving it.

"Looks like this angle is covered," I said. "Still want to go in?"

"Yes, but let's give them a few minutes," he said. Dad watched the building and the clock, as if frozen in place.

I rummaged through my purse and found a pack of cinnamon gum. I also encountered my nail file and spruced up my nails while we waited. I had just brushed the dust from my pant legs when Dad reached for the car door.

"Now," he said.

I scrambled to stuff everything back into my purse and had to run across the parking lot to keep up with him. By the time I got to the door, he was holding it open.

The receptionist in the modest anteroom looked up and smiled in recognition. "Liz McCall. Henry. How nice to see you." She shifted her attention to my father. "I was just thinking about you."

Dad leaned his elbows on the desk and raised an eyebrow. "Good thoughts, I hope."

The receptionist blushed, just a little. The rather plain fiftyish woman had been very concerned when I'd been there to contract help for Dad, and now, watching them grin at each other, I wondered if there'd been another reason. I checked the nameplate sitting on her desk. Edith Kingston. It would be helpful to know her name if she ended up being my stepmother someday.

"The police were here a few minutes ago," she said.

Dad had the gall to act surprised. "No trouble, I hope."

"I'm afraid so." Edith cocked her head and sighed. "It seems that one of our aides has apparently been killed."

"How dreadful!" Dad put on his most sympathetic expression. "I'm so sorry. Was it someone you knew well?"

And without even the hint of interrogation, out the information flew. The dead man was one Sullivan O'Grady. The police had presented Edith with a picture of the corpse.

"Can you imagine?" Edith's eyes glistened at the point of tears, and Dad murmured that he was sure it was all in the line of duty and my, wasn't she brave. This from the man who had told me to suck it up when I came down with chicken pox on my tenth birthday.

Sullivan, a.k.a. Sully to his friends and family, was a model employee, but not quite the model family man, apparently. He had two addresses on file, the first on a quiet street in a neighborhood of modest ranch houses just outside the village. This he had shared with his wife. The more recent address was a former fleabag motel, also just outside of town, recently converted to fleabag efficiency units, rented by the month, and populated primarily by the recently single.

"Sad how many marriages break up these days," Dad said. "I wonder what went wrong."

"Couldn't have been Sully," Edith said. "Everybody loved him. Military veteran. Hard worker. Faithful to a fault."

"You know, the service can change people. Some of our boys overseas have seen too much. I gather that O'Grady was injured over there?"

Edith's brows furrowed. "Not that I know about."

"Well, I thought it might explain something odd. See, the chief told us that O'Grady had no fingerprints, and I wondered if maybe his fingers were burned or something."

"I'd have no way of knowing that. Only . . . he'd have to be fingerprinted to become a licensed CNA in New York State. He must have had fingerprints at that point."

Dad nodded thoughtfully, then cocked his head. "O'Grady never had any problems with any of his other patients?"

By this point, I had kind of faded into the background. Edith only had eyes for my father, and I suspected that any contributions to the conversation from me would probably be construed as interference. Besides, I was good at fading into the background.

"Oh, no. Nothing like that. All the patients loved him," she said, then dropped her gaze. "Well, almost all. Some are never pleased. You could send out Mother Theresa, and they'd find something wrong with her."

"Any that we might talk with?" Dad said.

"I'm afraid not," Edith said.

"Privacy rules?" Dad inched closer. I wasn't sure if he was seriously interested in Edith or just playing James Bond to her Miss Moneypenny.

"I'm afraid their names wouldn't help. Sully worked mainly with terminal patients. It's not easy work, but he had a special gift."

"None of his former patients are alive?" Dad asked.

Edith shook her head, then dabbed at her eyes with a tissue. "And no complaints. At least not formal ones. He was very good with patients and their families."

"Never any hints of anything . . . missing or misplaced?"

"What do you mean?" She raised an eyebrow.

"Oh, you know how families can be sometimes." Dad adopted a casual air. "Aunt Matilda, who nobody has bothered with for years, supposedly left them an antique snuffbox dating back to the Revolutionary War, and it's gone missing. Good old Auntie probably hocked it for bingo money years ago, but the stranger who was in the house during those final days makes a good suspect."

Edith crossed her arms. "We've had that happen. Turns my stomach." She looked up at Dad. "But not with Sully. He was a dream employee. Going to be hard to replace that man."

"What can you tell me about the person you sent to replace him?"

"What do you mean?"

Dad leaned his elbows on the counter. "Well, when Sully didn't report for work, you must have sent someone out to cover his patient."

"No." Edith shook her head. "We never knew he wasn't working! Nobody told us he failed to show up. You could have knocked me over with a feather when the police said he'd been dead for days. And his client as well." She paused. "I suppose that's why nobody called." She bit her lip. "You don't think Mr. DuPont could have died of neglect, do you?" Her eyes went wild with panic. "That would be bad."

While Dad murmured vague reassurances, becoming more touchy-feely every moment, I sat back, literally, on the lumpy couch in the lobby and thumbed through a magazine while I unashamedly listened to the remainder of their conversation. Despite the privacy rules, Edith eventually let slip that Sully had also worked for the mayor's family when his father was terminal. Perhaps I could learn something about Sully from East Aurora's first lady.

By the time we left, Dad was loaded with potential leads and a possible love interest, while I'd sustained a paper cut and toxic exposure to a perfumed magazine insert.

"Home, James?" I said.

Dad shook his head. "Just beginning. How about the doughnut shop?"

"Back to your cop ways, huh? A peanut stick for your thoughts."

"Oh, they're not for me," he said. "We're going to pay a condolence call on the grieving widow."

# # #

Dad was good on his word and held the dozen dough-nuts he'd purchased unopened on his lap all the way to Mrs. O'Grady's house, outside of East Aurora, in a less historic—and more affordable—neighboring community. By the time we arrived, though, I'd downed half my coffee. I opened the car door and brushed the pieces of peanut that had fallen off my doughnut into the street. They'd make some enterprising chipmunk very happy.

The O'Grady house was like most of the other houses on the tree-lined street: modest two- or three-bedroom vinyl-sided ranches built in the 1950s, with asphalt driveways and large windows that looked into living rooms. They were popular with first-time buyers, and many of these houses were nesting grounds for young families, as evidenced by the explosion of half-buried Little Tikes cars and more than one perky snowman with rotting carrot noses.

Every square inch of the O'Grady's yard was trampled with tiny boot prints, and a snow disc lay half buried next to a mound of snow left from shoveling the drive. The sound of a crying child hit us before we made it to the door.

"Dad, maybe we shouldn't."

"Buck up, Lizzie," he said. "All part of the job."

I was about to remind him that my job was managing a toy store, but he was already half up the driveway. The front porch caught my attention. It was new and made of brick, while most of the others on the street were concrete with rusted railings. It was, however, untouched by a snow shovel, so we made our way to the more traveled side entry, and Dad rapped on the aluminum storm door. No way anyone could miss that racket.

By the time I caught up with him, a woman wearing a T-shirt, a stained, oversized cardigan, and yoga pants—and holding a howling toddler in her arms—answered the door. Her eyes were red and puffy. Apparently the police had recently given her the bad news.

"If you're selling doughnuts," she said, "I don't have the money right now."

"No, Mrs. O'Grady," Dad said. "I know this isn't a good time, but we're working with the police on the investigation. I was wondering if you had a few minutes to talk. Even if you don't, the doughnuts are for you."

The toddler unburied his head. Apparently he was familiar with the term "doughnuts." He lunged for the door handle.

Mrs. O'Grady wrestled the chubby wrist away from the door, then said, "Fine, come on in."

Dad ducked under a strand of low-hanging tinsel garland and followed her to a small landing, covered in shoes and boots. A handful of stairs led directly into the kitchen, where a few wet puddles, salt crystals, and dried footprints gave testimony to the fact that recent visitors hadn't removed their boots, so neither did we, although I did my best to dry mine on the sopping entry rug.

Mrs. O'Grady seated the child at a small table, where a slightly older girl sat coloring a picture of a reindeer. Soon both had doughnut halves in hand and the toddler was sucking down juice from a sippy cup.

Mrs. O'Grady gestured to the kitchen table, loaded with stacks of papers and riddled with scratches and dings, a few of which were filled in with dried food. Dishes overflowed the sink. The walls were decorated with crayon scrawls and food splatters, and the refrigerator was covered in magnets and artwork, featuring a green construction paper Christmas tree, its branches formed from traced child-sized handprints.

"Forgive the house," she said, then coughed into her sleeve. "We've been sick."

Meanwhile, the toddler left the table and was back at his mother's side, smearing a snotty face against her yoga pants before she picked him up and placed him on her lap. He rubbed one eye with his whole fist before leaning into his mother's chest. "I can't believe this is happening," Mrs. O'Grady said.

"I gather you were separated," Dad started.

That got the waterworks going. I found a box of tissues on a nearby table and slid them to her. She mouthed her thanks and grabbed a few. It took several minutes for her to regain her composure.

"Not because I didn't love Sully," she said. "He was a good dad. How am I going to . . . ?" She stopped talking while her breaths came quick and shallow.

Dad grabbed her arm. "Breathe slow and deep. It's okay."

When her breathing neared normal, Dad fetched her a glass of water from the sink.

She took several sips. "I told him I couldn't live like that anymore. I didn't think the separation would last forever. Sully's my soul mate. Was." She hiccupped and drank more water. "How am I going to do this without him?"

"Do this?" Dad said.

"Raise these kids. Alone." Her eyes widened, then she hugged the toddler even more frantically. "Sully always said he wanted a large family. I was an only child and lonely, so it sounded good to me. We got pregnant on our honeymoon, and that seemed to suit him fine."

"With your daughter?" I pointed to the girl still coloring silently at the table.

"Oh, no," she said. "Our son. Most of the kids are on a field trip with their home school group."

"Most of?" I said. "How many kids do you have?"

"Eight," she said. "I told him eight was my limit." She looked around the messy kitchen. "I should have put my foot down and stopped at six, but Sully could be so persuasive. Which is fine, but he wasn't carrying them for nine months, going through labor, and breastfeeding them while making sure the older ones kept up on their schoolwork. He was always at church or on mission trips, and he'd work long hours on that job of his. His clients were dying and needed him, he said. But sometimes we needed him here. Right?"

"He couldn't expect you to raise eight kids all by yourself," I said. Could he?

She sniffled twice, then blew her nose. "He didn't believe in divorce, either. I thought if he moved out for a little while, he'd see my point. But he wasn't moving back in until he realized that I wasn't going to have another baby.

"And now what am I going to do? Eight kids and all alone." Her breathing was becoming irregular again, so Dad coached her on how to calm down.

"Mrs. O'Grady," Dad said, "I have to ask. Was money an issue?"

She furrowed her brows. "As you can see, we don't live high off the hog, but we were never lacking for anything."

"It must have been difficult to support a family of eight children on what he earned as a home health aide. Food. Clothing. This house. Transportation." Since Mrs. O'Grady didn't answer, Dad rambled on. "I can see where it might be a temptation for some men to . . . supplement their income. Especially when maybe someone's not going to need money much longer . . . It makes sense, after all, to care for the living."

An entirely new expression overtook Mrs. O'Grady's face as she realized what my Dad was getting at.

"If you're saying my Sully stole anything, you're barking up the wrong tree." Her voice had risen, but when the toddler started stirring in her arms, she modulated her tone. "My husband was a very spiritual and moral man. If the Good Book was against it, Sully was against it, too. We might have been going through a rough stretch, but he would never steal from anyone, let alone a client who trusted him."

Dad was clearly now in the doghouse. Maybe it was time for some good cop/bad cop.

I gave Dad a disapproving stare and held it until I knew Mrs. O'Grady had seen it. Then I turned back to her. "I'm sure you're right. After all, there are other ways to make a budget balance."

"Exactly," she said. "Sully didn't believe in debt. He saved all the money for this house before we bought it. We got a good deal in a short sale and paid cash. Someone had totally trashed the place on the inside. We've been fixing it up little by little, using his military pension." She looked a little sheepish at the state of her house, then coughed into her sleeve, as if to remind us—or maybe herself—that she'd been sick.

"Did he, uh, build the front porch, by any chance?" I turned to Dad. "The *brick* porch?"

"Yeah, just before he left for his last mission trip. He was supposed to help lay the brick for a new clinic, and he said he wanted to practice. I wasn't about to complain. He did a beautiful job."

I nodded and sent Dad a look, just in case he was keeping score. This explained the bricklayer who wore scrubs. Just not who would want to kill him. I turned back to Mrs. O'Grady. "So he didn't leave you with a mortgage."

"Exactly. We didn't go out to eat, I clip more than my share of coupons, and yes, we believe in secondhand and hand-me-downs. But we were doing fine financially, so if you think he was tempted . . ."

I shook my head, as if that had been the last thought on my mind. Dad lowered his head to show suitable penance.

If Mrs. O'Grady had harbored any anger, it melted into reverie. "He could have had a better job, you know. He was smart. He was a combat medic in the army, and he could do just about anything the doctors could do. You should have seen the commendations he got. But Sully felt like it was his calling, working with folks who were about to . . . pass over." Her brow furrowed. "I guess those folks would be more vulnerable to theft, but not from Sully." Color rose in her cheeks. "They were blessed to have him there, I'm sure."

She closed her eyes. "Just more of a sacrifice than I was willing to make, him being gone those long hours and me here alone. There was never time for me. Or enough quality time for us. Sully had been talking about a date night, just the two of us. He hated that we were living apart. But I thought he was trying to talk me into more kids, so I stalled him. Now I feel selfish."

"No," I murmured. "I can see you have your hands full. And now with him gone . . . At least the house is paid for."

She sighed. "Sully made sure I would be taken care of. Financially, at least. We have a healthy bank account, money set aside for college and retirement. And I know he had decent life insurance in addition to the military survivor benefits." She blew out a breath. "I guess I need to call our lawyer and finance guy and start the ball rolling on all that." She forced a smile and brushed streaming tears away with the palm of her hand. "Sully always teased me that if something happened to him, I'd be a rich widow."

# # #

"A rich widow?" Cathy repeated with such excitement, she almost dropped her fork. We'd recounted the day's goings-on to Cathy and Parker over dinner. Or rather I did. Dad pretended to enjoy his meal.

Cathy had outdone herself in making dinner, and not in a good way. In the past, her meals had at least borne a resemblance to familiar foods. I was more likely to figure out who killed Sullivan O'Grady than to identify what she'd been aiming for when she'd assembled these ingredients in her casserole dish. At least the refrigerator biscuits were edible, if you peeled off the bottom layer of charcoal and skipped the doughy middles.

Cathy leaned both elbows on the table, sending her plethora of bracelets jingling as they slid down her arm. "Do you think she might have killed her husband? For the life insurance?"

"We asked where she was the night her husband was murdered," I said. "She claimed she was home with the kids."

"Unless she sneaked out and followed her husband," Cathy said, warming up. "Maybe she thought he was cheating on her." Cathy has a very active imagination.

Out of the corner of my eye, I spotted Othello get up from under the Christmas tree where he'd been lounging. He stretched, yawned, then stopped to sniff the air. We didn't give him a whole lot of table scraps, but if he came closer, tonight he was welcome to anything on my plate.

"She didn't say anything about an affair," Dad said.

"Well, he was a guy, right?" Cathy carried her empty plate to the sink.

"Hey," Parker objected. "Not all guys cheat."

Cathy came up behind him, putting her arms around him and doing her best sultry Marilyn Monroe impression. "Not even if the other woman is young and pretty and oh so interested in you?" She tapped his nose.

Parker froze for a moment, then said, "That depends. Can she cook?"

Dad shook with quiet laughter while Cathy snapped a dish towel at her husband. The skirmish ended when Parker managed to pull Cathy onto his lap.

I used the diversion to take a large forkful from my plate and drop it on the floor. Moments later, I was rewarded when Othello brushed up next to me on his way to the morsel I'd left him.

"But would she leave the kids home alone?" Dad asked, waving his butter knife in the air as he made his point. He was never that easy to sidetrack.

"How old is the oldest one?" Cathy asked.

I took a large sip of water. "Maybe twelve, but that's a guess from the picture tacked up on the fridge. Not old enough to watch over that brood."

"The oldest kids in large families tend to be very responsible," Cathy said, pushing herself back to her feet. "Like on that reality show with that big family."

"With legal problems of their own." Dad nudged his plate back as if he were full. "I don't think you'd be able to prove her alibi. If all the kids were sleeping, she could have sneaked out. I don't think you can name her as a suspect, though, unless you could place her nearer the scene. For instance, did anyone see her car out that night? Was she or her car captured on any of the security cameras on Main Street?"

"But she has a definite motive," Cathy said.

Dad rubbed the back of his neck. "He didn't force her into having all those kids. At one point, she felt the same way about it as he did. It might have been an issue that broke them up, but given time, who knows? Maybe they'd have worked through it."

"I also don't think she was following him," I said. "In all our talk, there was never the mention of another woman. So it's not like she was hoping to catch him in the act with some bimbo. What's the point in trailing him?"

"Unless she planned on killing him," Parker said.

"I don't think anyone was planning on killing him that night," I said.

Dad squinted at me but waited for me to supply the reason.

"Someone who had planned on killing Sullivan O'Grady would have brought a weapon, not hoped that those lawn darts were sharp enough and strong enough to do the job."

As my words sank in, Dad's smile grew broader, and I basked in the glow of his approval.

The moment was short lived. Cathy brought out dessert, a monstrosity of a gelatin salad. "I've been experimenting with vintage recipes," she said. "Not sure I'm going to make the tuna surprise again, but can you go wrong with Jell-O?"

Parker stared at the wriggling mass. "Are those turnips?"

Dad stopped her from scooping out a portion for him. "No thanks. I lived through the sixties. I think there's a law that says I don't have to do this again."

While the rest of us picked through our desserts, eating the Jell-O and leaving the odd contents on our plates, Dad gathered a pile of scratch paper and a mechanical pencil from the junk drawer.

"What are you doing?" I asked.

"I think it's time to make a suspect list."

"Is Mrs. O'Grady going on it?" Cathy asked.

Dad bobbed his head from left to right a few times. "For now. I did have another thought today when we were talking with her." He turned to me. "Did you catch it?"

"Another suspect?" I racked my brain trying to recall anything that Mrs. O'Grady might have said that pointed to anyone else. "She said she's the beneficiary of the life insurance. I don't recall her mentioning anyone else who would have profited from her husband's death."

Dad rapped his fingers on the table. "Not profited, exactly. But she said something a little odd. Her husband considered it his calling to help those who were about to cross over."

"Cross over what?" Parker said. "The River Styx? Death?"

"Wrong context," Dad said. "Crossing over Jordan, would be my guess. Still a metaphor for death. Crossing over Jordan into the Promised Land. One might question how much help he provided."

"I assume she meant that he helped make that transition as comfortable as possible," I said. "Not that he gave them a little push."

Dad shook his head gravely. "Never assume."

"Ooh," Cathy said. "A possible angel of death." I could tell she found this prospect even more titillating than a run-of-the-mill affair.

"So who would have had motive if that were the case?" Parker asked.

"His most recent client," I said. "Sy DuPont, if he felt his life was in danger. But why not just call the police?"

"You've messed up the timeline," Dad said. "By the time O'Grady was killed, Sy DuPont was already dead."

"He died when, exactly?" Cathy asked.

"We'd have to check the obit, but figure three days before the funeral, usually."

"A former client, then?" Cathy said. But when we all laughed, she amended it. "Okay, the *family* of a former client. Out of revenge or justice."

"Why at that moment and why with a lawn dart?" I asked.

"I still think the angel-of-death angle might be a good theory to share with Chief Young," Parker said. "It is his investigation. Make him chase it down."

I peered at Dad. "I guess we can do that. Just suggest the possibility to him. And we should make sure he knows about the bricklaying, so he doesn't waste too much time trying to figure out a more heinous reason for O'Grady's lack of fingerprints."

Dad pressed his lips together and closed his eyes, as if mentally weighing the idea. "Maybe after they do the autopsy on the old man."

"But Sullivan O'Grady would have been fired before Sy's death," Cathy said, using her fingers to make adjustments on an invisible timeline in front of her. "Hard to imagine him going back into the house, especially with Kimmie moved in and the snoop sisters watching the place."

"Let's not jump too far ahead of ourselves," Dad said. "First they need to figure out exactly how the old man died, but there are ways to kill someone that aren't instantaneous. So yes, it's possible that Sullivan O'Grady put some kind of plan in motion to kill Sy—poison, for example—before he got the boot."

"And before someone murdered him," I said.

Cathy pulled out a sheet of scrap paper for herself and jotted a few sentences down.

"Making your own suspect list?" I asked.

"No," she said, "but there's a mystery writer in my Thursday writers group. I thought the idea of someone killing the person who had already secretly poisoned them would be a great plot bunny for her."

Parker silently mouthed the words "Plot bunny?"

"But didn't we just prove that's not how it happened?" I asked.

Cathy finished her note with a flourish and folded the page. "That is why they call it fiction, dear."

After a brief silence, Dad stared up at the ceiling and rubbed the stubble on his chin. "I still feel that there should be a connection to the toys."

"Something you remember?" I asked.

He shook his head. "Just a gut feeling."

"Is your gut ever wrong?" Cathy asked.

"Frequently," he admitted, rubbing his stomach. I suspected dinner might be messing with it tonight. My stomach was also a little queasy. Or maybe just empty. Would anyone notice if I sneaked out for a pizza?

"I know what you're thinking," Cathy said.

I'd been considering whether I wanted the added calories of pepperoni, but I just said, "Oh, yeah?"

"It's what I've been thinking, too," she said. "It has to be one of those Wallaces." She folded her arms and sat back in her chair.

"Come to think of it, I had been thinking about the Wallaces," I said. Jack Wallace made the best pizza in town. "What brought them to your mind?"

"From what you told me about that whole wake, they thought they would have the most to gain from killing the old man, especially since they didn't know about Kimmie," she said, as if that explained everything.

Dad leaned forward. "But why would they kill Sullivan O'Grady?"

"Maybe," she said, her eyes flashing, "they needed to kill him because he was too protective of the old man, and getting him out of the house was the only way to get close enough. Or what if he was on to their plot, and they killed him to keep him quiet?"

"Still no connection to the toys," Parker said.

"What if they poisoned the toys?" she said. "You know, booby-trapped them so that they delivered a pinprick of curare or a cloud of toxic cyanide gas or something? Maybe he was bringing them to the shop because he suspected they were tampered with."

Dad stared at her.

Cathy took his shocked expression as proof that she'd offered up a profound theory. But when her back was turned to load the dishwasher, Dad shook the idea out of his ears like swimmers shake out pool water.

I got up and made a pot of coffee, then dug in the cupboard for a package of Oreos.

While the dishwasher was humming, we all recaffeinated and Parker hunted for his box of Apples to Apples for some evening fun. I tapped Dad on the arm. "You know, we need to think about that attempted break-in." I pointed to his suspect list. "Those kids who wanted to get into that house—why did they pick that morning? And what were they looking for?"

"Got it," he said, but he made no new additions to his papers. Rather, he stared up toward the ceiling again. Why did I have the feeling that he still wasn't sharing everything with me?

"Why don't we play in the family room?" Parker called.

"Coming!" When I stood up, a glob of tuna surprise squished its way through my sock. Othello hadn't eaten any of it.

# # #

My feet were frozen in place, and I could only watch the gigantic mechanism carry out its deadly dance. Gears meshed with gears, and a huge boot swung out in the darkness. A large silver ball, gleaming in what little light was in the room, started rolling and gained terrifying momentum. Suddenly I was trapped under a giant net with a horde of scurrying mice.

Then someone grabbed my foot.

I woke up screaming, or would have if not for the hand over my mouth.

"It's me," Dad said. "Shhh . . ."

As I fully gained consciousness, his face came into focus in the light from the hallway. I pushed myself up against the sofa back, pulled up my knees, and let my heart rate come back to normal.

Dad squeezed into the spot on the sofa vacated by my feet and put a comforting hand on my knee. "Sorry, Lizzie. I didn't mean to scare you."

Already the elements of my nightmare were beginning to fade, but I'd never see the game Mouse Trap the same way again. "What time is it?"

"Just before three in the morning. Sorry to wake you. I needed to talk."

Othello must have heard our voices because he hopped down from the oversized recliner and jumped up on the couch next to me. I put my feet on the floor, and he settled into my lap.

Despite Dad's professed need to talk, he was in no hurry. "I . . . remembered something," he said finally.

"About the man who died?"

He scrubbed his face with his hands. "I woke up, and I could see his face. He was standing outside the shop. The lights were off, but I could see his face from the streetlights. He was waiting at the door. And he was smiling at me, like nothing was wrong. I knew him, Liz. It's like I'd been expecting him. The next thing, I was opening the back door."

"And?"

"And then it fades again, as soon as I open the door. I remember, as I'm walking to the door, thinking that the alarm wasn't going to go off. It's something I knew."

"But you don't remember his name."

"Well, I know it now." His voice was growing agitated.

I took his hand. "It's okay. It's going to be okay. Could you have been trying to help him?"

"That's just it. I have no clue."

I leaned my head back to think and absent-mindedly began stroking Othello's fur. He responded with a contented and calming purr.

When I looked up, Dad's gaze had never left me. "When you see O'Grady at the door, what are you feeling? Are you happy? Scared? Angry? Do you remember that?"

Dad used his fingers to rake his hair back, then he closed his eyes and concentrated. "Nervous? Apprehensive?" Both were questions.

"Were you nervous because you were worried about what O'Grady might do?" What if O'Grady had attacked my dad, and Dad killed him in self-defense? But why would the apparently dedicated health aide and father of eight want to attack my father?

Dad grabbed the hair on both sides of his head as if he wanted to yank it out. "I. Don't. Know."

"Shh. Relax." I put my arm around him. "You'll remember. And if not, we'll figure out what happened."

"That's just it," he said. "I remember letting him in the shop. Just him and me alone in the shop, and that's exactly how you found us."

"Anything could have happened at that point. I refuse to believe you killed that man."

"On what evidence?" he said.

I took a finger and poked him in the chest. "On this evidence. You. I've known you all my life, and you may be a lot of things. Like everybody I know, a mix of good and bad, but you are not a killer."

He remained silent for perhaps a minute, then smiled sheepishly. He shook his head. "The judge would throw that out in a heartbeat."

"It won't come to that," I said, but we both knew I had nothing to back that up with.

"Hate to say it, Lizzie, but we're going to have to pencil my name in on that suspect list." He squeezed my hand. "Right at the top. Because if I was chief, I think I'd be in jail already."

Chapter 10

About four AM, a warm front blew through, and the wind shook the old house, sending creaks and groans through the infrastructure. About five AM, Bonnie and Clyde were making a racket on the back deck. And about six AM, Parker was humming in the shower. I know because I was awake for all of it.

When Cathy padded into the kitchen to make coffee, I was already on my third cup.

She collapsed into the oversized recliner and pulled her feet underneath her. After several sips, she croaked, "Good morning. You look like a wreck."

"Didn't sleep well." I resisted the urge to comment on her own early-morning appearance. Her hair was a study in static.

Moments later Parker joined us, appearing fresh and well rested, already dressed in his khakis and polo for work. The gang was all here. All but Dad, that is, whose measured snores gave us the assurance that at least someone could sleep.

"I hoped to ask another favor," I said. I hated imposing further on Parker and Cathy. We were already living in their home and eating their food. Not to mention, Othello was shedding all over their furniture, had knocked half the ornaments from their tree, and without his scratching post, I worried that he'd picked out a discreet portion of their sofa to dig his claws into.

"Sure," Cathy said, but at the same time, Parker said, "What is it?"

I wagged my eyebrows at him. "You're no fool." I took another sip of my coffee to fortify my nerves. "I'd like to swing by the police station this morning and talk to the chief, see how the investigation is going, and try to feel out if they have any suspects or new leads."

"Dad will love that," Cathy said. "He enjoys popping by the station."

I shook my head. "Here's the thing. I want to find out if they really consider Dad a suspect. They're not likely to tell me much anyway. Even less if he's around."

"He'll flip if he knows you're going behind his back," Parker said.

"Exactly. Which is why I was wondering if either of you could maybe distract Dad so he doesn't know what I'm doing."

"I was going to run some errands," Cathy said.

Parker shook his head. "Dad can come down to the center. We're having a school group in, and I could use the extra help with crowd control. He's good with the kids."

"Good with them?" I asked. "Or does he scare the living daylights out of them?"

"Both." Parker smiled. "Our father does have quite the multiple personalities. He can put the fear of God in any delinquent just with a glare."

"But he's such a teddy bear," Cathy said.

"That's because you've never been on the wrong side of the law," Parker said.

"Or broken curfew on a school night," I added, still smarting from the memory of a particular instance. Dad's temper had mellowed with the years. Or perhaps my formative years were spent with a parent working a stressful job and trying to compensate for an alcoholic wife. There had been occasional blowups at home. Nothing physically violent, but emotionally trying nonetheless. These were always followed by tearful apologies, hugs, and reconciliations. I knew my dad loved me. After the death of my mother and then later Dad's retirement, his temper had all but disappeared. His greatest frustration now was unsticking rusted gears on old toys and finding Barbie shoes that matched.

By the time we'd drained the coffee pot, we agreed that Cathy would drop Dad off at the wildlife center when she went out to run her errands, leaving me free to run mine. I was to continue to look tired—no problem—so Dad would assume I was home catching up on my sleep.

It worked like a charm. Dad might have been a tad suspicious, but he went with Cathy nonetheless. I leaned in the doorway and yawned as they backed out of the driveway, then I hit the showers, put heavy concealing makeup on my dark circles, then grabbed my coat and was out the door.

The combined police department for East Aurora and the neighboring town of Aurora was housed in the village's municipal building, a stone's throw from our shop on Main Street. The white-shuttered brick building had seen its share of history. The village's historian had also made the move, bringing the collection of murals that now filled up wall space in every hallway, making the offices a tourist attraction in their own right.

When I got to the police wing of the building, I spotted more than a few familiar faces, and officers waved or nodded to me as they milled around the area. I stopped at the front desk to explain why I was there, but the officer just pointed me to the door. I could hear it unlock as I approached. Apparently I hadn't worn out my welcome—at least not yet.

"I'm here to see Chief Young," I said to the officer, and she waved me to a group of chairs for the department's more welcome visitors, those not needing to be handcuffed to a bench, not that there was all that much of that in a town of our size.

I could already tell that the department was not operating at business-as-usual status. Trash cans overflowed with takeout bags, and stacks of cups dotted each desk, testifying that many here were working long hours. It didn't seem to be going well. Shoulders were hunched, chins unshaven, and a tinge of body odor permeated the air.

Even after the officer at the desk announced my arrival, nothing seemed to happen. When I'd visited the station when my dad was chief, generally only a minute or two passed before the door would open and he'd head out of his office smiling at me. But he was no longer behind that door, which now seemed impenetrable, and remained that way for the better part of an hour.

I got up to pace and stretch my back several times before sitting down again. When I was close to falling asleep in the chair, someone cleared his throat. I opened my eyes. Ken

Young stood in front of me, either smiling or smirking. I didn't know him well enough to know which one.

"You wanted to see me?" He still sported a stubbly beard, and I began to wonder if the department had made the decision not to shave until the case was solved, like hockey players who grow their beards when they start the play-offs. By the crumpled condition of his uniform and the amount of red in his eyes, I decided he just hadn't been home to sleep or shave.

I followed him back to his office and took an offered seat while he perched on the corner of his desk.

If I expected a greeting or pleasantries, I was going to be disappointed. "Shoot," he said.

"I came for a couple of reasons . . ." I stammered and stopped, a little taken aback. That was a mistake.

He gave me a shrug and a wry look, as if saying, "What am I supposed to do with that?" Or maybe that fabled line of Joe Friday, which Dad swears he never said: "Just the facts, ma'am."

I rallied. "First, I wanted to check if you'd gotten the autopsy results back for Sy DuPont."

Ken folded his arms in front of him and said, "Nope. I asked if we could hurry it up, and the medical examiner looked at me as if I was speaking Swahili." His guard was up. Where was the flirty guy who asked me to call him Ken? Seemed like this man had more than one personality, and I'd need the easygoing one if I was going to be able to pump him for information.

I tilted my head and hazarded a smile. "Dad and I were talking yesterday . . ."

"Did he reveal more about the incident?"

"Well, no. I mean, yes. But what I wanted to talk about was a few ideas we had. Like I said, Dad and I were talking, and we thought that maybe one of Sullivan O'Grady's former patients, or rather one of their family members, might have killed him. Perhaps because he was helping to usher them into the afterlife a little sooner than fate would have, if you get my point. Then there's Mrs. O'Grady. She had motive, and maybe if she was out driving when she said she was home with the kids—like if she was caught on a security camera . . . And then there's the matter of the missing toys, because they weren't in the apartment . . ." I trailed off, because if looks could kill, my body would be added to the medical examiner's backlog.

"Miss McCall," he said, then stopped. Something in his eyes told me he was counting to ten. "Miss McCall," he said again, then scratched his upper lip. "I appreciate you coming down here to supply more theories. However . . ." His head bobbed a couple of times. Counting again? "I have a whole department of active officers, all of whom are pretty good at coming up with theories." His voice was pleasant, but in a completely nonconvincing way. "Now, why don't you tell me about what your father said."

"I . . . maybe Dad should tell you." I was suddenly hesitant to share my dad's memory of letting the victim into the store.

"Fine," he said, putting his hand on the receiver of his desk telephone. "I can have him brought in."

"What is wrong with you?" I flew out of my seat. "Have him brought in?"

He walked to the open door and pushed it closed. Without saying a word, he resumed his perch at his desk.

My face was hot, and the words felt like they were still out there in the air, incriminating me, especially since he didn't answer. "Fine," I said. "He remembers letting O'Grady into the shop that night."

"And?"

"And he thinks he might have pulled the breakers, because he was sure the alarm wasn't going to sound."

"And?"

"That was it."

He sighed. "That we pretty much already knew."

"Look, the doctor thinks Dad may have some temporary memory. A concussion from that bump on the head."

He shoved his hands in his pockets.

I sat up straighter. "Your turn."

"Fair enough. Here's what we have. One Sullivan O'Grady shows up at the doorstep of your shop. Your father lets him in. A short time later, O'Grady is found dead in your shop. Your father is alone with the body. Yet somehow, he has no recollection of anything that happened. Just for that time in between." He uncrossed his arms and began a thorough examination of his cuticles. "It's too convenient."

"Too convenient?" The words drew the air out of my lungs and left me weak and limp, like I was about to slide off the chair and onto the floor like a melting ice cream cone—or a Dalí painting. "He can't pick and choose what he remembers." I was able to hold back the tears stinging my eyes, but my voice had grown husky.

Ken scratched his cheek. "I don't know what to tell you. Until he's more forthcoming, that's what we have to go on. Yes, we're doing our homework. We're checking the cameras up and down Main Street. Most are focused inside of the stores, but a few of them do provide some glimpses of the street. And yes, we're investigating Sy DuPont's death. Even though the family is less than thrilled with me."

"What about the woman who showed up? That Kimmie whatever."

"That might be the only entertaining facet of this case. That marriage license she was waving around appears legit."

"So this chick starts hanging around the house. Then the old man's health aide gets fired. Then she marries the old dude. Then both men die. How's that for a chronology?"

"And the motive would be . . . ?"

"She's an obvious gold digger. We learned from Mrs. O'Grady that Sullivan was very close to his clients. Maybe he was too protective and had to be disposed of."

"First, I'm not sure there was any real gold to be had."

"Then what were all those people shoving into their pockets?"

"Not the Hope Diamond, I can tell you that. This is real life, not *Antiques Roadshow*. We're talking a few bucks here and there for most of the small stuff."

"Surely a few genuine antiques were mixed in."

"I doubt Sy left enough of value to pay for the dumpster they'll need to haul in to clear all the junk out. No, that house was the only asset he had left. Not much gold worth digging."

"She might have *thought* there was gold. There's something fishy there. Maybe she's some black widow. *Maybe*," I said, "Sullivan O'Grady was taking his suspicions to my father to ask him for help."

"This is getting interesting. We have an angel of mercy *and* a black widow *and* an amnesiac *and* a beautiful amateur sleuth. This is where I usually walk out of the theater before the identical twins pop out of the secret passage. Liz . . ." He got up and pushed his rolling desk chair so that it faced mine, then sat down. He paused before starting to speak slowly and softly. "If you want to help, the best way isn't by driving around town asking questions that we've already asked. It's by getting your father to remember what happened. If you could work with him . . ."

"The doctor said it doesn't work like that," I said. "Memory is an elusive thing. It pops up when he's calm. And these last few days were anything but calm. If you could take down the crime scene tape, I could get him back in familiar surroundings . . ."

"I have another investigator going through the scene tomorrow."

"No," I said.

"No?"

Now my back was up. "You heard me. I'll hire a lawyer if I have to, but you've locked us out of our home and place of business long enough. Unless you're ready to arrest one of us, I want that yellow tape off our shop. You want Dad to remember? Let me take him back home. Let me get back to business. Now when can I have my shop back?"

He inhaled as if he was planning to let loose with a string of obscenities, but then he merely shrugged. "Tomorrow morning. Now, if you'll excuse me, I have to see if I can get my expert in earlier."

I left feeling oddly invigorated. I still worried for my father but was no longer terrified for him. Dad always said, "Truth will out." Then again, he lived his life making sure it did. Somehow I knew the truth would be revealed, if people worked hard enough. The police department clearly was not slacking off on this case, so it was only a matter of time. And I had no doubts whatsoever that the truth would vindicate my father.

I was so distracted with my thoughts as I walked through the station that I almost plowed right into Lori Briggs, the mayor's wife. She was wearing a cute little belted coat that somehow conveyed her figure. This was quite a feat, since most of us were bundled up, resembling Oompa Loompas in our insulated outerwear.

"Oh, Liz," she said. "I was just thinking about you. I'm assuming game night is canceled tonight. Too bad, because I was looking forward to a nice Pandemic." She was, of course, referring to the strategy game and not a global disease outbreak.

I walked with her to the exit. "Sorry, I should have called the regulars. I've learned we'll have our shop back tomorrow, so after that, the normal schedule resumes."

"If you'd like, I'll call everyone and let them know."

"That's okay. I'll take care of it," I said. Lori's tendency to gossip might end up costing us more than her kind offer would help.

"I guess they're releasing the name of that poor man who died in your shop," she said. Was that a dig, or was she probing for information? But since I wanted information from her . . .

"You know, I could go for a cup of coffee. Would you care to join me?"

"Coffee shop or cupcake place?" Her emphasis was definitely on the second. After mild protests on both sides (which we quickly overcame, especially when Lori discovered she had a coupon), we were sitting in the little cupcakery. She was working on a blueberry lemon concoction, while I gave in and finally tried the maple pancake and bacon cupcake. One bite and I wondered why I'd waited so long. Of course, when it came to flavors, this was now tied with seven others as my favorite.

"So you were coming from the police department." Lori rubbed a fork along her empty wrapper to nab the last bit of frosting. "Anything new in the investigation?"

"Just that they've identified the victim, as you said. Sullivan O'Grady." I looked up to catch her reaction. "Hey, didn't he work for your family?"

"Briefly," she said, as if to separate herself from him as much as possible.

"I've heard his patients were generally pleased with his assistance," I said. "I gather he was well-liked and trusted."

She pushed her plate aside and leaned in closer across the little table. "Actual results do vary. He was dedicated, I'll give him that much."

"But you weren't pleased."

"My father-in-law wasn't pleased. See, he always had a raucous sense of humor. A tad inappropriate at times."

"Sullivan O'Grady?"

"Oh, no! Dad. He liked the occasional bawdy joke. He was never one you invited to the better parties. Not that it bothered him. He'd rather sit in the basement, drink his beer, and smoke that foul pipe of his. Sullivan O'Grady didn't quite fit into Dad's world. And Dad wasn't ready to listen to any preaching about the world to come, either."

Something fell into place, like the right piece of the jigsaw puzzle when you've been trying to force the wrong one in for twenty minutes. "Sullivan O'Grady liked to talk to his patients about the hereafter."

"Like he had discount tickets," Lori said. "I don't think Dad ever talked about Jesus since he was confirmed—unless you count swearing. One afternoon of them alone together and Dad was ready to spit nails. The service replaced him with a nice older woman who was either partly deaf or pretended to be, because she wasn't offended at all by Dad's escapades."

"So O'Grady was a devout family man," I said. "Not the type who usually end up murdered."

Lori shrugged. "I don't know. They killed Jesus."

I drained the rest of my coffee. Lori's last statement may have been an attempt at humor, but it made me focus on the idea that Sullivan O'Grady wasn't killed because he was doing something bad, but perhaps because somebody didn't like how he did good.

# # #

My secret errands done, I headed out to the wildlife center to relieve Parker. Besides, I wanted to tell Dad the good news that we were getting our shop back. When I reached the end of the narrow drive, Miles's little Toyota was sitting in the parking lot.

I opened the gate as quietly as I could and just made out voices near the back cages. The wildlife center wasn't open to the public, at least not all the time. They were mainly in the business of caring for and rehabilitating injured wildlife, especially the area's plentiful hawk population. Usually animals stayed only until they'd healed and were then successfully released to the wild. Others survived their injuries but had lost the ability to defend themselves against predators and other dangers of the wilderness. These became permanent residents of the facility, along with a menagerie confiscated from illegal home zoos or surrendered by well-meaning animal lovers who could no longer care for them. These couldn't be sold or returned to the wild, so they lived out their days at the center, where visiting school and community groups could learn about them.

I crept toward the voices. Dad and Miles were in the middle of a quiet conversation, while Parker was working inside an empty cage. I ducked back behind a fence.

"So what about . . . ?" my dad asked.

Miles hushed him. "Just a minute. I want to see the hawk. That's the one I brought in." He raised his voice. "How's he doing?"

"The last X-rays on the wing looked pretty good," Parker said, "but he doesn't seem all that interested in flying." As if to argue the point, the hawk took off and fluttered a few feet, then started walking. "We'll keep working with him."

"Do you think he can ever go back to the res?" Miles asked.

"Not until we know he can fly," Parker said. "Too dangerous for him otherwise."

The hawk gave a few half-hearted hops across the pen.

Miles shook his head. "He's not going to get away from a bear that way."

"And he'd have difficulty hunting," Parker explained. "Or mating."

"Aw, man," Miles said. "You never said my boy lost . . . anything crucial."

Parker laughed. "His *crucial* parts are all there, as far as we can tell. I just meant that the female will choose the strongest, healthiest male." He tipped his head to where the hawk was still making his way across the floor. "I'm afraid Hopalong Cassidy here would be the wallflower at all the best bird dances."

While Parker gathered the hawk and went to take him wherever rehabilitating hawks spend the night, Dad elbowed Miles. "So what did you find out?"

"They were just being stupid," Miles said.

"That I knew," Dad said.

"Hey, I don't hang with those guys anymore, so they're not going to spill to me."

"Since when?"

"Since someone set me on the straight and narrow. As soon as they knew I was cooperating with you and then working for you and going to college, they dropped me like the proverbial sweltering spud."

"Sweltering spud?" Dad repeated.

"Hey, I'm a college boy now. Gotta exercise that vocabulary. From what I gather, they were probably back to their old tricks. They must have read the obituary in the paper and decided to hit the house. They were too dumb to realize that the new chief apparently had heard of that trick, too."

"Keep digging, if you can," Dad said.

"I don't think they know anything about the murder."

"Maybe they saw something at the house. You never know."

Miles saluted. "Sure, boss. I'll continue my association with known felons if it will help *you* out," he said with exaggerated sweetness. "After all, if not for you, I'd probably be getting my first jail tat."

Dad laughed. "Okay. Anything on the toy?"

"I keep getting shuffled from collector to collector. A few have offered to buy it, should it ever cross our hands again, but nobody seems to know exactly what it is or what it's worth. Last guy gave me the name of a specialty collector, but he's off on his honeymoon in Hawaii and apparently didn't leave his number with anyone, the slacker. I left my number with the nice lady taking care of his shih tzu, and she promised to give him my messages."

"Keep on it."

So apparently I wasn't the only one carrying out secret interviews. I backed up a few steps and approached them again, allowing my footsteps to crunch on the rocks. "Dad, are you back here?" When I rounded the corner, I said, "Oh, hi, Miles. I didn't know you were here."

"Hey, Lizzie," Dad said. "Did you catch up on your sleep?"

"It wasn't happening," I said, "so I decided to drive out and see what you were up to."

Miles seemed a little antsy, like he was ready to bolt. "I came to check on a hawk. It's from the reservation, and we have to look out for our own." He checked his phone. "But I should get to class." He started walking away. "Nice talking to you!"

"See you, Miles," I called after him, then squinted at my father. "He couldn't get out of here fast enough. He didn't come out here to check on a hawk, did he?"

Dad narrowed his eyes. "This is what I get for teaching you half my tricks. You're becoming too perceptive."

"Only half your tricks?"

"Hey, an old man's gotta protect himself."

I raised an eyebrow and continued to stare.

"Fine," he said. "I asked Miles to come out here. The young men who broke into Sy's house—or rather tried to? Miles used to hang with that gang."

"Oh, boy," I said. "So that's another connection that involves the toyshop. Do you think it's a coincidence that they picked that particular funeral from the obituary notices?"

"You were eavesdropping on me."

"Well, *you* were holding out on me." I poked my finger to his chest. "I thought I was your partner in this little investigation."

"You are, but Miles . . . I don't want too many people around the shop to know of his past. He's a good kid."

"So you hid your meeting with him from me. See, that's important. You also didn't tell me about the appointment you had with Sullivan O'Grady."

"That had nothing to do with Miles. There is no way he can be on the suspect list."

I stuck my hands into my coat pockets, then looked up at Dad. "How can you know that for sure? You've forgotten what that meeting was about. Can you be certain it wasn't about Miles? One hundred percent?"

Dad swallowed, his Adam's apple taking its good old time to bob in his throat. Then he sank down on a nearby bench and shook his head.

When he finally raised his eyes, they were watery. "I think I'd rather it be me."

Chapter 11

I couldn't quite make out the smell emanating from Cathy's oven, but when she went to the cupboard to pull out plates, she only grabbed two.

"This is for the boys," she said. "You and I are going out. See, I've been thinking."

"Sounds scary already," I said.

She hit me with a potholder, which I probably deserved. "I've been thinking about the murder and about everything you told us went on at that wake. I've decided the murder must have something to do with that Wallace family."

"And this merits a girls' night out?"

She wagged her finger at me. "Jack Wallace is the key."

"The key to . . . ?"

"To you getting closer to the family so you can figure out what is going on."

"So you and I are going to Jack's place to hang out and eat pizza and hope that something he says implicates his cousin George or his aunt Edna." It sounded ludicrous but more promising than whatever mystery was baking in the oven at three fifty. "Fine, I'm in."

# # #

Just after our pizza arrived, Jack made his first appearance.

"Sharon told me I had friends in the dining room . . ." he started to say. Then he apparently noticed the getup and extra makeup that Cathy had insisted I wear, because his voice cracked and his jaw dropped.

"Hi, Jack." I gave him a little wave.

"We were just having a girls' night," Cathy said, fooling no one. At least I think that's what she said, because Jack was gazing into my eyes, and I was staring into his, and she could have been reciting the Gettysburg Address backward and I wouldn't have noticed.

Finally, he broke eye contact. "I . . . probably shouldn't keep you from your dinner."

"Join us if you can," Cathy said.

"Well, I am due for a break." Jack pulled up another chair and helped himself to a slice of pizza. "The pizza's on me tonight, especially if I'm going to help you eat it."

"Why do you think we invited you?" Cathy quipped, then winked at me.

I took one bite of pizza and melted.

"That's the reaction I like to see," he said. He went on to illuminate us on aging the yeast dough to produce bubbles, then cooking it at the right temperature to achieve a "char" without burning anything. The right kind of tomatoes imported from Italy. Fresh mozzarella. Virgin olive oil. And the basil was grown in the basement under special lights he bought at a police auction.

Delivered by someone else, it might have been a boring lecture. From Jack, who spoke with such magnetism, the food became even more alluring. Even sexy. Like the audition tape he'd sent into one of the food networks last year, where he'd cooked another Buffalo favorite: beef on weck. The video, which they showed one night at the public library, was surreptitiously renamed *Fifty Shades of Gravy*.

After we'd talked food for almost twenty minutes, Cathy kicked me in the shin, not that it helped. I had no idea how to change the topic of conversation to his family.

"Hey, do you know what would be fun?" she said to Jack. "You should give Liz a cooking lesson. You're both so enthusiastic. You'd have all kinds of fun."

Jack's eyes narrowed momentarily, then he quirked his head, as if studying me. "I'd be game."

"Uh, yeah. I'm sure we could do that. Sometime."

"Tomorrow's my day off," he said. "Unless you're busy."

"That's perfect!" Cathy said.

"Good," Jack said. "Speaking of cooking, I should get back to the kitchen. Six o'clock? You remember where the house is, right?"

"The house?" Here I discovered the fatal flaw in Cathy's plan, even before Jack's next words left his lips.

"I'll let my mother know you're coming."

As Jack made his way back to the kitchen, Cathy smiled smugly. "See, just like I planned. Tomorrow you'll spend more time with Jack and his family. It couldn't have worked out more perfectly."

I glared at her. "You've never had dinner with Jack's mother. The only thing she hates more than me is the idea of Jack and me together."

# # #

The next morning, Dad was chipper and raring to go. I don't know what he was more excited about, getting the shop back or that I said I'd make breakfast for him when we got home.

Despite my apparent desperate need for cooking lessons from Jack Wallace, I was a fair hand in the kitchen. Nothing fancy, but I conquered the basics and could read a recipe. I could make eggs that were neither rubbery nor slimy nor brown, a skill that had eluded Cathy. Nor did I go on health food benders, suddenly making everything with black beans, beet greens, or tofu. Don't even get me started on the Thanksgiving fiasco of 2015: kale done nine ways.

We avoided the front of the shop at first by parking in the back alley. The alarm was off. Apparently having a long string of cops and forensic people traipsing through the building at all hours was deemed protection enough.

The upstairs apartment felt weird. While Dad and I put away the groceries that Cathy had sent home with us, Othello inched out of his carrier to sniff the air. This was our home, the place where I could walk around in my pajamas with my hair messed up, put my bare feet on the coffee table, and drink too much coffee. A place where I'd been free to be myself. Only it didn't feel free. It felt scary and tense, like all that hominess had been sucked out of the building.

Othello went to check out any changes. He circumnavigated the entire apartment, sniffing, then swiped his cheek against corners and odd surfaces he found important. I wished reclaiming my life could be as easy.

In truth, the murder in our shop, followed by Dad's subsequent amnesia, cast strong doubt on whether our lives would ever be the same.

As I busied myself scrambling eggs, the worries kept scrambling my brain. Was Dad's memory loss a harbinger of more problems to come? How long would he be able to keep working? Would we need to find alternate living arrangements for him? I couldn't even think the words. *Nursing home.* There, I thought it. But tears threatened to tumble out, and my throat felt as if I was trying to swallow a llama.

Still, I forced a smile as I set two plates of sunny yellow eggs on the table for Dad and me. We had this moment. We were together right now, and I was going to enjoy every bit of it.

"Keep your *sunny side up*, Lizzie," Dad said, as he dug into his eggs. "Things will work out yet. Come out of your *shell* and be *eggs*-cited about the possibilities."

"I guess the *yolk's* on me," I said.

"*Omelet* you get away with that one." He picked up the newspaper.

"What is it with you and the papers lately? You were practically buried in a stack of them at Parker's house."

He folded the paper and set it back on the table. "I'm going to wager that you won't buy that I was catching up on the funny pages."

"At another time, maybe."

"Too bad, because I did catch up on the funnies. I also reread the news stories about the murder. The newspapers are woefully behind what we know from our little investigation. But . . ."

"But?"

"A bit of an anomaly kept cropping up when I thought about the wake. It's why I wanted to talk to Miles about the attempted break-in and why I'm not ready to let that go as coincidence."

"Why's that?"

"See, when you get to be my age, sometimes you find yourself reading the obituaries. I hadn't recalled seeing Sy DuPont's. So I went back and checked. Good thing Parker had all the old issues in his recycle bin. But Sy's obituary wasn't in the *Advertiser* or in the *Buffalo News*."

"Could it have been in some other paper?" I asked.

He shrugged. "If it was, I can't find it."

"So the guys who tried to break in learned the old man had died and that the house would be empty, but not from the newspapers," I said. "Funeral parlor? Online notices?"

"They told Miles they had read it in the obituaries." Dad scratched his cheek. "It's why I want Miles to find out a bit more. There might be nothing there, but . . ."

I got up to clear Dad's plate but stopped to press my finger into his stomach like he was the Pillsbury Doughboy. "I know. You feel it in your gut."

By the time Cathy arrived for her shift at the shop, we'd made all the yellow tape disappear, although Dad had insisted on rolling it up and keeping it, saying it might make for a great Halloween display next year. I put his macabre souvenir into the cupboard while mouthing a prayer that next October would find us all here, still in business.

Someone had already mopped up the pool of blood where Sullivan O'Grady had died, but I thought I could still make out a sticky residue between the tiles. After I'd mopped over the same area seven or eight times, Cathy came up behind me.

"I don't think you can wash away what happened with a mop," she said.

"Does the shop feel different to you? It's like something changed. A stain I can't get out."

"Maybe Sully's still here," she said. "That would be cool."

"Cool?" I couldn't hide the disdain in my voice.

"Not that he died here. But think about it. Every other business on this block is haunted. Strange footsteps. Shadows. Some say Millard Fillmore still goes to the office every day and his door swings open. Visitors to Jack's place say they've heard children playing and laughing when nobody is there."

"Not this again," I said. When it came to hauntings, I was happy to be labeled a skeptic. None of the businesses had been haunted until ghost hunting became popular on the cable channels.

"I know," Cathy said, apparently not getting my meaning. "Why don't any of those kids ever come over here? You'd think they'd want to play with all the toys. Like maybe we'd come in sometime to find the old rocking horse moving, at least. Something."

"Some people have all the luck." I checked the aisles again to make sure everything was ready for the hopefully paying public. More than once, I felt edgy, as if I were being watched. When I spun around, nothing was there. Nothing except that infernal monkey with the cymbals.

We flipped the "closed" sign to "open" three minutes before our normal opening time of ten AM. Then we waited.

Dad headed back upstairs to tinker with some recent acquisitions, which the police had accepted from the UPS man and left just inside the door. Perhaps he was psychic, because the first time the bell sounded, Peggy Trent walked in, carrying a basket.

I was tempted to sic her on my father, but he'd been through enough these past few days, so I explained that Dad wasn't working this morning and left it at that.

"But he is doing okay?" she asked. "I heard he blanked out the night that poor man died."

"Concussion, the doctor said. His memory is starting to come back, little by little."

"One can only hope," she said. "I wanted you to know that the town is here for you. For you both. If you need anything, please let me know."

"I'll do that." I took the basket she held out. Somehow she'd transported a gorgeous batch of blueberry muffins halfway across town while they were still warm. Despite not liking Peggy, I would admit that the woman could cook. "And thanks for the muffins."

"You're welcome." She paused at the door. "I will need the basket back. Maybe you and your father could return it, and then stay for dinner, when he's feeling better."

"I can ask if he's up to it. And I'll make sure you get your basket back. Thanks."

And the persistence award goes to Peggy Trent.

Shortly after she left, a couple of customers wandered into the shop. Out-of-towners, I think. They'd *ooh*ed and *aah*ed and got their fingerprints all over a bunch of our most expensive merchandise, sniffed all the Strawberry Shortcake paraphernalia, and then purchased a vintage Lite-Brite for twenty bucks.

The next time the door opened, Ken walked in. He removed his hat and looked around, then came to the counter. I'd been so bored, I was going through our candy display, checking expiration dates. It's a tough job, but I considered it my duty to dispose of any expired candy appropriately. So far I'd consumed two giant Pixy Stix and three packets of Pop Rocks and could barely stand still.

"Everything okay this morning?" he asked.

"Just ducky," I said. "We've been swamped, can't you tell?" I waved my hand around the empty shop.

"Folks will come back when they're ready. You'll probably see a few lookie loos, too. Some are morbid that way. Don't let them get to you."

"Thanks for the heads-up."

"Now that he's back home, has your father remembered anything?"

"You mean, did he walk into the place and have a eureka moment, suddenly recalling whodunit? Oh, absolutely. But we didn't want to bother you with the details." I rolled my eyes. "I would have called you if he had."

"I deserved that. You've given me no reason to believe you've been anything but candid with me. But I did want to check in. It's not always easy to return to what has become a crime scene."

"I admit," I said, "the place feels weird. Like some wax museum exhibit of what was once home. Everything looks the same, but it feels like a cold, lifeless copy."

"Give it time," he said.

I bit my lip and nodded. "In the spirit of full disclosure, I should say that Dad's come up with something. Not a memory. It's another theory, and I know you said . . ." I paused, wondering if I could verbalize Dad's idea about the missing obituary without implicating Miles.

Ken exhaled loudly. Or was that a sigh? "Listen, I'm sorry about that, too. I was tired and the investigation wasn't going well. I should have been more patient yesterday. So, yes, I would be interested in your father's little theory."

His *little* theory? I ignored the suggested slight and told him about Dad's discovery about there being no obituary. I almost had Ken out of the door when Dad came hobbling down the stairs, shouting, "I remember!" His face blanched when he rounded the corner and saw the new chief listening intently.

A few minutes later, the three of us were gathered around the kitchen table while Cathy watched the shop. Not that we had many customers to watch for.

"So what exactly did you remember?" Ken had opened his notebook and held his pen at the ready.

"Relax, Dad." I put a comforting hand on his shoulder.

Dad closed his eyes as he began talking, probably to help his concentration. "I was down working in the shop when the phone rang. I picked it up, and the voice on the other end said, 'Hello, this is Sullivan O'Grady.'"

"When was this?" Ken asked. "How did you respond?"

"I don't remember," Dad said.

"Had you ever talked to him before?" Ken asked.

"I don't think so," Dad said.

Ken scribbled that down. "You don't know when this was?"

Dad shook his head, then looked at me. "I answered the phone quickly because I didn't want to wake up Betsy. I mean Liz." Dad leaned aside to Ken. "She hates the name Betsy."

"So probably during the night," Ken said.

"I'm not much of a napper," I said, "so you can pretty much bank on it being during the night." If Dad's slip of that nickname was meant as a diversionary tactic, it wasn't going to work. I pressed him further. "Do you remember why you didn't want to wake me? Was there something you didn't want me to see or know about?"

Dad thought about this for a second, then shook his head. "I think it's just because you get grumpy when you wake up in the middle of the night. Always have." He turned to Ken. "Once she stomped around for days . . ." He trailed off when Ken didn't smile.

"This was the night he was killed?" Ken asked. "Did you ask him to come to the shop?"

Dad shrugged.

Ken stared down at his notebook. "Well, I can recheck the phone records from the shop. Nothing stood out the first time, but now that we know O'Grady phoned here, maybe we can identify the number he was calling from." He closed his notebook. "Might be something to go on."

# # #

The rest of the day brought just a handful of customers and even fewer sales. The coupon would run in the evening paper and hopefully draw a few bargain hunters out. At the end of the day, instead of kicking my feet up to spend time with Dad and Othello, a nice bowl of popcorn, and our well-worn DVD of *The Muppet Christmas Carol*, I was getting ready for an unnecessary cooking lesson with my ex and his mother, a woman who thought of me the same way a chicken farmer might regard a bird flu epidemic.

In fact, when I got there, Mrs. Wallace had taken a supervisory position on a stool at the kitchen island with a stack of magazines next to her. She nodded and said, "Hello, Elizabeth." She then proceeded to ignore me. That, I could handle. In fact, I preferred it to conversation.

Jack tied an apron around his waist and then tossed me one. "I wasn't sure what you wanted to learn to cook, so I thought I'd start with something I knew you liked to eat. Cheese ravioli," he said, in his luscious food porn voice.

My stomach gurgled and my heart started racing. "Ooooh."

His mother sighed and flipped the page of her magazine.

I'd cooked a passable cheese ravioli at home before, opting for premade pasta and a sauce I whipped up in a slow cooker. But that wasn't what Jack had in mind as he made a well in a pile of semolina for fresh eggs and we made our own pasta. If real life were a Hallmark movie, I'd have fumbled trying to roll the dough, and Jack would have come up behind me and put his arms around me to help roll it out perfectly. Then we'd kiss and both end up covered in flour. He must have seen the movie too, because that's exactly what happened. All except the kiss. And *that* might have happened if Jack's mother hadn't been sighing and slamming magazine pages.

The cooking lesson was interesting, though, from the zig-zag pasta cutter and the sauce made from fresh tomatoes and herbs. Hours passed before we—all three of us—sat down to sample our creation, but the ravioli was scrumptious. I couldn't get enough of the sauce, heaping it on my pasta and dipping my bread into it.

I think we were halfway through dinner before I realized that none of us was talking. I glanced up from my clean plate and Jack was smiling. I set my fork down. "This is wonderful."

"You were the cook tonight," he said. "So all compliments go to you."

"No, it's this recipe and those ingredients. I've never cooked anything like this in my life."

"With a little more practice," Mrs. Wallace said, "you'll learn not to overwork your pasta."

And right then I knew two reasons why a long-term relationship with Jack would be impossible. The first was, of course, his mother. The second was that I was sure to get incredibly fat. The first was the deal-breaker. I was willing to risk the second.

"I was surprised to see you at Uncle Sy's wake, Elizabeth," Mrs. Wallace said. "How did you say you knew him again?"

"It was really Dad who had wanted to go," I said.

Mrs. Wallace pushed her half-eaten plate of food away. Her loss. She folded her hands in front of her. "And how did your father know him?"

Oh, great. So much for me trawling for information. Instead I was going to get the third degree. "I gather Dad had answered a number of calls at Sy's address throughout the years."

"Of course," she said, then shook her head. "Uncle Sy always did have an active imagination. Sometimes he called the police. Sometimes he called the family, and we'd have to go walk around the whole house to make sure nobody was trying to break in, then hold his hand until he got his wits about him. The old coot. It became insufferable near the end."

"Is that why you hired a home health aide?" I asked.

She put her hand on her chest. "*I* didn't hire him. Sy did that on his own."

Jack shifted a piece of ravioli around on his plate. I had a feeling I had hit upon a sore subject. He looked up. "Actually, we hadn't seen Uncle Sy in quite some time."

"How long is some time?" I asked.

"I don't see why that should matter," Mrs. Wallace said. "We're a family, and all families have difficult members, right? No need to go airing our dirty laundry to just anybody."

Jack sat up straighter. "I'd hardly call Liz just anybody."

"I didn't mean to pry," I said. "Only I have to admit I'm curious about your uncle and his relationship to Sullivan O'Grady." I dipped the serving spoon back onto the plate and chose two plump raviolis.

"Oh, so now they're supposed to have had a *relationship*?" she said, raising her volume.

"I didn't mean to suggest . . ."

Jack pushed back from the table. "Not fair, Mother."

She glared back at him for several moments, and I worried I was about to witness something akin to Godzilla and Mothra doing battle over Tokyo. I'd be playing the part of Tokyo. Finally, her shoulders slumped. "Guess I'm still burnt up over that whole situation. When I think of what we did for that man over the years. And then . . ."

And then what? I was afraid to ask it aloud, for fear of being accused of more prying. So I dug into my ravioli instead.

"I spent the better part of my life at that man's beck and call," she said. "Shovel his walk? Call Gladys. Need someone to drive him for his colonoscopy and endure his flatulence in the car all the way home? Why not call Gladys?"

Gladys? So that was her first name.

"Mother, you haven't shoveled in years," Jack said, "and I hardly think Liz expects an explanation."

"No." She put up her hand. "I won't have anybody questioning what happened between us and Uncle Sy. Let's get it *all* into the open."

"Mrs. Wallace, you really don't need to . . ." I purposefully trailed off. I felt guilty for my little deception, because I did want her to go on.

"I suppose you think we're all a bunch of greedy relatives, poised to jump on whatever we can get out of his death." She turned again to me. "If that's what it looks like, there's no one to blame except Sy. I remember the first time I shoveled his walk. I must have been ten years old. I would have been happy for a quarter. But what does dear *Uncly Sy* do? He winks at me and says, 'I'll remember that, sweetheart. And when this old man is dead and gone, you'll know how much I appreciated it.' It's like he was conditioning us—all of us— to take care of him, with promises of something nice when he kicked off."

"He couldn't have been that old when you were ten," Jack said.

His mother's face froze. "That geezer was always old."

"I'm sorry you had so much difficulty." I tried to keep my voice suitably meek. "I didn't mean to make you rehash any of this. I'm more interested in the aide."

"I'm getting there," she said. "Eventually his pleasant personality had whittled the group down to just a couple of us he could still count on to run errands. Then the phone call came. Two AM, mind you. Could I come right over? He heard a noise. Well, that old house has been groaning, popping, and settling for decades. I hadn't been sleeping well, and I'd just had a procedure of my own." She leaned closer to me and whispered, "A female thing."

Jack rolled his eyes.

"I wasn't about to leave my nice, warm house, clean a foot of snow off my car, and drive over to Sy's. So I did what I should have done years ago. I told him no." She shook her head. "He told me I'd be sorry, and that's the last I heard from him. He didn't call me or answer my calls, or anybody's from the entire family."

"When was this?" I asked.

"Almost a year ago," she said. "Apparently that's when he hired the aides. I gather there's been more than one. Which makes sense." An unaccustomed smile tickled the corner of her lips. "No stranger is going to put up with Uncle Sy for a whole year."

"So there's nothing you can tell me about the aide who died," I said.

"Only what I read in the papers," she said. "That he died in your shop. What was he doing there? Was he trying to sell something? Something of Sy's?"

I glanced around the room. Unfortunately the answer to this question wasn't woven into the drapes or spelled out on their popcorn ceiling. Finally, I met her gaze. "I wish I knew."

# # #

The heated conversation seemed to clear the air, at least between Mrs. Wallace and me. She went to bed, leaving her son unprotected from my supposed feminine wiles. As Jack and I cleaned up and did the dishes, he was pensive.

Finally, as he slapped a cloth against the counter, I could no longer pretend not to notice.

"Are you okay?" I asked.

He stared down at the soapy rag and shook his head. "I'm fine." Then he turned to face me. "It's *us* who's not fine. Maybe I'm wrong, but you and your sister-in-law come into my place, and you in that . . . outfit. Suddenly you need cooking lessons. I assumed you were coming on to me. I thought maybe you wanted to rekindle something."

"I . . ." What could I say? Was I still interested in Jack?

"You came for something else," he said. "Evidence. Clues. You think that my family might have something to do with this murder. And instead of talking with me, instead of coming right out and asking me, you put on some elaborate hoax to wrangle an invitation."

Not since Patty Wriggly and I cut class in middle school and sneaked into an R-rated movie had I been caught quite as red-handed and given such a severe dressing down. That time it had been by my mother, who had wandered into the theater waiting for her afternoon buzz to wear off. You never forget being dragged by the ear out of a public place by a woman too drunk to stand and too angry to sit.

"I'm sorry," I said. It was the only response left. I swallowed hard. "It's my dad, you see. I'm worried about him. I don't like that he can't remember what happened. I don't know what the chief believes or what the town will decide happened if he can never remember."

"So you're looking for someone else to blame? Well, you can cross my name off your list. Cross Mom's off, too, while you're at it. We won't be your scapegoats. Do you have any idea what's going on in this family? They've exhumed Uncle Sy. Everybody's whispering."

"I said I was sorry."

"Let me get your coat."

"I don't blame you. I'm going."

"No," he said. "You don't understand." He put his hands in his pockets. "I *get* family. You're worried for your dad. I don't like what's going on with my own family. But if you really want to find the killer, I've got a good suspect in mind." He pulled his keys from his pocket, tossed them into the air, and caught them again. "And I'm going to help."

Chapter 12

I shivered, then used my glove to clear a circle in the fogged-up passenger window of Jack's pickup. We were parked outside his Uncle Sy's house and no hanky-panky was going on, not that I hadn't given it a stray thought.

"I don't understand what we're doing here," I said. "Nothing's happening."

"Nothing yet, but I know that woman has to be involved somehow."

"Oh, you're talking about *Aunt* Kimmie." I thought the conversation needed a little comic relief.

But he was all drama tonight. "Think about it," he said. "Who is this woman? Uncle Sy never went anywhere. Where did she meet him? Why would he marry her? And why would she marry him?"

"I think the term 'gold digger' was bandied about a little."

"Liz, look at the place." He gestured in the general direction of the house, then switched on the engine and the defroster. "It needs a new roof. Hasn't been painted in years. The lawn's a mess. It has the curb appeal of a junkyard. And despite Uncle Sy's promises to his relatives, I'm pretty sure that house was his only asset. No competent gold digger would mess with him."

I held my cold fingers over the vents. "Maybe he convinced her that he had more money than he did."

"I'm not sure I buy that."

"So what's your idea?" I asked.

"My idea is to watch her and try to figure out what she's up to."

I cleared a little more fog from the window, using a fingernail to scratch off a bit that had frozen. I stared up at the house. One pale light shone through the living room window, but nothing moved. "Is she even home?"

We sat watching for another half an hour, idling the engine on occasion. Then Jack drove to the Tim Hortons around the corner, where we both used the facilities and bought large coffees to warm our hands and stomachs. Ten minutes later, we were sitting in the same place watching the same silent house.

I couldn't argue with Jack's logic. Why would such a young woman basically elope with a guy four times her age just days before he died?

"What motive would Kimmie have to kill O'Grady?" I asked.

"Maybe he knew what she was up to and threatened to stop it."

"Makes sense. I was talking to Chief Young, and he said the marriage license was legit. Is your family going to do anything to fight her claim to the estate?"

"Maybe," he said. "It depends on a couple of things. First, we want to know what the estate is worth, to see if it even makes sense to fight it. Yeah, houses around here, even in disrepair, aren't cheap. But there's rumors he'd taken out a reverse mortgage on it. Once the value has been determined, we'll decide if it's even worth pursuing."

"You sound pretty sure it won't be."

Jack shook his head. "It's not news Mom wants to hear, after falling for his promises all her life. But old Uncle Sy was nothing more than a hoarder of cheap junk and a con man. And not even a very pleasant con man." He raised his cup in a toast. "To family."

I tapped my cup to his and took a sip. "You know, this is a lot different from how we use to park in high school, down by the creek." I rubbed a spot on the fogged-up window again so I could see out. "The steamy windows are pretty much the same though."

"Like that time your father caught us and I pretended to have car trouble."

"And he insisted that you try to start it."

"Started right up that time," he said. "That old clunker used to stall out at every traffic light. When your Dad was right there, it worked like a charm."

"He always did have a way with cars." I leaned back against the headrest. "What ever happened to us?"

"I should have told you." Jack tapped the steering wheel with his thumbs, then let out a frosty breath. "I chickened out."

"You chickened out of our relationship? Or you chickened out of telling me?"

He looked up, his features just visible in the light from the streetlamps and his eyes glistening. "I was wrong to just not show up. I thought I could. Then suddenly, I just couldn't."

"Couldn't what?"

"Liz, we'd been dating ever since our sophomore year. Back then, much as I imagine it is now, when you're dating that long, people expect a relationship to take a certain . . . direction."

"If you think I was expecting a commitment, you're off your rocker. We were too young to think of, well, marriage or any of that stuff."

He swallowed, and his Adam's apple bobbed. "But there are often other expectations, specifically prom."

I stared up at the windshield. "I think the expectations are that I bought a dress and you rented a tux. Flowers are optional, as is a limo."

He blew out a frosty breath. "You know. *After* the prom. What did you think was going to happen?"

Suddenly my lips went dry. "Oh, *those* expectations." I glanced up at him. "You were nervous?"

He flung his head back into the seat. "You're still not getting it. We had already registered at different colleges, with separate futures mapped out."

I studied what I could see of his face in the glow of the streetlights.

"I knew that if you and I crossed that line . . ." He reached up and gently pulled a strand of hair from my face. "There'd be no going back. See, I thought we were always more than childhood sweethearts. If I was going to spend my life with a home and family, I kind of pictured you there. Liz . . ." He cupped his hand around my cheek and drew me closer.

I closed my eyes.

Then someone knocked on the car window.

I opened my eyes, as did Jack, the spell broken.

"Does your father still do that?" Jack said.

I rolled down my window. But it wasn't Dad standing in the snow. It was Irene. Or was it Lenora? No, I was pretty sure it was Irene. "Why, hello!" I said.

"I'm sorry to bug you," she said. "I didn't see that you were making out until I got close to the car. I thought you were here to spy on that Kimmie woman."

I was speechless. Jack shrugged and said, "Maybe we were."

"In that case," Irene said, "you two might want to come to our house. You can see Squiggy's house pretty good, and it's a lot warmer."

I turned to Jack. He looked at me. Moments later we followed Irene up the walk to her house, next door to Uncle Sy's old place.

Lenora met us at the door. "Oh, thank heavens," she said. "It's freezing out there. Wouldn't want to find two popsicles in the morning. Come on in and warm up."

The blast of hot air hit as soon as I crossed the threshold. Their place was as warm and humid as a hospital. The little entry foyer led into a proverbial parlor, with high-backed chairs in muted and feminine pastels. A miniature evergreen tree with tiny decorations sat on the table between them. Bing Crosby crooned softly from their old-fashioned console stereo. And there were crocheted doilies everywhere.

"They were watching Sy's house," Irene explained.

"Oh, tsk," said Lenora. "That ditz isn't even home to be watched. Come in and wait awhile. You'll know when she pulls in."

Irene pointed to the front window. "When anyone turns into that driveway, the headlights shine right into the parlor. So have a seat and visit with us while you wait."

Lenora clasped her hands together. "How about I put on the teakettle. We have cookies." She stopped. "Sorry for getting so excited, but we rarely have visitors these days. Have a seat, and we'll be right back."

As they hustled off to the kitchen, Jack and I found seats in the wingback chairs with a good view of the road.

I smiled at Jack as Irene's and Lenora's happy voices filtered from the kitchen.

He shook his head and then leaned closer and whispered, "If they offer you elderberry wine, don't drink it."

I raised my eyebrows. "Should we open the window seat?"

He shook his head. "I think there's been enough bodies, don't you?"

Lenora bustled in with a tray of bright red-and-green iced cookies. "You might need to let them defrost for a few minutes so you don't chip a tooth," she said. "We always start our holiday baking early and put our cookies in the freezer."

Jack leaned forward. "You don't find it odd that we were outside watching the house?"

"Odd?" she said. "Of course not. We've been watching it for years. As far as houses go, it's an interesting one to watch. Not that we have anything to compare it to. We've lived here all our lives, just as your Uncle Sy has. Had. Oh, dear, I hate referring to people we know in the past tense."

Irene shuffled in with an old-fashioned tea service. A definite antique and probably worth a pretty penny. After closer inspection, I realized that this was a well-loved collection and used regularly, as evidenced by the hairline cracks, occasional chips, and dull or even missing finish. I suspected they'd gotten much joy from it through the years.

The tea was hot and good.

"So you used to watch Uncle Sy, too?" Jack said.

"Oh, yes. No more than neighbors should, though," Irene amended. Then she winked. "Wouldn't want him to get the wrong idea."

"Not to worry," Lenora said. "Apparently we were too old for him anyway."

Irene laughed at her sister's joke.

"So when did this Kimmie character start hanging around?" I asked.

"She was a fairly recent development," Irene said. "Started coming around a couple months ago. She and those odd friends of hers, having orgies in the house."

"Orgies?" Jack coughed on his cookie. "With Uncle Sy?"

Lenora threw her hands up. "I know. It sounds absurd, but we know what we saw."

I leaned forward. "What exactly *did* you see?"

"Well, it would always be late at night," Lenora said.

"Ten or eleven. What kind of time is that to start a decent party?" Irene said.

"Then a whole bunch of cars would drive up, people laughing and talking and heading into the house," Lenora said.

"Young people mostly," Irene said, "with a few older ones mixed in. Men *and* women." She nodded knowingly.

"And then the house," Lenora said, "which was lit up like a Christmas tree, started going dark. They'd pull all the shades and switch off *all* the lights until it was pitch black. What else could it be but one of those orgies you read about?"

"What indeed?" Irene said.

"Is Kimmie still having these . . . orgies?" Jack asked.

"Oh, yes," Irene said. "She's had at least two of them since Sy died."

"Not very discreet, that one," Lenora said.

I turned to Jack. "Could she have wanted to get your Uncle Sy out of the way so she could have a permanent . . ."

"Party pad?" Irene said brightly.

"See," Jack said, "I told you she was up to something."

"Then there are the boxes," Lenora said. "FedEx and UPS have been doing double duty beating a path to her door."

"Delivering what?" Jack asked.

The sisters shared a conspiratorial glance, then Irene leaned in closer. "We were wondering if they were some of those sex toys."

A cookie stuck in Jack's throat again.

"Just guessing," Lenora said. "She could be redecorating, but that's not nearly as exciting, is it?"

"We've seen boxes going out, too," Irene said pointedly at Jack.

"She's liquidating Sy's assets before the will is even read," he said.

"That's supposition," I said. But Jack was up and pacing. Sore subject.

I turned back to the sisters. "Any idea where these boxes came from? Like, maybe you got a peek at a return address?"

"I never thought of that." Lenora's shoulders sank, as if she was disappointed with herself. Then her eyes lit up. "But there's some on her porch right now."

"I'm going to check it out," Jack said, already heading toward the hook where his coat was hanging.

"What if she comes home?" I stood up and met him at the door.

"She won't be home until after eleven tonight," Irene said.

I checked the time on my cell phone. It was only a little after ten PM.

Jack paused at the door. "You coming?"

I didn't answer but caught my coat when he tossed it.

"Do let us know if you find anything interesting," Irene said as she and her sister waited inside the door.

I followed Jack down the sisters' walk, but my feet balked as he headed up Sy's driveway. I remained on the sidewalk. "Is this tampering with the mail? That might be a federal offence."

But Jack was already at the door, darting from box to box. "Some of this is AV equipment. Cameras. Recorders." He picked up one box and tried to shine a light from his cell phone on the address. "It's too dark. I can't make it out." He jogged it out to where I was standing, under the streetlight. "Can you make out the return address?"

That's when the police car, sirens blaring, pulled out from a spot in the darkness with the high-powered headlights focused on us.

Chapter 13

"So what was it like in the big house?" Parker asked as I slid into the passenger seat of his car. "Did you get to keep the orange jumpsuit and the flip-flops?"

"Orange isn't my color." I took a cleansing breath. "Thanks for picking me up."

"You're welcome, but it's not something I ever thought I'd have to do. What happened?"

"I was with Jack Wallace . . ."

"Ah."

"What do you mean, 'Ah'?"

"Why were you with him? After how he treated you?"

"Ask your wife. She set it up."

"That makes me feel a lot better." We drove the next couple of blocks in silence. Then he said, "It was a theft charge?"

"I didn't steal anything. And neither did Jack. He simply carried a package to the streetlight to figure out where it came from. He wasn't going to take it anywhere. How were we to know that the chief was watching the house?"

"Ken Young?" Parker said. "Your boyfriend arrested you?"

"He's not my boyfriend." I crossed my arms in front of me. "Especially not now. When they finally got in touch with Kimmie Kaminski, she declined to press charges, so it's a moot point."

"You always did have all the luck." When he pulled up behind the shop, he turned off the engine. "Liz, I didn't tell Dad what happened. And I suggest you don't, either."

"Not a problem," I said.

"I'll wait here for Cathy. She stayed with Dad."

I leaned over and gave Parker a hug. Sometimes it can be awkward hugging your brother, even more so while he's wearing a parka and buckled into a motor vehicle. But I think he got the point.

When I got upstairs, the apartment was dark. Cathy switched off the television.

Othello hopped up, arched his back in a lazy stretch, and ambled over, rubbing against my booted legs.

"Thank heavens," Cathy whispered, coming over to hug me. "I felt awful when I heard what happened."

"Dad doesn't know, right?" I picked up Othello, and he rested against my shoulder, a prickly whisker scratching against my chin.

Cathy shook her head. "Parker texted me. Dad's sleeping now, so for all he knows, you were out late on a date."

I breathed out a relieved sigh.

"So, except for the whole getting arrested part, how did it go?"

"Are you asking about the date or the investigation?"

"Do I have to pick one?"

"Parker's waiting for you. Pick one, and I promise to fill you in on all the other details tomorrow at work."

"Spoilsport. Okay, the investigation. No, the date."

"Final answer?"

She wrinkled her nose and then nodded.

"There might be something there. We had a long talk and got some things out in the open. We ended on a good note. That is, until the sirens started."

"That is exciting!" She grabbed my arm. "Unless he's a killer."

"I don't think Jack killed anybody."

"I hope not. I can't wait until work tomorrow!" She shoved her arms into her coat and headed down the stairs.

I followed her to double-check the locks and alarm system. I must have been holding onto Othello too tightly, because he squirmed out of my arms at the bottom of the steps and took off running into the shop.

I wasn't ready to settle down for the night either, so I flipped on the shop lights, grabbed a bag of Pop Rocks from the candy display—for strength—and booted up my laptop, which I'd left at the counter. Despite the slap on the wrist we'd gotten from Chief Young, I was still curious about the boxes that we'd found on Kimmie's doorstep.

Cameras and audio equipment, Jack had said. Immediately my brain had erupted with possibilities. The first was that they were using the house to film pornos, but that might have been inspired by the sisters' lurid imaginings. They could be shooting a documentary. Or some kind of commercial. Or a low-budget independent film, using Sy's worldly goods to fund their production. Or trying really, really hard to get on *America's Funniest Home Videos*.

The box Jack dragged to the streetlight didn't have a company name on it, just three initials and a logo. It didn't take long to find the logo on Google. The company website was slow in loading, and in the meantime, Othello decided I was more interesting than his favorite stuffed terrier pull toy that sat in the store window, because he jumped on my lap.

There in the darkness, as I stroked his sleek fur, we learned that Kimmie had received a package from one of the foremost manufacturers of infrared cameras.

Huh?

\# \# \#

"Infrared?" Dad said the next morning while buttering his toast. A little too much butter, but I wasn't ready to fight the cholesterol battle. I'd told him everything about the previous evening except some of the juicier details about Jack and me and the whole part about being arrested.

"Could be making a movie of some sort," I said. "But I don't get the infrared part."

"Some law enforcement use infrared," he said. "That's how they catch people trying to enter illegally from Canada, not to mention human trafficking, at the border. Might she be filming some kind of documentary?"

"I wondered the same thing."

"You didn't ask her?" he said.

"Well, the . . . circumstances made it a little awkward." I dug into my fried egg, hoping he wouldn't press further. And if he did, at least I could take the time it took to chew and swallow to think of a response.

Dad didn't answer right away. Instead, he watched me. After I swallowed, then washed down the last bite of egg with my coffee, he attacked. "Awkward, why?" He squinted at me, and I knew I was done for.

"Fine," I said. "Jack took one of the boxes off the front porch, trying to read the return address, and we both got busted for attempted theft. Ms. Kaminski was kind enough not to press charges, but it didn't seem like a good time to give her the third degree about her shopping habits."

Dad blinked. His lips began to quiver. Then he threw back his head in laughter.

I fumed for about four seconds, then I couldn't help but smile.

"I can see why that would have been difficult." He wiped his eye. "But here's what we're going to do. When Cathy gets here, you and I are going to head over to Kimmie's house, and you are going to apologize."

"Dad, I'm not ten years old. I don't know that I owe her an apology, and I certainly won't be hauled over there like some juvenile delinquent and made to act contrite on cue. Jack's right. She's up to something."

"Of course she is," Dad said. "Lizzie, you're missing the point. How are we going to find out what she's up to unless we go over there and ask her?"

"The apology is merely a ruse," I said.

Dad winked at me. "Now, I recommend you go into the bathroom, look in the mirror, and practice your apology."

# # #

Cathy arrived early, primed with double caffeine and eager to hear what happened the evening before. It was too early to pay a social call, so while Dad showered and dressed upstairs, I filled her in and let her know of our plans for the day.

"You be careful," she said. "Dad is right. She's up to something."

"I thought you said the Wallaces were up to something."

"Is it the day for true confessions?" she said.

"As good a day as any." Then it dawned on me. "Wait, do you mean . . . ?"

She winced. "I really didn't think the Wallaces had anything to do with the murder. I thought maybe you and Jack needed time together, to see if sparks flew. Maybe fan the flames."

"Sparks did fly, and something caught. We had time to discuss what really happened years ago. I'm glad we got everything out into the open." I wagged a finger at her. "But no more deception. No more pushes, okay? I'm not a desperate spinster, at least not yet."

"Fine," she said. "Let nature take its course. Just don't sabotage it."

I nodded, but as I worked around the shop that morning, stocking inventory and waiting on customers—yes, Miles's coupon drew them in—I couldn't help thinking about what she meant.

I certainly didn't sabotage my relationships. They just didn't work out. In most cases, I ended them after I couldn't picture the two of us doing the whole starter home and picket fence together. It didn't pay to jump into things. Some of my high school friends were already onto their second husbands. I wanted a happily-ever-after kind of guy. Someone I could count on, who would tough out the rough patches with me. Someone who didn't wear his emotions on his sleeve but didn't hide them, either. He'd be strong but compassionate. A leader but benevolent.

I stopped in my tracks, staring down at the superhero action figures. I wasn't looking for a man with X-ray vision or superhuman strength. When had my ideal husband become a clone of my father?

# # #

I felt a prickle up my back, as if I was being watched, as Dad and I walked back up Kimmie's sidewalk. I glanced at the house next door, then waved to Irene and Lenora, who were standing at their window.

"Do you know what you're going to say?" Dad asked.

I squared my shoulders and nodded, although my stomach was either unhappy with lunch or nervous about this bogus apology. I took a deep breath, then pressed the bell. Just in case, I lifted the old doorknocker and rapped it a few times.

A series of bumps and footsteps followed, growing closer to the door until it finally inched open, and Kimmie, still in her pajamas, peeked out.

She blinked at me, then recognition set in. "You!" She started to close the door.

"I've come to apologize!" I said quickly. The door stopped, now cracked open about two inches. "And explain."

"Go ahead," she said.

Dad signaled me to go on, so I poured my "apology" into the two-inch gap of space. Somehow, by the time my story ended, I had morphed into some innocent bystander who practically threw herself on the doorstep to prevent Jack from absconding with Kimmie's mail. "Of course, you can't really blame him," I insisted. "He was distraught over his uncle's death."

The gap in the door neither widened nor closed. Nor was there any verbal response from Kimmie. I hazarded a look at Dad, but he rolled his eyes at my story.

Finally, the answer came. "Apology accepted. I don't want problems with Sy's family. But tell your friend the next time, I will press charges."

Dad fingered the Christmas wreath on Kimmie's door. "Wow, real evergreen!" he said, then leaned in to sniff it. "Very nice." He sounded genuinely impressed. "Wherever did you find it?"

The door opened another inch. "At the farmer's market. Have to go early though. They sell out."

"Sy never bothered much with Christmas. I don't remember him ever putting up decorations, not any of the times I answered calls here."

The door opened a couple of more inches. "Are you a cop?"

"Retired now," he said, "but I came out here quite a bit when Sy was alive. Seems he used to hear things."

A few more inches, and we could now see her face. "Strange sounds? Footsteps?"

"Sounds about right," Dad said. "Although I can't say I ever discovered the source."

Kimmie flung the door fully open now and eyed my father up and down. "Would you like to come in?"

Chapter 14

The late Sy DuPont's living room was even more cluttered than it had been the day of the wake. Cardboard boxes had been ripped open, and packing peanuts skittered in our wake like tumbleweeds. Electronic components sat on shelves that once held Sy's hoarded bric-a-brac, much of which had been cleared out. An online auction packing slip did give some credence to the claim that Kimmie was selling off Sy's possessions. Meanwhile, sparkling new cameras, recorders, and other unidentified electronic equipment were sitting on the same dining room table that a few days ago had held Jack's deviled eggs.

Kimmie removed a few boxes from the chairs at the dining room table and gestured for us to sit. "I'm most curious about the calls Sy made to the police." Before she sat down, she slipped several pieces of equipment back into their boxes. To make room? To protect it? To conceal its purpose?

Dad sat primly with his hands folded. "My, you've been busy in here. Redecorating?"

"I . . ." Kimmie paused. "Making a few changes. But about the calls that brought you here . . ."

"Oh, those," Dad said. "So many years ago. All water under the bridge now. Say, I was surprised to learn that you'd married old Sy. How did you say you met him?"

Dad sat there and blinked innocently, as if he were oblivious to her curiosity. I was on to his game. The longer it took to wrangle the information out of him, the longer we'd stay in the house and the more likely we were to learn something.

Meanwhile, my phone buzzed, and I reached to check it. It was just a spam e-mail—seems I won the Irish sweepstakes yet again—but it gave me an idea. I clicked on the camera, toggled off the flash, and nonchalantly took a few pictures of the equipment still on the table.

"I didn't say how I met him." Kimmie leaned back and folded her arms in front of her. "It's rather painful to talk about now, I'm afraid." She made a point of staring wistfully off into the distance. Apparently she was up for a match of wits with Dad.

"It must have taken a lot of courage to go through with that marriage," Dad said. "With him being so much older. I'm sure your family tried to dissuade you."

Kimmie sat up straighter. "Not at all."

"Supportive, were they?"

"Actually," Kimmie said, "I never told them. It happened so fast."

"Your mother wasn't at the wedding?" Dad asked. "Your father didn't walk you down the aisle?"

"We, uh, had a private ceremony, here at the house. Very simple."

"How refreshing," Dad said. "Most girls today want a big dream wedding." He elbowed me in the arm. "When my daughter gets married, I think she'll want me to rent out the Taj Mahal."

I sent him an adoring look. At the moment, the sentiment was faked.

"Of course, nothing is too good for my little girl when she marries that man of her dreams."

"We didn't want that kind of wedding," Kimmie said.

"How pragmatic of you," Dad replied.

She nodded, but Dad's comments about her parents had hit emotional pay dirt.

"Was it love at first sight?" Dad asked.

Kimmie didn't answer. Instead, she sent him a sly smile and said, "Would either of you care for a glass of water? Tea? Hot cocoa?"

"Hot cocoa would be lovely," Dad said.

When she left the room, I leaned forward and whispered, "Why are you letting her off the hook? Hot chocolate is going to take a while, and you know as well as I do that she's in the kitchen concocting a story."

"Meanwhile, we're in here with all her stuff." He pointed at the boxes holding the equipment she had put away.

"Oh!" I said, then started taking pictures again of every bit of equipment in sight, along with all the company logos and return addresses I could find. By the time Kimmie returned with three cups of steaming cocoa, I was back in my seat, trying to feign calmness while my heart was racing.

Dad went back to blinking innocently. "That's going to hit the spot, thank you."

"I was thinking," Kimmie said, "that I'm really not up to chatting about Sy and our relationship."

Dad leaned forward, put his hand on hers, and looked her flat in the eyes. "I understand. I lost my wife, too, some years ago." He maintained his gaze and kept his hand on hers. If anything, the pressure increased, as if he was waiting for her to cry uncle.

Moments later, she pulled her hand back and averted her gaze. "Thank you. But I still am curious to know about the calls at the house."

Dad took his time to answer. "Nothing much to report. False alarms."

"Specifically, what did he call about?" she asked.

"I fail to see why that's important now," Dad said.

"It's important to me!" Kimmie stood and began to pace, apparently growing frustrated with Dad's verbal gymnastics. "You said footsteps?"

"Why? Are you hearing footsteps?" Dad asked.

Kimmie gritted her teeth. If Dad didn't stop soon, the death toll wouldn't end at two. She was sure to strangle him. "Let's just say that I'm not sure that Sy's spirit is completely at rest."

"His spirit?" Then he stopped. For once, Dad was at a loss for words.

"Yes, I feel him here." She crossed her arms over her heart. "Close to me."

Suddenly the equipment began to make more sense. A chill ran up my back and goose bumps broke out on my arms, despite the heavy sweater I wore.

I'd figured out exactly why Kimmie had married Sy and why she wanted that house.

"You know what, Dad?" I said. "It's late. We lost track of the time, and you have that appointment at your proctologist."

"My . . ." Dad gaped at me like I'd lost my mind. For once, I was one step ahead of him.

"Get your coat. We'll be late, and if we miss it, they'll still charge us for the appointment."

Dad glared at me while he shrugged on his coat but then shifted his focus back to Kimmie and reached for her hand. "I know how difficult those first few weeks alone can be. If you need to talk to anyone in your time of grief, call me." He paused, staring intently into her eyes.

Was he coming on to Kimmie?

That was the first question I asked as we climbed into the car.

"Yes, I was coming on to Kimmie, to test a theory," he said. "Believe it or not, there are young women who are attracted to older, more mature men. I wanted to see if she was one of them."

"By setting yourself as romantic bait?"

"Well, I am younger and more virile than Sy."

"This is good, because Sy is dead," I said. "You could hardly be less virile."

"Look how fast she recoiled from one touch from a slightly wrinkled hand. No way she was romantically attracted to Sy. She married him for some other reason."

"I know exactly why she married him. She wanted the house."

"That house is a money pit," he said.

I started whistling a Christmas carol and just drove. I was enjoying my secret a little too much.

Finally, when we pulled into the alley behind the shop, Dad noticed. "Okay, smarty-pants, why did she want the house?"

I unbuckled my seat belt and twisted to face him.

"Kimmie wants the house because it's haunted."

# # #

"Have you lost your mind?" Dad said as I pushed open the back door of the shop.

Cathy stood just inside, pouring herself a cup of coffee. She looked up and smiled. "This sounds promising."

"How was business?" I asked.

"Pretty good, actually. I'm more curious how your day went."

"Apparently ghosts have now entered the picture," Dad said, with more than a hint of scorn.

"For the record," I said, "I never claimed I believed there were actual ghosts in Sy's old house. I'm saying that Kimmie Kaminski thinks there are, and that is why she wanted the house. I suspect that's the prime motivator behind all that equipment she's ordering."

"Why would she want a haunted house?" Dad asked. "Wouldn't that lower the value of the property?"

Cathy and I both shook our heads.

"Ghost hunting is big business these days," Cathy said. "Like I've been telling Liz, I think we need a ghost in the shop."

"I'm still taking applications," I said, echoing Dad's sarcasm.

Cathy laughed. "You know, you don't have to actually believe it. But many people out there do, or are at least interested enough to pay attention to the claims. That brings in more tourists."

"It doesn't scare people away?" Dad asked.

Cathy shook her head. "Skeptics don't believe, so they ignore it. The ghost chasers love that kind of thing, though, and so do a lot of the historians, if you can put a name and date and a good story to the haunting."

Dad stared at the floor for a few moments. I assumed the gears in his head were turning. "What does that have to do with the investigation?"

"Let's think about this," I said. "So Kimmie is a ghost hunter. How does she find out about Sy's house, if he's such a hermit?"

"He didn't hesitate calling the police when he heard odd noises," said Dad. "Maybe he got tired of us not doing anything about them and decided to go in another direction."

"That makes a lot of sense," Cathy said. "One of the things these ghost hunting shows on television do is try to restore a sense of safety to people. Reassure them that the spirits are friendly and there's not some ancient demon ready to strike."

"You watch the shows?" I said.

"I might have seen one or two." Cathy stopped and adjusted the collection of bracelets on her arm. "One of the women in my poetry group is involved in that kind of thing."

"Hunting ghosts?" Dad said.

"Well, she's more of a medium," Cathy said. "At the last meeting, she remarked that I had a very powerful aura."

Dad shook his head. "Please tell me you're not planning to leave your day job. You'd make a terrible medium."

I buried my head in my hands, anticipating his next remark.

"You're more of a large," Dad said.

He was saved by the bell as the front door opened. Cathy glared at him, then went to wait on the new customer.

"Welcome to Well Played," I could hear her say as she went back into the shop.

"Why do you antagonize her?" I asked.

"Too good of a line to pass up," he said.

"What if we need her help?" I moved closer to Dad so my voice couldn't be overheard. "I wonder if Cathy's medium friend might know anything about Kimmie, or even the history of the house. Maybe shed some objective light on this whole thing."

"You're seriously considering going to a medium for information?"

"Not from the beyond," I said. "I'm more interested in who was in the house the week or so before Sy and Sully died. Besides, I don't even have to make an appointment."

Dad raised his eyebrow in question.

I tapped my forehead. "Tonight's Cathy's poetry group. I sure hope they're open to visitors."

# # #

Cathy's group met in a tight space in the small bookstore. I had my handwritten poem folded in my hands but set it in my lap when my sweaty palms started to dampen the paper.

The group that gathered was eclectic, indeed. Matronly women in frumpy mom-jeans. Young hipster types. The wardrobe stretched from business casual to tie-dye to Goth black.

The first offering was a group performing something they called "sound poetry." To my untrained ears, it sounded like a barbershop quartet record played backward and at the wrong speed. The next few readers offered similar fare. Poetry had sure changed a lot since Edna St. Vincent Millay.

When it came my turn to read the poem Cathy insisted I attempt, I was both confused and intimidated.

"I'm afraid it's not very good," I said.

"We all have to start somewhere, dear," the leader encouraged.

I unfolded the page and read:

ODE TO A TOY MONKEY

On a shelf alone I stay
Frozen out of time.
Once active and prone to play,
I no more can chime.

For silent are the gears
And rusted are the springs,
A victim of the years:
The decay that adulthood brings.

But the mind is not decayed
And should my works be wound,
What terror will be wrought!
And what evil will be found!

The part about evil was a last-minute addition. As I'd stared at the grinning cymbal fiend, the verse seemed to fit. Now I wasn't so sure.

"Did you intend it to rhyme?" someone asked. And for the next forty-six minutes, the group discussed my use of point of view, then hotly debated nature versus nurture and the goodness of man and how that applied to toy monkeys. Finally, the leader put an end to it by announcing that time was up. "Please, everybody, stay and have cookies."

"But I didn't get to read," Cathy said.

"Save it for next time, dear," the leader said before turning back to me. "And, Liz, I loved your poem. Very evocative."

"Beginner's luck," Cathy grumbled as we headed over to the snack table. "Here, let me introduce you to Althena."

She never got to make the introduction. Althena came at me with both arms extended. "Elizabeth. I got the name right, haven't I? I loved your poem."

"Beginner's luck?" I said.

"No, the way you caught a spiritual element in the old toy. So many times those impressions linger on in artifacts from the past. I'd very much like to see it sometime."

"Certainly," I said. "It's in my family's toyshop. But if you're into that kind of thing, you'd probably be more interested in a house I've come across that's apparently having some spirit activity. The owner just died, you see."

"Are you talking about Sy's old house?" she said. "I'd heard that he'd passed away."

"You knew Sy?"

"Professionally," she said. "He claimed to be troubled by the spirits that inhabited the place. Old Scrooge was under the impression that I provide some kind of free pest removal service. It doesn't work like that. I'm more interested in making connections."

"Do you know if he contacted any of the local paranormal societies?" I asked.

"That sounds more his speed," she said. "Those guys are nuts, but they work for free."

"Have you ever met someone named Kimmie Kaminski?" I asked.

"Kimmie? Sure, I used to read for her all the time. Wait, are you saying Kimmie has something to do with one of those whackadoodle paranormal teams?"

"She might," I said. "I know she's been acquiring equipment. I thought perhaps she was part of one of the local groups."

"Hmm, I doubt it's that simple," Althena said. "See, Kimmie is . . . sensitive. She's drawn to spirit activity. But she's also smart. She's working on her own advanced degree in paranormal studies. Maybe that's why she has the equipment."

"Right now all that equipment is in Sy's house. She married him," I said, and then waited for a reaction.

"Married him? I wonder if her parents know," she said. "I'll have to ask them next time we talk."

"You know Kimmie's parents?"

"In a manner of speaking," she said. "When I did Kimmie's readings, who do you think she wanted to reach?"

"Her parents are dead?" Cathy said.

That explained why Kimmie hadn't told her parents she had gotten married. I took Althena by the arm. "If I could set it up with Kimmie, would you try to . . . make a connection at Sy's house? I'd like to be there."

Althena agreed. On our way to the door, she leaned back and squinted at me. "Has anyone told you that you have a very powerful aura? More than any I've ever seen."

Trailing behind us, Cathy sighed.

Chapter 15

"All set," I said, hanging up the receiver in the shop. "Althena is going to meet me there at eleven PM, and Kimmie sounded excited about the idea of a séance at the old house."

"This is a major rabbit trail," Dad said. "I don't see what you expect to accomplish."

Our conversation paused while a couple entered the shop and started wandering the aisles. A few minutes later, they left with a couple of jigsaw puzzles and a dozen vintage View-Master slides.

When they were out the door, I turned to Dad. "Hey, it doesn't matter if ghosts exist or not."

"I think that's quite relevant, if you don't want to waste a whole boatload of time. It's hard to believe what normal, sane people can talk themselves into. I don't want you marching headlong into that woman's delusions."

"No, Dad. Don't worry. You raised a firm skeptic."

"That's my girl." That familiar childish gleam returned to his eyes. "Just do me one favor, if you come across a ghost?"

"What's that?"

"Try not to think of the Stay Puft Marshmallow Man."

I smiled. "Here I was in the mood for s'mores. Still, I don't think the ghost angle is a dead end."

Dad raised an eyebrow.

"Pun unintentional," I said. "I think Kimmie's beliefs matter because they give her a motive. Look, she wants to get into the haunted house. Sy wants to find out what is going on with his house. There's the basis for a match made in heaven. Or at least some quickie Niagara Falls wedding chapel. It's simple symbiosis. But Sy has an aide. Sully O'Grady is a religious man, and he's not likely to go along with all this ghost hunting business. So . . ."

"So Kimmie whacks him?" Dad said. "Why in the shop?"

"If she'd killed him in the house," I said, thinking on my feet, "who's the main suspect? She wanted distance. So maybe she sends him out with the toys to be evaluated, and she follows him. She finds you two alone in the store, then she strikes."

Dad thought for a moment. "How does she plan to overpower two men, one an ex-cop and the other a veteran?"

"Element of surprise?" I said.

"I guess that makes more sense than a ghost did it." He scratched his cheek. "If you're right, you're walking into the house of a killer tonight." He drew in a long breath through his teeth. "I'm going with you."

"The more the merrier," I said.

"Speaking of marriage . . ." Cathy said.

"We weren't speaking of marriage," I said.

"Close enough," Cathy said. "Anyway, I decided to treat us all to lunch today!"

I eyed her suspiciously.

She winked at me. "All you have to do is pick it up."

I rolled my eyes. "Jack's place?"

"It will be ready in five minutes."

# # #

Of course, grabbing my takeout and running was not going to be an option. When I arrived, Jack was at the counter clutching my bag.

"On the house," he said. "Peace offering." He stepped from behind the counter and gestured toward a small table by the window. "How much trouble did you get in last night?"

"Not as much as you might think," I said. "Dad thought it was hysterical. He dragged me back over to Kimmie's house to apologize."

"I'm sorry for involving you in this."

"Not a problem. In fact, we have a lead thanks to you. It seems Kimmie's interest in the house isn't primarily financial. She thinks it's haunted. We're going back tonight for a séance."

Jack's face drained of all emotion, and he stared straight ahead. I wasn't even sure he was focusing on me anymore.

"Jack?"

"That . . ." he said. "That kind of makes sense. Uncle Sy used to call all the time talking about strange noises. We assumed that he wanted attention, that he was lonely, cooped up in that old place."

"Apparently he was convinced that something other-worldly was going on, enough to enter into an arrangement with Kimmie."

He raked a hand through his hair. "If she's some kind of ghost hunter and thinks the house is haunted, she's not going to let it go, is she?"

"Not without a fight," I said.

"Do you think you could get me into this séance thing?"

"Why?"

"Because I don't believe the haunting is real. Uncle Sy just had an overactive imagination, and he freaked himself out. I mean, if you sit in the dark all alone and listen long enough, anybody is going to start hearing things. If someone can explain the noises, maybe she'll move on."

"I think it's going to be harder than that to get the house back for the family."

"Then again, you never know . . ."

"What are you grinning about?"

"Maybe Uncle Sy will show up, rattle a few doors, and personally tell us who is supposed to get the Hummel."

# # #

Othello was snoozing on my pillow when I went upstairs to change for the evening. I sat on the foot of my bed and stared at the open closet. He crawled into my lap, and I scratched under his chin, then worked my way to that magic spot behind his ears. He became Silly Putty in my hand.

"What does one wear to a séance?" I didn't have any real-life experience to draw from. In the old movies I'd seen, generally people wore black, including black pillbox hats with trim black veils. And here I was fresh out of pillbox hats of any color.

I did, however, pull a pair of black jeans from the closet. I resisted the urge to dig out my *Ghostbusters* T-shirt. Or Scooby-Doo. I picked out an orange tunic, thinking it reminded me of Velma without being too overt. I held it up to Othello. "What do you think, buddy? Does it make me look smart?"

He meowed once and hopped off the bed.

A few minutes later, I knocked on Dad's door. "Last train heading out in five minutes."

He stepped out of his room in the midst of straightening his tie. "How formal is this thing?" He took in my outfit and ripped off the tie. "Isn't it a little early?"

"I wanted to stop at the house next door," I said. "Those old biddies keep a good eye on the place, and if anything new happened, they'd know about it."

"Then I'm ready." He picked up his chief of police coat.

I pointed at it. "Should you be . . . ?"

"Oh." He rolled his eyes. "Force of habit." He put it back and pulled out his short wool car coat. "Better?"

I kissed him on the cheek. "I think you're the bee's knees."

# # #

Irene and Lenora opened the door. "We're pleased as punch to see you," Lenora said. "Something odd is happening over at that house tonight."

"Something big," Irene said. "People have been in and out all day."

"I know." I kicked off my boots on their entry rug. "You remember my dad, right?"

He stepped out of the shadows.

"For a second there," Irene said, "I thought you had your young man with you again."

"Your young man?" Dad said as he shook hands with both Lenora and Irene.

"They mean Jack," I said.

Dad left it alone but winked at me.

I turned back to the sisters. "No orgies to worry about. There's a séance next door tonight."

Silence reigned, although I caught their widened eyes and a furtive glance.

"Good heavens," Lenora said finally. "Why would they want to do that?"

"Apparently," I said, "Sy was under the impression that his house was haunted. That's why Kimmie wanted the place."

"She *wanted* a haunted house?" Irene placed a hand on her cheek, as if that was the most absurd thing she'd ever heard.

"Have either of you heard any stories of hauntings next door?"

Again, the sisters shared a look, then Lenora said, "Maybe you'd better come in."

Soon Dad and I were sitting in their front parlor while they hustled to the kitchen to make tea, despite our insistence that we didn't care for any. I could make out hurried whispers but couldn't hear what they were saying.

"They're up to something," I said to Dad.

He dipped his chin once. "In spades."

When they returned with a tray, I watched their faces carefully.

Irene exhaled, then said, "I'm afraid we haven't been candid with you. We do know about the odd occurrences next door."

"But you didn't mention them?" I asked.

The sisters shared another glance, then Irene answered. "When young folks talk about things that go bump in the night, it's all eerie and mysterious." She sighed. "When older folks do, people think we're dotty."

"I'm beginning to find that out myself," Dad said. "What do you know? About the house next door, I mean."

Lenora set down her cup and cleared her throat. "Mainly what we told Sy, back when he started seeing and hearing things."

"I thought you didn't talk to him," I said.

"Not recently," Lenora said. "This was way back. In the seventies or eighties."

"It would have to be the eighties," Irene said. "I remember having big hair at the time." She turned to me. "You're too young to remember the Aqua Net generation, aren't you? Perhaps it's safer. All those fumes. But I do kind of miss shoulder pads."

Lenora shook her head. "Made me look like a linebacker."

"What exactly was Sy seeing and hearing?" I asked.

"Footsteps," Irene said. "Crashes, unexplained whispers."

"What did you think of this?" I asked.

"Well, considering the history of the house . . ." Lenora began, and then let her comment hang in the air.

"What history?" Dad asked.

"The murder, for instance," Irene said.

Chapter 16

Half an hour later, we arrived at Kimmie Kaminski's doorstep, armed with the oral history of the house—some eighty-plus years of it.

Kimmie—wearing a black T-shirt emblazoned with the slogan "Ghost Hunters Are My Rock Stars!"—opened the door. She introduced us to several young men: Chuck, Zack, and Spook (which I really hoped was a nickname), all members of her paranormal team. They were similarly dressed and generously tattooed and were in the process of setting up various electronic devices.

Many of the boxes had been cleared away. One large box, perhaps from a refrigerator, was in the center of the room. The seams were sealed with duct tape and the inside lined with aluminum foil.

"Never mind that," Kimmie said. "Just a little experiment I'm working on."

Dad did a double take as he walked by.

"Althena isn't here yet." Kimmie rubbed her hands together. "I'm excited about tonight. There's this energy that something is going to happen."

"I feel it," Chuck said. Or maybe it was Zack. They both were young men and wore black baseball caps pulled low over their scruffy faces. Spook was the only one who stood out, with his completely bald head and wide eyes.

"In addition to whoever was in the house before," Kimmie said, "it's possible that Sy and Sully could be here now, too. Especially since Sully won't be completely at rest. And Sy always wanted to know what spirits were in the house. He might stick around for those answers."

"Do you know the history of the house?" I asked.

"Just bits and pieces," she said. "Sy was a bit scattered near the end. Wait, do you know more?"

"From the neighbors," I said. "I gather this house has quite a history."

"We should document this," Zack said. Or maybe it was Chuck.

"Can we record you telling the story?" Kimmie asked.

Dad put his hand up. "Not me. Camera shy." Except I knew he was lying. "But Liz would be happy to."

"I . . . sure." I was fitted with a microphone and posed in a threadbare armchair. Lights shone and cameras rolled. While all attention was on me, Dad wandered around the house, poking and prodding and looking around. Apparently I was his search warrant.

"So what can you tell us about the history of the old DuPont house?" Kimmie asked, her voice taking on a journalistic timbre. "Is it true that old William DuPont died of malaria in the master bedroom?"

"I don't know about that," I said. "From what I heard, the house was built by a Dr. Leonard DuPont, but of no clear relation to the industrialist millionaire." I heard a quiet sigh but kept going. "According to local sources, Doctor DuPont used the home not only as his residence but also as his hospital and operating room."

A bright smile spread across Kimmie's face. "So it's possible that some of the patients died here as well."

Unless he was very good, I thought. But I bit back the snarky comment. "Several years passed before a regular office and hospital were set up, so yes, it's likely that more than one patient died here."

"I wonder if we'll hear from any of them tonight. Some residual moans, perhaps," Kimmie said, and then she started talking to the walls. Loudly. "Are any of Doctor DuPont's patients here? Did you die in this house of a disease people didn't understand? Or did you have an operation and die on a bloody operating table?" She got up and spun around, taking in every nook and cranny in the room.

Fortunately, nobody answered. She sat down. "That's a good start. Anything else?"

"The ladies next door did mention a murder."

Kimmie's jaw dropped and her eyes glittered. "A murder!" she repeated with the same tone that game show announcers used to say, "A new car!"

"Back around the turn of the century . . . not this century . . . the oldest son, a young man of dubious character, died suddenly, days after making unwanted advances toward the cook's daughter. The family suspected poison."

"And?" Kimmie was on the edge of her chair.

"Murder could not be proved," I said, supplying the second- and third-hand information the sisters had given me.

"No poison was found, so they weren't convicted. From there the story diverges. Some say the cook and her daughter were fired and left penniless. Nobody wanted to hire them, considering the allegations."

Kimmie was now smiling like the cat that ate the canary. If I tried hard, I could see yellow feathers dangling from her mouth. "So the spirit of the young man wouldn't be at rest, and the cook and her daughter might have returned seeking vengeance." I doubted anyone could be more delighted about the idea of a vengeful spirit inhabiting her house than Kimmie Kaminski.

"That's one version of the story." I was almost afraid to tell the alternate version.

Kimmie was perched so far forward in her chair that she was in danger of falling off.

I continued the tale. "The other story suggested that the cook's daughter became pregnant by the young man, and the cook and her daughter were kept prisoner in the house until she gave birth, so as not to sully the family's reputation. The baby was stillborn, and the family buried it in the walls of the house. Only then did they allow the cook and her daughter to leave. They were provided a generous stipend to relocate to the West." I sighed. "Although some say that was a story made up by the family, and both mother and daughter are also buried on the property."

Kimmie leaned back in her chair as if exhausted and gazed up wide-eyed at the cracked ceiling. "This just gets better." She sat up to face her crew. "We'll have to keep our ears open for a crying baby." Her voice crackled with enthusiasm. "Skeptics think that sort of thing can be debunked as stray signals from baby monitors." She turned back to me. "Tragic stories like that seem to echo from the walls in places like this. So many spirits not finding rest."

"Of course, these are just stories," I said.

"I'll check it all out," she said. "I have friends in the history department at the university. Never let it be said that Kimmie Kaminski ever relied on hearsay. I believe in historical documentation and the scientific method." She was producing so much saliva she could have given Pavlov's dogs a run for their money. "Was there anything else?"

"Apparently," I said, "Millard Fillmore had dinner here on more than one occasion." That wasn't unusual, since he lived in the community and, by all accounts, liked to eat.

Kimmie was off and running. "Mr. President?" she said loudly to the walls. "Mr. President, can you knock on something and let us know you're here?"

Dad had completed his circle of the room and came up behind me. "Apparently the spirit of Millard Fillmore is quite deaf," he whispered.

But Kimmie wasn't. She silenced him with a finger to her lips.

Dad stepped back toward the staircase and casually rested an arm on the cracked varnished banister, which creaked a little in the process.

Kimmie shot him a warning glare.

Everyone in the room was stock-still as she listened.

Suddenly a faint rattle seemed to come from somewhere upstairs. Kimmie and her fellow ghost hunters abandoned the interview and, along with all their equipment, scrambled up the stairs. The ceiling shook with their footsteps.

Dad wandered over to me, looking suspiciously innocent with his hands jingling something in his pockets.

I squinted at him. "Did you do that?"

He ignored my question and handed me a business card. "See what I found."

The card read,

Kimberly Kaminski
Paranormal Investigator and Relocation Specialist
Demons Exercised

"I think she was going for 'exorcised,'" I said.

"Could be exercised." Dad's lips twisted into a quirky half smile. "Have you ever seen a flabby demon?"

"I can't say I've seen one at all, and I hope to keep it that way." I slapped his arm and a couple of tiddlywinks—what purists call "tiddledywinks"—fell onto the floor. I suspected the ghost the group was currently chasing was less of an ethereal orb and more of a plastic disk.

"Wait!" I tapped the card. "This would imply that Kimmie doesn't just intend to investigate ghosts. She wants to relocate them? Move them around? Why, that would make her . . ."

"A real female ghostbuster," Dad said. "I bet that's what the chamber of foil is all about."

Moments later I was startled by a clear, definite knocking sound. It was coming from the front door, so I opened it. Jack stood on the doorstep, a few flakes of snow in his dark, curly hair. Behind him, Althena was coming up the walk.

"Where is everybody?" she said as she shrugged off her coat.

"I believe they're upstairs with Millard Fillmore." Dad managed to avoid the smile on his lips, but I could see it in his eyes. He was having an awful lot of fun.

The paranormal team came down the stairs, congratulating each other over various spikes and readings on their equipment. "I think we got an EVP," Chuck (or Zack) said.

Kimmie briefly greeted Althena and the new arrivals, then went straight to the computer, where Spook played around with the equipment.

I helped Althena find a spot to hang her coat, then asked, "What exactly is an EVP?"

"Electronic voice phenomena," Althena said, but she sounded bored when she said it. "Many paranormal groups believe that spirits can talk to them through sensitive electronic recorders or white noise."

By this point, the group had isolated the voice and were replaying it repeatedly. "I hear temperature," Zack (or Chuck) said.

"T'sure," is what I heard. They played the audio five more times.

"It could be tincture," Kimmie said. "Remember this was a doctor's office."

"Tincture," Spook said. "I think you're right."

Althena rolled her eyes, made her way to the dining room, and dropped her bag on the table with a thud. She removed a black cloth and covered the table.

"Oh, sorry," Kimmie said. "That was the first EVP I heard in this house, although Sy claimed he often heard disembodied voices."

"Perhaps we could put away the equipment for a time?" Althena said.

"Can we leave one camera on to collect evidence?" Kimmie asked.

Althena nodded, then Kimmie called for us all to gather around the dining room table.

"I hope this isn't Millard Fillmore's seat," Dad said as he pulled out a chair.

"I do sense a spirit," Althena said, "but I'm feeling a playfulness." She raised her voice. "Is there a child here?" It seemed to be a universally understood truth that spirits were deaf.

"A child or a baby?" Kimmie asked.

Althena breathed in. "A child."

"Did you hear that?" Kimmie said.

We all looked at each other.

"I heard a child's laugh upstairs," Kimmie said.

Zack and Chuck went running upstairs with their equipment.

Althena sighed heavily. "The spirits are disturbed by all this running around. The child is gone now. A girl, I believe. I got the impression that she was searching for something. 'Where's my toy?'"

I kicked Dad's foot under the table.

Althena sensed the disturbance. "Does the toy have significance?"

"Maybe." I turned to Kimmie. "Do you know if Sy has any toys in the house?"

"He was like eighty. Why would he have toys?" she answered.

"Old toys," Dad said. "Very old toys."

"Come to think of it," Kimmie said, "I think I did see some when I first came here. One was an elephant. I didn't pay much attention."

Dad leaned forward. "When was the last time you saw them?"

"Not since I moved in, I know that much." She eyed Jack Wallace. "But a lot of things went missing after the wake."

"None of my family took any toys from this house," Jack said.

"These would have gone missing before Sy's death." I felt like a rat, but now that we were on the topic, I took my opportunity. "What can you tell us about Sy's aide?"

Kimmie squinted at me. "You mean the one that died in your shop? Sully? That's one reason I wanted you here tonight. Murder causes a strong disturbance in the energy." She circled to face an empty corner. "Sully, are you here tonight? Did you come back to check on Sy?"

I decided to try a bolder tact. "Why would Sully take toys out of this house? For what purpose?"

"Were they valuable?" Jack asked.

"We're not talking millions or anything," I said.

"Old toys aren't typically objects of theft," Dad explained. "Not by people who know what they're doing. The most valuable ones are usually worth hundreds. Only the rarest can achieve values in the thousands."

"Maybe he didn't know what he was doing, then," Kimmie said. "Maybe he just wanted them for himself."

I shook my head. "Sully seemed to be a man of faith and character, from what everybody else has told me."

Kimmie snorted. "He was a self-righteous jerk. The only reason Sy kept him on as long as he did was because they were both veterans, and Sully was the only one up for one more retelling of the Battle of Triangle Hill."

Dad sent her a sympathetic look. "I don't imagine you and he got along all that well. Sully would have been against ghost hunting and communing with spirits."

Kimmie's jaw set. "Some people don't understand our research and what we are trying to do."

I pulled out Kimmie's business card that Dad had found. "Do you mean cash in on the transfer or removal of spirits?"

Kimmie put her hands on her hips. "I see someone has been snooping. Those cards are old. Experiments didn't exactly work out the way I'd hoped."

"You mean the tinfoil chamber of doom wouldn't contain them?" I asked.

Kimmie rolled her eyes. "It's just a prototype. But no, it doesn't contain them. Mostly because it's impossible to tell when they're actually inside the thing."

"Wait, did you really think people were going to pay you to get rid of their ghosts?" Jack said.

Kimmie closed her eyes, trembling like a firecracker about to go off. "That was only part of it. Yes, some people are freaked out by having ghosts in their houses."

"What were you going to do with them?" Jack said. "Put them all in a foil box?"

"Will you stop with the box?" Kimmie said. "The box was only temporary. See, for every person who wants to get rid of a spirit, there's at least one person out there who would like one."

"You wanted to . . . sell ghosts?" Jack threw his head back in laughter, but Althena was appalled.

"It doesn't matter much anyway, because I haven't figured out how to trap them, so don't worry. However, if this house is as active as it seems, I don't even need to go that far. I can open up the place for tours and use that to fund my experiments."

"Sully would have tried to dissuade Sy from inviting you and your team to investigate the house," Dad said, his voice soft but distinct. "He certainly wouldn't want you marrying the man and moving in." Dad squinted at Kimmie, whether for effect or because of the dim light, I wasn't sure. "What happened between the two of you?"

"Look, I didn't invite you here to interrogate me," Kimmie said. "The truth is, Sy did invite me, and he liked what I had to say so much, he made sure I got the house so I could continue my work."

"But why marry him?" Jack said.

Kimmie laughed. "It suited both our purposes. Even though he made sure he changed his will, leaving his house to a stranger would always be suspect. Had I somehow swindled the old dude? Was he really of sound mind and body? Besides, Sy lived here a long time. The spirits surely were comfortable with him. As his wife, the relationship gave me a clear connection that they would understand." She smiled at Jack. "Mostly Sy was for the idea because he wanted to see how the family would react. Too bad he never got a chance to tell them."

Jack tipped his head. "There's still the second autopsy."

"Do you seriously think I offed your dear Uncle Sy?" Kimmie said.

"You didn't have to," Jack said. "But if evidence comes back that suggests he might have suffered neglect in his final days, expect a good fight in court." He held up his hands. "Not from me, mind you."

Kimmie smirked at him, and her voice came out dripping saccharine. "Of course not."

Suddenly Althena, who had been silently listening to us all this time, put her hands up, as if to quiet us. "Somebody's here. Sully, is that you?"

I distinctly heard a cough.

"Who was that?" I said.

Everybody at the table shook their heads. Zack and Chuck were still upstairs.

"Sully," Kimmie said loudly, "are you angry at me for getting you fired?"

"Uncle Sy," Jack called out, mocking her tone, "are you angry at Kimmie for making a mockery of your death?"

"No," Althena said. "I'm sensing—"

Before she could finish, a whispered voice said, "Yesssss." As the final consonant faded into a hiss, we all looked at each other, wide-eyed and barely breathing.

Chapter 17

"Did someone move the monkey?" I stood at the register and stared, transfixed, at the toy with the cymbals. I wasn't sure what was different, but a shiver ran down my spine anyway. I had a macabre sense that, when nobody was in the shop, it hopped down from the shelf and banged its cymbals together, sending a message in Morse code to all the other demonic monkeys, thus furthering their plot for world domination. Or, at least, my personal demise.

Cathy waved a hand in front of my face. "Don't freak out, Liz. I dusted the shelf this morning."

I closed my eyes and sighed in relief. When I looked up, Cathy was grinning at me.

"I don't blame you for freaking out," she said. "Last night sounded bizarre."

"Do you believe all that ghost stuff?" I asked. "I mean, somebody could have faked the voices."

"You mean like *someone* faked the noises?" She waved at Dad.

He looked up from where he was trying to patch his prized toy soldier and sent her a sheepish grin.

"Jury's still out," she said, "and I don't expect them to reach a verdict anytime soon. Is there anything so wrong about wanting to reconnect with those you lost?"

"It's not natural," Dad said. He and I exchanged glances. While living with Mom had been tough, losing her had been just as hard on Dad. On all of us, really. I think there's a sense of missing not only someone but also what that relationship could have been and never would be.

"Of course it's not natural," Cathy repeated, oblivious to our moment. "That's why they call it the *super*natural."

"I'm still more interested in what we learned about real, flesh-and-blood people last night," Dad said. He pushed his mound of plastic and patches aside before setting up a portable table in an open space near the register. "Let's concentrate on the normal rather than the paranormal." He pulled open a folding chair and sat down.

"We certainly learned a lot about Kimmie Kaminski." I opened another chair.

"Are we calling Kimmie normal?" Cathy said as she set another chair at the table for herself.

"I need something to write with," Dad said. "I miss my board at the station."

Cathy handed him an Etch A Sketch.

He stared at it blankly, as if he were considering it.

"We don't have twelve years." I went to the counter and retrieved some old scrap paper and a jelly jar full of mismatched pens we keep for scoring our game tournaments.

Dad fished out a colorful pen bearing the name of a local dentist and started writing. "So Kimmie Kaminski. Maybe not normal, but at least she'd register on an infrared camera,"

Dad said, then paused. Apparently it was up to us to fill in the gaps.

"She seems to think she will inherit Sy DuPont's house," Cathy said. "She might have wanted to kill the old man so she could claim her inheritance quicker."

"We need to focus on O'Grady's death," Dad said. "Unless the medical examiner finds anything to suggest that Sy DuPont's death was caused by anything unnatural. I suppose she had means and opportunity. Anyone, really, might have followed Sullivan O'Grady here. My question is, *why* would Kimmie follow him, and why would she choose this shop as a location to commit murder?"

I found myself sucking on my chapped lower lip. "It's still unclear to me why Sully came here." I broke eye contact with Dad before continuing. This would be so much easier if he remembered what had happened the night O'Grady died, even if he remembered why they'd met in the closed shop at night in the first place. "What if it wasn't about the toys? What if he came to tell you something, maybe about Kimmie? What if he sought you out because you were once the chief of police?"

"Why not go to the current chief?" Dad asked.

"Because he trusted you more," Cathy said. "What do we really know about Ken Young, anyway?"

"If that were the case, perhaps the toys were merely a ruse to give him a reason to see you," I said. "But why would he need one?"

Dad nodded. "The truth is usually simpler. It's safer to work with the assumption that O'Grady came for an evaluation of the toys."

BARBARA EARLY

"The toys that belonged to his employer," Cathy said.

"Or to Sy's neighbors," I said, "if we believe Irene and Lenora. And eventually to the toy museum, unless Sy changed his mind about donating them posthumously when he reworked his will to include Kimmie."

Dad leaned his elbows on the table. "That's a lot of claims on a collection of old tin." He scratched his brow. "So assuming O'Grady didn't steal them, which jibes with what others have said about him, it's possible that Sy initially sent his aide here to get an evaluation of the toys. Maybe he was trying to decide what to do with them and wanted to know what they were worth."

"Do we even know that yet?" Cathy asked.

"Mostly," Dad said. "A few hundred each, give or take. Except the mystery one nobody can identify. Miles was hoping to hear from the expert later today."

"Fred and Ginger," I said. "I don't think it's as simple as O'Grady being sent here by his employer. He seemed awfully nervous. Then he gave us the fake name. If he was here on a legitimate errand, he'd have no reason to be so stressed, certainly not enough to hide his identity."

"The question is, from whom?" Dad said. "That opens up a whole 'nuther list of suspects: people who feel they'd have some claim to the toys."

"The Wallace family, for instance," Cathy said. "Dear old Uncle Sy had been making them promises for years. They can't have been happy to learn he was stringing them along."

"They were all ready to clear that place out, until Kimmie walked in," I said. "I suppose they might have resented O'Grady if they saw him walking around town with a box of their uncle's things and thought he was trying to abscond with part of their inheritance. But enough to kill? So far, beyond a few snarky remarks, the Wallaces seem to be channeling their anger into litigation."

"*Channeling?*" Cathy repeated.

"That's the spirit," Dad said. "You're possessed by a great talent, but you don't have a ghost of a chance of surpassing me in the pun department."

"I'm haunted by that reality. Sorry, the pun wasn't intentional," I said. "I just mean that the Wallaces might be ticked enough to take dear Kimmie to court, but they're far from homicidal. Jack seems to find it downright amusing."

Dad tapped the pen on the table. Just then a mother and young daughter came into the shop. He shuffled his paper into a neat pile, with blank sheets on top. I guessed a murder investigation might scare away customers. While the pair strolled into the doll room, Cathy hovered nearby, ready to be of assistance. I went back to the counter, and Dad drained his coffee cup and headed to the back room for a refill.

His timing was again impeccable, because no sooner had he cleared the threshold than Peggy Trent entered with a covered plate. She glanced around the room and the corners of her mouth fell. "Don't tell me I missed him again! One of these days I'm going to lay eyes on that man. I suppose I can leave these with you."

As soon as she put the plate on the counter, a delightful aroma of ginger and nutmeg wafted all around me. She peeled back the foil to reveal perfectly plump and gorgeously decorated gingerbread men. "I just have to share my holiday baking," she said, "and with your mom gone these many years, I can't imagine anyone I'd rather share with. You'll make sure that elusive father of yours gets at least one, right?"

"I'm sure he'll enjoy these," I said. That much was true. He loved her cooking. It was merely Peggy he couldn't stand.

"Will the shop be open for game night tonight?" she asked, tapping the table where Dad had left his stack of notes.

"Absolutely," I said.

"Maybe I'll see him there." She lingered a few more moments, pretending to peruse our inventory, but her gaze didn't move far from the door to the back room. Eventually she gave up the pretense and drifted out.

No sooner was she out of sight than Dad returned with his coffee.

"How do you do that?" I said. "It's like a superpower."

"Do what?" he asked.

I held out the plate of gingerbread cookies. He winked, then helped himself to a cookie. As did Cathy and I. The cookies were soft, chewy, and sweet, with just the right amount of molasses without being overpowering.

"That woman can bake," I said. "I've changed my mind. I want her to be my new mommy."

Dad shook off the idea like a dog shakes off bath water.

"Besides," Cathy said, then paused to bite off the head of another gingerbread man. "How do you know that the baking wouldn't stop the moment she thinks she has him, huh? Your best bet is to keep stringing her along."

"I haven't given her one ounce of encouragement," Dad said.

I licked my finger. "Cathy's right. Just keep doing what you're doing."

Cathy had to swallow quickly. Her customers had exited the doll room and were headed to the register with several vintage Barbies. "This was my first Barbie," the mother said, smoothing the doll's hair, "and now I can share it with my little girl."

I smiled at Dad. That's what we were all about: helping adults rediscover the joys of play and passing the traditions on to future generations.

As soon as the customers left, Dad pulled out his papers again. "Where were we? Oh, yeah, people who might have had claim to the toys. I have the Wallace family, and I suppose we need to add *Arsenic and Old Lace*."

"Those sweet old biddies?" I said.

"Which is why I called them *Arsenic and Old Lace*," Dad said. "To remind you that not all old maids are sweet and innocent. The sisters do have a prior claim on the toys, at least the boxers."

"True," I said, "but they seemed genuinely surprised that Sy still had their toy."

"Surprise can be faked," Cathy said, helping herself to one more cookie.

"Even so," I said, "how would Irene and Lenora have known that O'Grady had the toys and was bringing them here? Do they even have the mobility to follow him? Would either one of them have had the strength to drive a lawn dart into a man's chest?"

"Don't know. Don't know. Don't know." Dad put three question marks on the page next to their names. "Whenever I talk with them, I get the feeling that they know far more than they're letting on."

I was about to argue with him, but I'd entertained the same impression, and on more than one occasion. "The only other folks with any kind of claim to the toys would be the museum. But they didn't have to kill to get them. As far as they were concerned, the toys were going to be added to their collection upon Sy DuPont's death."

"Unless," Cathy said, "he changed the will and everything went to Kimmie."

"How would they know that?" I said.

"Too bad." Dad shook his head. "Can you imagine how much fun it would be to frame Peggy Trent?"

I didn't want to encourage Dad's bad behavior. "So the only other suspect I can think of is Mrs. O'Grady."

Othello picked that moment to jump on the table, only there were no game pieces to swat around. He seemed disappointed. He gave the plate of cookies a sniff, but then backed off. Perhaps the intense spices messed with the super-sniffer cats were born with. Dad scratched him behind the ears, and Othello climbed onto his shoulder to snuggle.

"It's usually the spouse," Dad said. "So much simpler that way."

"And the O'Gradys were separated," I said.

The bell over the door rang again, but this time Miles walked in. Dad waved him over and offered him a cookie. Miles took one but leaned against the display while he ate it rather than taking a seat at the table.

"We were discussing the murder," Dad explained. "I'm sure Mrs. O'Grady's at or near the center of the official investigation." He stroked Othello's tail, which the cat then swished in his face. Dad was unfazed. "I could be wrong, but I still don't think she did it."

"Because she's a woman?" Miles asked.

"I think a woman could have killed him," Dad said. "I have no illusions that the fairer sex is incapable of violence. And if it's a question of strength, those blades were sharp. Back in the day, lots of folks with clay soil used to sharpen the points even more. I knew we couldn't sell the darts. Still, I thought they'd be safe locked in the case. I should have chopped off the points or thrown the whole set away. Here's a new company policy: no more lethal toys. Period."

"You couldn't have predicted what happened," I said.

"I also can't see Mrs. O'Grady using a lawn dart to kill her husband." He held his hands up to stave off any protest from us. "Life insurance aside, I don't think that Mrs. O'Grady really wanted to have to raise that brood of kids all by herself."

"She might have forgotten that in the heat of anger," I said.

"What was there to be so angry about here? If she'd caught him cheating with another woman, then maybe. But he was meeting an old man in a toyshop. What could have happened to set her off?" Dad shook his head. "It doesn't work for me."

"Is there anyone you like better for it?" I asked.

"What about the people who tried to break into the house?" Cathy was keeping up with the conversation, but her eyes were glued to the cookies.

"Let's protect these from Othello." I secured the foil over the plate. But Othello just blinked at me from Dad's shoulder. "The break-in was the day of Sy's funeral," I said. "If whoever tried to gain entry into the DuPont house was the same person or group of people who killed Sully, they would have already had the toys. So what then? They figured out where the toys had come from and decided to go back for more. But how would they have known about the connection between O'Grady and DuPont?"

"Does the attempted break-in even have anything to do with O'Grady's death?" Dad said, but I doubted he was talking to me. His eyes were on Miles.

"I wouldn't rule it out." The cookies now out of sight, Cathy swept back into the doll room.

Some strange vibe was passing between my father and Miles. "Is there something you two would like to tell me?" I asked.

Dad stared down at his paper while Miles leaned back and studied his sneakers for a good ten seconds. Finally, he looked up. "I might know who tried to break into the dead guy's house."

Dad set his pen down.

"Some dudes I used to hang with. Only they swore they were done with that kind of thing. Said they were only doing a favor for someone."

"A favor?" I said. "Someone asked them to break into the house?"

"It's not like they wanted to talk to me about it, considering they know who I work for. They beat around the bush, said that the only way they'd do a job like that is with some inside connection." Miles shrugged as if he thought the idea crazy too. "They kept telling me they weren't breaking in. They had a key."

"A key?" Dad leaned back, grimacing.

"Where'd they get a key?" I asked.

"That they're being tight-lipped about. Asked me why I was so curious all of a sudden. I didn't want to push."

"You were right to stop." Dad flipped to a clean sheet of paper. "Let's think about this for a minute. Does anything connect the break-in with Sully's death?"

"Okay," I said, trying to follow where he might be leading with this. "When the attempted break-in occurred, Sully was already dead, but nobody knew the victim was Sully."

"Except the killer," Dad said. "Presuming he even knew whom he had killed."

"That's a scary thought," Cathy called out. She peeked her head back in the door. "If the attack was random, any of us could have been killed."

"Doesn't feel random," Dad said.

"How do they even investigate a random attack?" I asked.

"Forensics, hopefully," Dad said. "But all those tests take time. For now, they have to assume that the killer was someone who knew the victim and had a motive. I think we should, too." He tapped the paper. "Now, back to the time of the break-in."

"Sy was being buried," I said, "but the obituary was never printed in the paper. Yet somehow, Miles's . . . former associates knew the house was unoccupied, which was unusual, since everybody I've talked to has told me that Sy never went anywhere."

"They found out from someone," Miles said. "Maybe this mystery person who gave them the key?"

Cathy peeked her head back out. "An inside job? One of the relatives wanting a jump on things?"

"That doesn't entirely make sense, either," Dad said. "Why involve these young men when almost everyone had opportunity to get into the house and retrieve whatever they wanted? The relatives all had keys. Kimmie had a key. Presumably, O'Grady had a key. By the look of things, Sy hadn't changed the lock in years."

"The preservation folks frown on modern-looking locks," Cathy said.

"Perhaps Sy was too cheap to invest in a more secure reproduction when the original worked just fine," I said. "You don't suppose O'Grady could have been killed for his key, do you?"

"Oh, they wouldn't have . . ." Miles started, but his brow creased in worry.

Dad jerked his head up suddenly. "Now there's a sixty-four-thousand-dollar question. I'd like to know if a key was found on him." His gaze fixed on Miles. "It would be better for your friends if Sully had a key among his possessions." He turned and gave me one of his mischievous grins. "One of us should probably make nice with Ken Young and see if we can find out."

"Why me?"

"He likes you more," Dad said.

"He *so* likes you," Cathy said, leaving me blushing while she went back to her work.

"Fine, I will endeavor to evoke my wiles tonight, *if* he comes to game night. Which I doubt, since he's working a murder case."

"He'll be here," Cathy said. "Because you're here."

Dad grinned. "If it were me, I'd be here."

"You're blowing this out of proportion," I said. "Don't go renting a hall or anything. He smiled at me a couple of times. That's all."

Cathy whistled the first few bars of the wedding march from the other room.

I pointed a finger at Dad. "You lie. You'd be out working the case."

"Yes, Lizzie, I'd be working the case. But I'd still be here." His voice grew more solemn as he hazarded a glance to the spot where Sullivan O'Grady took his last breath. "This is the scene of the crime."

Chapter 18

It was Monopoly night at Well Played, and by six thirty, Cathy and I had pushed aside all the moveable displays and set up four folding tables. These supplied enough room for eight vintage boards—including a variety of game tokens, real estate, houses and hotels (both wood and plastic), and a king's ransom in colorful fake currency.

"You'd better lock up Othello." Cathy slipped on her gloves, getting ready to leave.

"Right," I said. Monopoly was one of his favorites. One sprint across the boards would send everything flying.

After a brief hunt, I found the cat sitting in the shop window, expressing amorous attentions to a Scottish terrier pull toy, which now had a little white cat fur mingling with his synthetic black variety. "You nut." I lifted him gently into my arms. That is, I tried, but he stuck his claws into the carpet lining the window, and I had to pry him up. "An office romance is always a bad idea. Trust me on this."

As he steadied himself on my shoulder, digging in his claws, I looked out onto the street and wondered how the weather would affect attendance. A light, dusty snow had fallen, and a circuitous breeze swirled and rippled it across the brick street and sidewalks like sand in a desert. It would be easy to get lost in that, mesmerized by the changing patterns. I wrenched myself away and carried Othello upstairs.

When I came back down, Dad had cranked up the Christmas music and picked up a miniature cannon, one of the retired tokens that still graced our boards. "Funny how games change over time."

I nodded, not just thinking about the quality of the playing pieces. That Monopoly started out as The Landlord's Game is a sad bit of game history. The original purpose was to expose the greed of property owners who took unfair advantage of their tenants and *not* to celebrate their cunning. Others eventually took the game, improved upon it, and sold it to Parker Brothers, while the original developer got nothing. Lessons in greed well-learned.

Soon the bell over the door started chiming at regular intervals. Our friends and neighbors greeted us, some giving Dad a hug at the door, or at least a smile and a wave, before they took up their positions at the gaming tables.

Dad's prediction was correct: Ken came. He scanned the store from one end to the other before claiming a chair on the outskirts of the room, giving him a full view of everyone present. Only then did he wave at me and slip off his jacket.

Even Dad decided not to lock himself up in his garret. He shoehorned himself in at a nearly full table just before Peggy Trent arrived. She claimed the last spot one table over to join a game with Jack Wallace and Glenda, the owner of the yarn shop. Peggy briefly acknowledged her opponents, then concentrated all her attention on my father.

"There you are, Hank!" She followed this up with her best come-hither look. If she wasn't careful, Dad was going to start running in the opposite direction. She reached into her tote bag and pulled out another covered plate. "I brought more cookies," she practically sang out.

I came to Dad's rescue. "Thanks for the ones you sent over earlier. But . . ." I paused and put on my fake contrite voice. "We don't allow outside food brought in during game night." I shrugged, hoping I came across as a little bit sweet.

"Oh, sorry." She pushed the plate into her bag and fished out her knitting. "Remind me to give them to your father before I leave."

Like Peggy, Glenda had brought her knitting, and the click of needles soon blended with the sounds of dice rolling, deal-making, and general conversation.

Jack caught my arm. "Are you playing, Liz?" His expression said, "Rescue me."

"Sorry, not in a playful mood, I guess." Instead, I went to the candy counter, grabbed an assorted armful, and started making the rounds.

All our gaming tables were at or near capacity. Maybe some of the morbid types wanted to ogle the crime scene and hear the latest gossip about the murder, but I'd like to think that at least a few had come to show their support. They were buying snacks, at least, and a congenial mood prevailed, even while players scarfed up properties and tried to drive each other into bankruptcy.

Lori Briggs had assumed a spot at Ken's table, and I think she was regretting it. If there was any truth to Peggy's unveiled accusation of Lori flirting with the chief, he wasn't reciprocating, at least not tonight. Not engaged in the game or in conversation, he mechanically rolled the dice, moved his racecar, and then returned to watch the crowd.

I tried to follow his gaze. Who was he watching? These were our friends and neighbors, playing games and having fun. Surely none of them was a cold-blooded killer returning to the scene of the crime. And were criminals even drawn back to the scenes of their crimes? Or was that just old movie fodder?

A shout drew my attention. Jack was performing a rather nerdy celebratory dance, fanning his face with Park Place and Boardwalk. I couldn't help but wince when Peggy tucked States Avenue and St. James Place under her corner of the board. Bad trade.

Jack apparently mistook my wince for admiration of his gamesmanship. "Pull up a chair, Liz. Come watch me win."

Jack was making one of the biggest mistakes you can make: selling off everything for a pricy monopoly, leaving himself cash poor and unable to build on it. Meanwhile, Peggy started adding cheap houses to hers. From those she'd collect regular rents, keeping Jack cash poor. Peggy had this one all but locked up.

Despite the train wreck I knew was coming, I set up another folding chair where I could watch this game as well as Dad's. Unfortunately, it also left me staring straight at my nemesis, that little monkey with the cymbals. Tonight they seemed ready to strike.

While Glenda dithered over whether or not to buy Marvin Gardens, Jack leaned over. "I don't know if you got a chance to hear yet. The second autopsy results came back on Uncle Sy."

Even though his tone was low, heads turned in our direction, necks craning to hear.

"Natural causes," he said. "Same as before. Now the cousins want another service. Only nobody wants to pay for it." He eyed Ken.

The chief's jaw tightened. "The village is paying for the diggers and all the complications involved since the ground is frozen. A service is the responsibility of the family."

"Wouldn't that be Kimmie's job this time?" I asked.

Peggy leaned forward. "Is Kimmie the new wife I heard about?"

"Yup," Glenda said.

"You guys know about Kimmie?" I asked.

"Been the topic of the town for days," Glenda said. She must have seen our startled expressions. "Well, when a college student up and marries an octogenarian bachelor in a community our size, people are going to talk about it. A few of the ladies in my morning crochet class have decided that the . . . unusual excitement did him in." She paused for effect. "Mostly, they're asking why. What was she hoping to gain?"

"A haunted house," Jack said. Excited whispers rippled across the room, like a stone tossed into a pond.

Glenda and Peggy both stopped their knitting in midstitch.

"Haunted?" Peggy asked. "And she still wanted it?"

"Oh, haunted places mean tourist dollars now," Glenda said. "Why, we have our own ghost at the yarn shop."

"How do you know?" I asked. "Have you seen it?" I wondered if Dad had gone all across town with his tiddlywinks.

Glenda continued her knitting. "One of the local paranormal groups caught some men's voices or something like that, so we tell the tourists that it's Millard Fillmore."

"Apparently he likes to make the rounds," Jack said.

"Oh, dear," Glenda said. "Is he taken already? Maybe I could say it's William McKinley. Is he taken?"

"I don't think so," Peggy said, "but has he ever been to East Aurora?"

This question sparked a general discussion. The conclusion was that although there was no direct proof, at least without a visit to the historical society, that William McKinley ever visited East Aurora, it was well documented that the druggist who supplied McKinley's medicine eventually settled in the village. So the footsteps above the yarn shop might easily belong to the druggist, pacing over some mistake, or McKinley himself, seeking retribution for the ineffective medicine.

Once that was settled, Peggy turned to Jack. "Do you think Kimmie Kaminski's claim on the house will hold up?"

Jack pushed up the sleeves of his sweater. "Personally, I'm up for letting her keep that spooky old place." Jack squinted at my father. "Actually, it wouldn't surprise me if half of what happened the other night was faked."

"The other night?" Ken asked from across the room.

"Séance at the old DuPont house," someone said. I wasn't even sure where the voice had come from. That's one thing about small towns—not many secrets. Except for who had killed Sullivan O'Grady, that is.

"A séance?" Ken was apparently the only one in the room that hadn't heard, not having lived in town long enough to be a part of the gossip network. I wasn't sure if that would help or hinder his investigations. "Who all was at this shindig?" he asked.

"Kimmie and her paranormal team," I said. "Althena, the psychic."

"I was there," Jack said.

"Dad and me," I added.

"Don't forget Millard Fillmore," Dad said.

"I'm sticking with McKinley," Glenda said.

Ken put his hands to his temples. "What were you trying to accomplish with a séance?"

"For one thing," Dad said, "I wanted to see Kimmie in the house. Get a feel for what she was up to. She seems sincere in wanting the house for her paranormal investigations."

"Perhaps Sullivan O'Grady was a threat to her plans," Peggy said.

"Sully wasn't a threat to anyone," Glenda said, "unless you had Saturday morning plans and he was headed up your driveway for a little impromptu Bible study."

"That doesn't, however, mix with ghost hunting," Peggy said.

"I'm just ready for all this murder business to be over," Lori Briggs said, then let two dice fly from her hand. One of them fell (accidentally?) on the floor, so she got up to retrieve it, managing to expose quite a bit of cleavage from her V-neck sweater. In Ken's direction, of course. "When are you going to make an arrest?"

"When I have enough evidence to make a case," Ken said, his ears coloring.

"Does that mean you know who did it?" I asked.

He was wise enough not to answer.

Glenda laughed. "Maybe we should have played Clue instead of Monopoly tonight. Was it Kimmie Kaminski in the toyshop with a lawn dart?"

A few titters of laughter ensued, but the quip hung in the air, like smoke at a cigar convention. Sullivan O'Grady had been killed here, in the shop. With a weapon that was also here, in the shop. So all anyone needed to do to complete his card and make an accusation was decide whodunit. Although those gathered here were too kind to say it, the most likely explanation was that he was killed by someone associated with the shop. Like my father, for instance. Or me. Or Miles. Or Cathy. Or Parker. But any of these possible solutions would destroy life as I knew it, so I wasn't ready to lend credibility to any of them. I had emotionally eliminated the five most likely suspects. I wondered if Dad had as well.

Ken's game wrapped up first. He lost, badly, which, come to think of it, is generally how you lose Monopoly. I went to his table to help put the pieces away.

"Thanks," Lori said, with more than a hint of insincerity. With nothing left to do, she made a remark about getting home before the weather got worse.

Ken dawdled over the game board, absentmindedly flipping the racecar between his fingers while he continued to study the other players.

"Chief?" I said, then waited until he looked up, almost as if coming out of a dream.

"Sorry, Liz. Woolgathering, I guess."

"I was wondering . . ." I kept my voice low, but above a whisper. Whispering indicated that what you were trying to say was secret, or at least private. And human nature made people all the more eager to hear. If you spoke in a normal voice, like you didn't mind being overheard, people tended to filter you out. Something I'd learned from Dad, but I couldn't recall when.

"Do you know if any keys were found on Sullivan O'Grady's body?"

"Any number of them," he said. "Did you have any particular one in mind?"

"How about a key to Sy DuPont's house?"

"You're wondering if whoever tried to get into the DuPont house the morning of the funeral might have taken it." Ken leaned back in his chair, crossed his arms, and tilted his head. "Not a bad theory, except . . ."

"Except?"

"O'Grady turned in his key when he was fired. I learned that by talking with Kimmie Kaminski about something other than things that go bump in the night. She witnessed the old man giving him the boot and saw Sully hand his key back to Sy."

So the young men who showed up at the DuPont house didn't get a key from the corpse. So where did they get it?

Still, the relief on Dad's face was palpable. By dismantling that last connection between the young men and the murder victim, he had removed any sinew connecting Miles to the murder.

The rest of the games eventually wrapped up, and people tugged on their coats, gloves, and hats and left without a lot of chatter or threats of rematches. The talk of the murder had perhaps cleared the air a bit while simultaneously muddying it.

Finally, Dad excused himself and climbed the stairs toward his bed, carrying, of course, the plate of cookies from Peggy.

Jack lingered behind, helping to break down the tables and chairs and push the portable display shelves back into place. "Liz?" He sheepishly bobbed from foot to foot. "Do you have a moment to talk?"

I still had the last two folding chairs tucked under my arm, so I handed him one. I opened the other and sat down.

"I wanted to ask about the other night." He pushed his chair open and straddled it, facing me. "Am I right in thinking that your father rigged a lot of that stuff at the séance?"

"Some of it. I'm never letting that man near a set of tiddlywinks again. But not the voices."

"Do you think the place really could be haunted?"

"Something is going on over there. Whether it's a portal to the underworld remains to be seen."

"Liz, nobody thinks your Dad killed Sully O'Grady." The expression in his eyes was intense and sympathetic. He laid a comforting hand on my leg. Then, as if he realized what he was doing, yanked it back. "We're in the same boat, you know."

"And me without my passport."

He sent me a wry smile. "Just because you can laugh about something, it doesn't make the problem go away."

"Sorry, just my coping mechanism."

"I can see that," he said, grabbing my hand. "Only I think there are better ways to cope. Together."

"Jack Wallace, are you propositioning me? It's a little cold right now for a cruise on that boat of yours."

"We can talk about *that* later." He gave me a shy smile. "I just meant that until they figure out who killed this Sullivan O'Grady, people are going to look at us both a little funny."

"Everybody seemed fine tonight."

He waited while my words hung in the air, hollow and false.

"Fine, you're right," I said. "What are you proposing?"

"Now who's doing the propositioning?" he said. "See, two can play at that game."

"Now we're back to playing games. Checkers? Chess? More Monopoly?"

"Clue," he said. "I think you and I should team up again and figure out who did this thing."

"Because that worked out so well last time," I quipped.

"And if the chief decides at the end that your father did it? Or my mother? Liz, I know you and your dad are working the case. I'd like to help."

"How exactly would you like to help?"

"I beg your pardon?"

"You're interviewing for the position of amateur sleuth slash sidekick. We'll dispense with the written résumé, but next time come more prepared. Now, Mr. Wallace, tell me your qualifications. What can you add to this investigation?"

He straightened up in his chair, as if he were at a real job interview. I gave him bonus points for playing along. "I'm a hard worker and very enthusiastic."

"That's what they all say. Honestly, Mr. Wallace, you're going to have to bring more to the table than that. Otherwise, you're wasting my time."

"I can give you unrivaled access to the Wallace family secrets."

"I thought you said your family wasn't involved. Then what advantage would there be in knowing their secrets?"

"You have a point." He rubbed his hands together. "I also could offer some degree of protection. Investigating a murder carries a bit of danger, I would think."

"You're volunteering to protect me? Do you pack a rod, Mr. Wallace?"

"No, but I can look pretty intimidating in a pinch."

"I see." I steepled my fingers. "Well, Mr. Wallace, I'm not sure I have any immediate needs for muscle, but we'd be happy to keep you in mind should an opening arise."

"Liz, I'm serious. It could be dangerous, and you shouldn't be working this alone."

"I'm not alone. I have my father."

Jack remained in his chair without speaking, and the tension between us grew until you could cut it with a knife. Only I had no idea what kind of tension it was. Or what would happen if it kept tugging at us.

"Fine," I said. "What exactly would you expect from me in this partnership?"

"I'd like to know what you've found out, for starters. I mean, I can see Kimmie Kaminski is on your radar."

"And the Wallace family would be grateful if I could dig up more evidence against her, right?"

"Mother, for one, would be ecstatic. But only if it's real evidence."

"Would someone manufacture evidence against her?" I immediately sobered. "Your family? They mustn't do that. It will cloud any real evidence that remains."

He looked down. "I'm doing my best, Liz. But Sy's rumored spoon collection from various state fairs is a siren's song to certain relatives. They want her out of the house."

"Did many of your family members have keys to Sy's place?"

"You mean are they planning on sneaking in there and cleaning it out? There's been talk. But only talk."

"Any of them desperate enough to hire someone to do it for them? The attempted break-in the morning of the funeral. They didn't break in. Rumor is they had a key."

"So you think one of the family hired a gang of punk kids to break into the place?"

"It certainly sounds like somebody did. Who else would want to get in there that badly? Not Kimmie. She was already living in the house."

"I don't know if I like where this is going."

"Hey, you promised me insight into the Wallace family secrets. That's one of two things I'd like to know."

He set his jaw, then nodded in agreement. "A promise is a promise. I'll see what I can find out. What is the other thing you want?"

"The recipe for your secret sauce."

# # #

My conversation with Jack was the kind I was likely to replay in my head multiple times, which I did while I checked the locks, switched off all extraneous lights, and made sure the coffee maker was off. I was still reviewing our talk when I climbed the stairs to the apartment, avoiding the creaky one. I didn't need to worry about disturbing Dad. His reassuring snores were vibrating the timbers. *That's probably why we don't have ghosts*, I thought as I secured the locks on our apartment door. We'd never hear them over the din.

I poured milk into a small bowl of Frosted Flakes and carried it to my bedroom, wincing at the recollection of my conversation with Jack. At the time, I was being playful. But the more I rehearsed it in my head, the more it sounded like blatant flirtation. I groaned, and Othello jumped up to comfort me—or was he aiming for the leftover milk in my bowl? Only a few drops remained, so I let him have it while I stroked his fur.

What if involving Jack was a mistake? Still, his suggestion to think of this as a game of Clue had merit. I found a pad of Post-it notes on my nightstand and scrounged up a pen from the drawer. I then made up a "card," Clue-style, for each suspect. Except I dispensed with the corny pictures. If I could eliminate all the suspects except for one, then I'd know who did it. Right?

To be thorough, or so I told myself, I first made a card for my father. I couldn't breathe while I was writing his name on the top. Dad had an appointment with the victim and access to the site and the murder weapon. I was about to draw a line through his name, but Dad's inability to fully recall the event made it impossible to cross him off as a suspect, if I was doing this exercise objectively. Was I deluding myself? Surely a lot of killers out there have friends and family who would swear on a stack of Bibles that their loved one was incapable of murder. But what motive might Dad have had to kill Sullivan O'Grady? Was it over the toys? Or were the toys just an excuse for the two of them to meet? What if the meeting escalated into anger? Or violence? What if Dad grabbed the nearest weapon in self-defense?

This idea didn't sit well with me. I couldn't imagine my father thrusting a lawn dart through anyone's chest. It also went against everything I'd learned about Sullivan O'Grady. He was a health care aide, apparently because he liked to help people. The biggest scratches on his character were that sometimes he came off as a bit overzealous and didn't always get his priorities right concerning his family. I had no idea how either of these flaws could put him in conflict with my father.

The next card I made was for Mrs. O'Grady. She and her husband were going through marital issues, bitter enough to warrant a separation. Had she been so resentful at her husband's neglect that she followed him? And got angry at what? Him carrying a box of toys into a toyshop? Or maybe she had more of a cold-blooded plan to benefit from his death. No crossing her off the list.

I then made a card for Kimmie Kaminski. She was a ghost hunter. Sullivan O'Grady was a skeptic and in a position where he might have forewarned Sy DuPont and his family of her intentions. Had she prevented him so that she could carry out her plans and inherit the house? Yes, apparently Sy's second autopsy showed no signs of foul play, but he was an old man. By marrying him, Kimmie gained a place of residence and a claim on the supposedly haunted house, and she just had to wait until he kicked off. If Sully stood in the way of her plans . . .

A thought tickled at my subconscious just as Othello curled up next to me and his whiskers tickled my leg. Would a sincere ghost hunter kill someone? Or would she be afraid that person would come back to haunt her? I tapped my pen on the Post-it. Or would she *want* that person to come back? A psycho ghost hunter who killed people to haunt her house? Sounds like a made-for-TV movie you'd watch at three AM during a bout of insomnia. But I wrote "Psycho??" under her name for future reference.

Then I made a card for Kimmie's associates: Chuck, Zach, and Spook. Since they were part of her paranormal investigative team, they would have been in the house, presumably before Sy's death. They might have seen Sully as a stumbling block. Had one—or more than one—of them followed him, saw him enter the toyshop, worried that he was spilling the beans to a former chief of police, and then capitalized on an opportunity to kill him?

This created an even more bizarre image. Instead of a made-for-TV movie, Kimmie and her henchmen almost seemed like a group of villains from *Batman* (the Adam West version—the best version, in my opinion). I couldn't see Kimmie standing back in high heels and a catsuit, hands on her hips, saying, "Get 'em boys," while her gang of thugs went at Sullivan O'Grady, causing sound effects to pop on a screen in bright comic bubbles. Well, apparently I could see it. But it made me laugh. Not that I could completely rule them out.

I ripped off that sheet and set it aside. Who were the other suspects in this game of Clue?

On the next page, I simply wrote, "Kids." They'd tried to break into—or rather, let themselves into—Sy's house on the day of the funeral. Miles's connection with this group also forced me to make a card for him. I didn't like the coincidence that his former gang might have been involved, but coincidences like this abounded in a village our size. One couldn't count on six degrees of separation in East Aurora. I forced myself, again trying to be objective, to imagine a scenario where Miles and/or his former gang could have been guilty of murder.

The gang I could see. Gangs of nameless, faceless people were handy to blame for just about anything. Perhaps they had somehow come under the impression that the toys Sully had been carrying were worth something and followed him. But Sully hadn't been carrying the toys at the time. They were already in the shop.

But Miles knew about them. We'd e-mailed him pictures. Had he let them know, or perhaps let slip, that the toys were at the shop? Had they targeted the shop to steal them? Given their value, at least of the ones that we knew about, was it worth the risk? Then again, Miles was the one with the Internet contacts. He's the one who told us he couldn't find the value of Fred and Ginger. Maybe that was a lie. Maybe the thing was worth oodles, and he was cashing in. The thought made my stomach churn. It seemed out of character, both for Miles and for my father, who was normally a good judge of character.

But where did this group get the key, if they even had one? They'd need a connection to someone else who had access to the house, and that thought made me breathe a little easier.

The Wallace/DuPont family? What if they spotted Sullivan O'Grady with the toys? They might have jumped to the conclusion that he was absconding with their inheritance. So had one of them killed Sully, taken the toys, then contracted with this gang to break into Sy's house while everyone was at the funeral? Perhaps to remove something else of value before the other family members could get their claws into it?

And where did Jack Wallace figure into this? Was he trying to be helpful? Or was he trying to discover what I had learned? That thought sent chills through me. Had I been sitting, face-to-face and knee-to-knee, with a cold-blooded killer trying to thwart our investigation?

My major suspects accounted for, I made a few more cards, taking into account some of our neighbors who had come to game night.

I made one for Peggy Trent, just because she had some connection to the toys via her work at the museum. I wasn't sure she even knew Sully, and I doubted she had keys to Sy's house or contact with a gang of thugs. Maybe writing her name on a card was just fun.

I also made one for Chief Young. What if Sully had discovered something unsavory about the current chief? It wouldn't take much of a stretch of the imagination to think that he'd come to my father, a much loved and revered former chief, for advice, using the toys simply as a diversion. He had no clear connection to the gang, but he was the one who caught them, thus conveniently diverting attention further from himself.

I even made a card for Lori Briggs. Her family didn't care much for O'Grady, firing him when he was caring for their relative. Maybe there was more to this story. As the mayor's wife, she had connections to a lot of people.

The last name I wrote down before I fell asleep was Glenda's. I just wrote "Glenda," because I wasn't sure I'd heard her last name. What did we know about her? She was getting on to be Sy's age. Perhaps they had some connection that we didn't know about.

As I started to doze off, with the lights on and surrounded by one purring cat and a host of Post-its, my brain tried to solve the puzzle. Only Clue swirled together and mixed with Monopoly and Batman, transforming East Aurora into a hotbed of crime and greed, where nameless, faceless thugs roamed free, and archcriminals sauntered around town in catsuits, building houses and hotels, every one of which was haunted by the ghost of Millard Fillmore.

Chapter 19

When I stumbled down the hall the next morning, Dad greeted me with the smell of coffee and a cheerful hello. I grunted a response, and he turned down the way-too-joyous Christmas music blasting from his portable radio before he bent down and peeled a Post-it note from Othello's nether parts. He placed it on the table with the others that apparently the cat had dragged in.

"Glenda?" He rolled his eyes.

I pushed my disheveled hair from my face and stumbled toward the coffee pot. "Well, you never know. Perhaps she stabbed him with a knitting needle and then figured the weapon would give her away, so she removed it and used the lawn dart."

"And her motive?"

"He'd been telling too many yarns?"

"Try again."

"Crewel fate. He caused that accident that left her in stitches."

He sucked air through his teeth.

I took a long draft of the coffee. "And he'd stolen her purls."

"Drink faster." He pulled out a chair for me, then settled back down with his paper.

The coffee was strong for my taste, but I added sugar and it did the job. Mom always said that Dad's coffee could peel wallpaper. But when Parker and I had put it to the test on the wall in his bedroom—and verified her theory—she hadn't been pleased at all.

Of course, Dad had poured gallons of it down Mom's throat through the years. I can't honestly say it sobered her up any. I suspect coffee just makes for a more alert and agitated drunk. Maybe that's not always a good thing.

As the caffeine kicked in and my eyelids opened, I noticed that the note bearing Dad's name was already on the table. I snatched up the incriminating paper.

Dad grabbed my wrist. "It's okay, you know."

I crumpled up the note and tossed it on the floor for the cat. Othello jumped for it, then batted it with his paws, weaving it around the table legs like a hockey puck until he got it clear and chased it down the hall.

"Maybe I should be a suspect in this case," Dad said.

"You'd never kill anyone. And you'd never lie to me."

"I wouldn't lie to you," he repeated and cradled his mug in two hands. "Come to think of it, I never told you that I didn't kill him, just that I don't remember doing it."

I leaned my elbows on the table and rested my chin on my hand. "Dad, how can you tell if someone is lying?"

"You mean interrogation techniques?" He rubbed his bristly eyebrows. "There are a few tricks, but nothing foolproof."

"Such as?"

"When people are telling lies, sometimes they won't look you in the eye. Or they'll focus off to the left or above your head. But some people do that when they're trying to remember something."

"So they don't look you in the eye."

"It's not definitive. Maybe they're shy. Or ashamed of something else. Or attracted, even. I interrogated one guy for three hours. Didn't look me in the eye once. Kept looking at my shirt. When I got home, I realized I had a huge jelly stain down the front. Of course, the real bold ones, the pathological liars, will stare you straight in the eye and let anything fly."

"How else, then?" I tried to recall if Jack had looked me in the eyes at all.

Dad got up to refill his coffee. "Sometimes when people add too much detail, it's a giveaway. If they're making it up on the fly, you can sometimes catch them because they forget what story they told. So you keep asking the same questions over again, in slightly different ways, to see if the story changes. Can be a long process."

"So that's why you were always late for dinner." I sipped my coffee thinking that this conversation had occurred a decade or two later than it should have. Dad might have been easier to live with if I'd known a little more about what he did all day. I was also beginning to understand his attraction to the job. It was more puzzle solving than cops and robbers. And like Dad, I was awfully fond of puzzles.

Dad wasn't done sharing. "If someone insists on telling a story the same way each time, using the same words, you know they rehearsed it. Or if they're too helpful."

"Like volunteering too much? Offering to help?"

Dad turned the page of his newspaper and peered over the top of his reading glasses. "Might be trying to cover up something. Then again, they might have thrived on gold stars in elementary school and never outgrew the compulsion."

"Jack Wallace offered to help us poke around in this case."

"He did, did he? Now you're wondering why. Does he really want to be helpful? Or is he hiding some deep, dark secret?"

"What do you think?"

"I think maybe I'll make us some eggs. You're going to need the protein. You've got a lot of thinking to do."

# # #

Since I had closed the shop late after the game tournament, Dad and Cathy both insisted I needed some time off. I climbed into my car and started driving and thinking. It was one of those crisp, sunny days that put a crust on the snow, and I found myself squinting against the glare as I left downtown and headed toward the house where Sullivan O'Grady had once lived with his wife and kids.

I parked on the street a few houses down from theirs and waited. I wasn't sure what I was waiting for. A yellow bus came by and picked up all the neighboring kids. I remembered that the O'Grady kids were homeschooled. That had to be a lot of work.

Only today, they did leave the house. A smaller bus stopped right in front, and four older kids, all wearing stiff, new private school plaid, left the house. They looked intimidated as they trotted carefully between the snowbanks piled on each side of the sidewalk, as if they were running some frozen gauntlet. Their mother followed them outside and had to peel the youngest away from her bathrobe to deposit the child on the bus. Said child was sending up a wail that would drive banshees away.

The door closed and the bus departed, leaving Mrs. O'Grady staring after them.

I got out of my car and rushed up to her, cheerfully asking, "Getting the kids off to school?"

She wiped away a tear with a knuckle. "First day. Sully was all for homeschooling, but I wasn't sure I could keep up with it. Their grandfather offered to pay for private school." She squinted at me. "You were here with the police, right?"

Only this time without my father, I didn't have the guts, or perhaps stupidity, to feign a police connection. "My father is the former chief of police, but I've never been on the force." I looked her straight in the eye, hoping that she'd conclude she'd made some kind of assumption the first time. Did that make me a pathological liar?

She seemed overwhelmed and confused. "I have to get back inside."

God forgive me, I followed her in without an invitation.

In the days since Sully's death, she'd managed a little housework. Clean casserole dishes lined the counters, probably once containing food brought by friends and family. An infant I didn't see last time was in a swing and the older one in a playpen. Or rather, halfway over the top of the playpen. She rushed to put him back in, which he thought was great fun. He giggled and jumped and slapped his hands against the top railing.

"Sorry, I don't recall your name," she said.

"Elizabeth McCall."

"Betsy?" She smiled. "Like the old paper dolls?"

I winced. "My dad was a fan. Only I don't go by the name Betsy. I'm impressed, though. Usually it's the older folks who try to call me that."

She collapsed into a chair at the kitchen table and gestured to an empty seat. "My grandmother gave me her old paper dolls to play with when I was a kid. She'd never cut them out. It was great fun then. I guess they'd probably be worth something now. Wasted."

"No, not wasted." I sat across from her, taking care not to lean against the sticky chair back. "Play is worth something. Happy kids are worth something."

"I suppose." Then she paused. Apparently this is where I was supposed to fill in the reason I came.

"Hey, I'm sorry if you had the wrong impression of who we were when Dad and I visited last time. Truth is, I manage the toyshop . . ."

"Where Sully . . ." She ran a fingernail along a scratch in the table.

I swallowed the lump in my throat. "We're still trying to make sense out of what happened."

"I don't know how I can help. I don't even know why he was there." She bit her lip. "Was he buying something for the kids? Because I don't know if I could bear the thought that he died doing something for the children."

"Earlier in the week, he brought in a box of old toys. Antiques. He came in asking for an estimate of their value.

We later learned they belonged to his employer, Sy DuPont. Did your husband ever mention him?"

She sank back into her chair, then clasped the neckline of her robe a little closer. "He rarely talked about his clients. I did get the impression that Sully wasn't enjoying his work much lately."

"I've heard that Sy DuPont could be rather abrasive."

"That could explain it. Whether clients were kind to him or not, Sully had a strong work ethic. If anything, he'd work harder to please them, and he certainly wouldn't abscond with anything that belonged to his employer, if that's what you're getting at."

"No, I wasn't going there at all. But it would help quite a bit if I could figure out what he was doing at the shop with those toys."

"Perhaps Mr. DuPont wanted to sell them?"

"That's where it gets a little tricky. He's not around to give his side of the story. And your husband deliberately gave us a false name."

"Sully wouldn't lie."

"He didn't actually say his name. Just handed me a business card that belonged to someone else. He seemed nervous. Any idea why?"

She stared into space, somewhere in the direction of the butter dish on the table, then shook her head. "I have no idea what he might have been doing. If he was being deceptive at all, he would have been nervous. That wasn't his nature."

"And you don't know what he might have been doing with the old toys?"

"Occasionally, if an employer didn't have enough to pay his salary, Sully would barter. He's come home with all kinds of old junk—broken-down furniture, dishes, once this really nice quilt."

"I guess we can check to see whether your husband's normal salary was being paid."

"Sometimes people would give him things for doing odd jobs after work. Things that weren't part of his job description, like cleaning out attics and basements. Painting and that sort of thing."

"So perhaps Sy DuPont hired him for odd jobs and paid him with the toys?"

"Maybe." But she didn't sound convinced.

"Then why would he have been so nervous about it?"

"I don't know." She paused to brush a handful of crumbs from the table. "I'm guessing."

"The other odd thing was that these particular toys were already promised to somebody else. DuPont had planned to donate them to the toy museum. Are you familiar with the place?"

"I've never been there. But Sully used to take the kids there on days when I needed a break. Well, he acted like he was giving me a break. I think Sully was looking for an excuse to go there himself. He'd go whenever he scrounged up a coupon. He loved that place." Her brows pinched. "Could he have been taking the toys there?"

"Then why would he be meeting with my father in the middle of the night?"

"He met with your father?" Her head jerked up. "What does your father have to say about it?"

Apparently Chief Young didn't share many details of O'Grady's death with his widow. "Dad doesn't remember." When her jaw started to slack, I rushed to explain. "It's a long story, but my father suffered a concussion. He's still hazy about some of the details."

She leaned forward, her elbows on the table. "So what you're saying is that my husband had a secret middle-of-the-night meeting alone with your father, and you're trying to figure out what happened?" Her tone had grown accusatory.

I closed my eyes, bit my tongue, counted to ten, and did whatever else I could to control my temper. "I . . ." Then I repeated the cycle and started over. "My father was chief of police for many years, served with honor, and was the kindest, most patient father a girl could have asked for. I don't believe he could have killed your husband."

"But you're here because you're not sure."

"I'm here because I am sure, but I'm not so positive the current chief will accept my character witness. Until the real killer is caught, my father is under a cloud of suspicion."

"What if you're wrong? What if he did it?"

I swallowed. "Then the evidence will bear it out and justice will be done. I'm trying to find the truth."

"Not just someone else to pin it on? Because that chief was here asking me a whole lot of questions, too. I know it doesn't look good, with us separated and all."

"I'm not trying to pin it on you. That is, unless you killed him."

She leaned forward, her head bowed as if she was in deep thought or prayer. She remained there as several interminable minutes ticked by on her food-splattered kitchen clock.

Finally, she looked up. "I think if you wanted to pin it on me, you wouldn't be here. And if you really thought I did it, you probably wouldn't be here alone with me in my kitchen. Am I right?"

Now it was my turn to sit back in my chair and think. This was unfortunate, because as soon as I did, I remembered the sticky spot on the chair back. "I haven't taken my father off the suspect list. I couldn't take you off, either."

"But what you want is the truth?" She studied my face, as if the answer were scrawled on my forehead. "I hope in this case, the truth sets all of us free. Is there anything else you want to know?"

"Were you or your husband acquainted with anyone in the Wallace family? Or anyone else in the DuPont family?"

"Wallace, like the restaurant?" She shrugged. "We got wings there once for some out-of-town guests. But we can't afford to eat out much."

"What about teenagers? Well, they'd be a little older now. Young men in their late teens, early twenties perhaps. That's an awfully vague question, I'm afraid." How does one ask someone if they're acquainted with a gang?

She leaned forward. "I can answer it, though. We only have contact with the kids from the church youth group. Much to their dismay, the group is one hundred percent girls."

Right about then, I ran out of questions to ask, which was good, because the toddler grew more demanding of her attention. When I vacated the O'Grady house, I left with a spot of a syrup-like substance clinging to the back of my sweater, a new appreciation for Mrs. O'Grady, and a five-by-seven portrait of her husband from happier days.

When I climbed back into my Civic, I set the photo on the passenger seat. "Who are you, Sullivan O'Grady? And what was it about you that made someone kill you?"

I started up the car, checked my mirror, and pulled away from the curb.

If I were going to retrace Sullivan O'Grady's steps, the toy museum would be a stop I wanted to make. Jillian Hatley, the assistant curator, was the person who had sent us to Sy DuPont's house in the first place. What would happen if I showed her the picture of Sully?

A new feeling of unease started growing in my gut. There was yet another connection involving toys. I didn't want this murder to be about the toys. I wanted it to be about greedy relatives and ghost hunters, not something that would turn the focus one-eighty back onto the shop. Or perhaps on the biggest toy expert in East Aurora, Hank McCall.

There were plenty of open parking spots by the toy museum, and I learned why when I tried the door. Locked. I considered stopping at the bakery for a muffin to absorb some of the acid sloshing around my nervous stomach when Jillian rushed up to the door.

She pushed it open a couple of inches, waited her usual few seconds, then said, "Good morning, Liz. I'm sorry you had to wait." Then she pushed open the door for me to enter.

"You don't have to open up on my account," I said. "I see I'm here before the official hours."

Her head bobbed a little, as if she was listening to some translator over an earpiece. "No, that's fine. I'm here anyway. You might as well come in, too."

I followed her inside, resisting the urge to apologize.

She walked back to a vacuum cleaner parked in the middle of the room, unplugged it, and began coiling the cord. "Are you here to see something in particular?"

"Actually, I have another question. When you recognized the toy I showed you, it helped us and the police to identify the man who was killed in our shop. I'd like to show you a picture of that man. I believe he's been to the museum, and I was wondering if you or Peggy might remember anything unusual about him or his visits here."

She scrunched up her nose, just a little, and her eyebrows drew closer. "All right. If I have to, I will."

I wondered at her reaction until I slid the photograph out of my purse and handed it to her. She placed one hand flat against her chest and closed her eyes.

"Jillian, what's wrong?"

"He's still alive."

"I'm afraid to say this man is very much dead." Did he have a doppelgänger? That would add a whole new dimension to this mystery.

"No, I mean in the photograph. I thought you were showing me a picture of the dead man, after he was killed."

"Sorry to scare you. No wonder you didn't want to see it. You were very brave."

"No, I'm sorry," she said. "I didn't mean to appear unhelpful."

I let it go; otherwise, we'd be apologizing to each other all day.

She took the photograph and studied it. "I remember this man. He came in with a lot of kids. That's pretty unusual."

"People don't bring their kids here?"

She tilted her head, as if I'd asked a particularly difficult question. "I guess kids like the new children's museum, where they can touch things." She gestured to the museum's sealed displays. "Kids get bored just looking at toys locked away in glass cases. I asked Peggy if she could talk with the board about expanding, finding a bigger place where we could add a room where kids can play. I thought we could put some of the less valuable toys in there. So many of our donations end up in storage now because we don't have the space to display them. But Peggy was against the plan. Said real estate was too expensive and that going through all the old toys would be too much work."

"There's probably something to that. They'd have to be tested for lead paint. So many children's toys of the past wouldn't be considered safe by today's standards." Like lawn darts.

"I suppose you're right. It seems such a shame to see children leave here unhappy."

I bet Jillian apologized to all their parents.

She tapped O'Grady's picture. "His kids were well-behaved. As I recall, he showed them some toys that belonged to people he'd worked for. He'd taken some of our cards. He said he knew a few people who might have old toys to donate." She tipped her head, then remained frozen that way for what seemed like forever.

"What are you thinking?" I finally asked.

"He was a bit agitated the last time he was here. He asked about a toy that someone had recently donated, and it wasn't on display."

"Not yet?"

"We don't have room for every toy. Most of them are archived. Peggy picks out the best toys to display. Many don't make the cut, I'm afraid."

"By donated, do you mean bequeathed? Was Sully . . . this man . . . looking for a toy donated to the museum after its owner died?"

She nodded. "That's how we get many of our donations."

A few things suddenly fell into place with a satisfying snap. Sullivan O'Grady worked for terminally ill patients. He liked the museum. He took cards, probably using them to help convince some of his patients to donate their toys to the museum. Perhaps he'd convinced Sy DuPont to do the same. But Sully was apparently upset about the museum's archival policies that last time he'd come. Was that what he was doing with the toys? Did he want an evaluation of them to determine if Sy's toys should make the cut and be displayed in the museum?

"If I give you a list of names of donors, do you keep information on the toys they donated?"

"Of course," Jillian said. "On the computer." She pointed toward the back room.

"You going to be here a while?"

\# \# \#

I swung by the toyshop and picked up Dad, promising him lunch if he'd help me with one small errand. As we parked in front of the health care agency again, he said, "That's not exactly a small favor. It probably violates all kinds of company policies. Maybe even laws."

I just smirked at him and he unbuckled his seat belt. "Fine," he said, "but this is going to cost you dessert as well." When I didn't move, he stopped. "Aren't you coming?"

"From the way that receptionist looked at you last time, I think you have a better chance if you go in alone."

"You mean?" His eyes grew wide in what I suspected was feigned surprise. To prove it, he batted his eyelashes.

I socked him in the arm. "I don't understand it, but yes."

Dad reached for the door handle. "My fault for being such a chick magnet, I guess."

"At least among the AARP set."

He felt his chest. "My ego is crushed."

"I wouldn't want to see you give up your day job to become a gigolo or something. Now go work that charm of yours for a good cause."

He saluted, climbed out of the car, and leaned back in. "If I have to take my shirt off, it's going to cost you extra." He winked and then headed to the front door, his limp nearly invisible. I bit my lip as I considered the implications. Dad found police work invigorating. There was no arguing the light in his eyes or the animation in his face. It was like a tonic to him. A deadly medicine.

I waited in the car for about half an hour, wondering exactly what Dad had to do to get the information, but he came out with a slip of paper and a silly grin.

"Oh, brother," I said when he got back into the car.

"What, it was your idea." He reached for his seat belt. "And it's going to cost you. Big time."

"You don't mean you had to take off your shirt?"

"No." He sent me a pleading look. "I have a dinner date for Friday night."

I pulled away from the curb. "I'll make sure you have a freshly ironed shirt."

Chapter 20

Jillian was busy with visitors when I dropped off the list of names of Sully's former clients, and the kids in her tour group did indeed look bored. She promised to fax something over later that afternoon. After a leisurely and expensive lunch, Dad and I went back to the shop and tried to figure out, among our huge pile of outdated office equipment, if we had anything that would receive a fax.

"Yes, you do," Cathy said. "The old printer. I had to fax a poem to a contest, and I remember hooking it up. Not that it was worth the effort."

"Didn't win?" Dad asked.

She folded her arms in front of her. "I won, all right. The poem was published in their anthology, but they didn't pay me anything for it, and the book cost me forty-five bucks."

I winced.

"But I am a published poet. One of the better ones in the book, if I say so myself. I had been considering submitting another one this year, but it seems the attorney general shut them down."

Dad spun away so she couldn't see his face. "What a pity."

I dusted off the old printer and found it a place on the counter within reach of our landline—which took a bit of finagling, since this thing was a behemoth of old technology. I figured out how to send a fax from my laptop, and it printed out, so we were in business.

Then we waited. And waited. By late afternoon, Dad was yawning and stretching, so I sent him up for a nap. Othello followed him, as if he was seconding my suggestion. By five, Cathy was ready to head home to make dinner for Parker and then out to another of her writing groups.

"Are you sure you don't need me?" She wrapped her scarf around her neck. "I can swing back after dinner . . ." Her hesitant expression indicated she'd be making an extreme sacrifice.

I gestured toward the empty shop. "I think I can keep the hordes at bay." With no game tournaments bringing customers in and no tourists in town, especially after dark, I'd likely have the shop to myself tonight. Which would work out well, if Jillian ever managed to send that fax.

I stared out the window after Cathy left. At five, the sun had already been down for about twenty minutes, making it seem later than the hour. The days were short and still getting shorter. One could almost imagine the darkness growing stronger, plotting and scheming to obliterate the day entirely in one long night of darkness, cold, and snow.

I threw that thought aside as the Christmas lights along Main Street started popping on. I flipped the switch for our own Christmas display in the window, and it lit up as well. No, the darkness would not win. Not tonight, anyway.

For good measure, I found a radio station playing holiday music and piped it through the store. I wondered how many of the items on our shelves had once been encased in holiday wrapping paper and opened by bright-eyed, excited children on Christmas morning.

I leaned against the counter and continued staring. Despite their collectability now, the items in our shop were probably not the cherished items from the tops of letters to Santa. Those had been ripped open first and played to death. The action figures still in their cases and the games still in their shrink-wrap, most prized by collectors today, were the items kids unwrapped and said "thank you" for (at least if they were taught manners) before they were shoved aside in favor of a more desired toy. Maybe this shop was really an island of misfit toys.

"Who needs therapy?" I'd just figured out why I felt so at home in this place.

A couple of holiday shoppers did venture in from the cold. One walked the store slowly, smiling over objects she recognized. After letting her know I was there to help if she needed anything, I left her to her reminiscences. While she was still making her circle through the store, another gentleman entered and picked up a few things to check price tags. He grimaced and left. A disappointed bargain hunter. But the woman purchased a couple of unopened blister packs of now-vintage Barbie clothes and an older sixties version of the board game Acquire—a highly collectable version since the newer ones are cardboard. Of course, any time we can get our hands on a 1999 version, with its molded hotels, it's snatched up online almost as soon as Miles can put it on eBay.

The last customer had been gone five minutes when the phone rang. It was Jillian.

"Liz, sorry it's so late. It took me a few minutes to get everything together, and we've been rather busy today."

"Not a problem, Jillian. I appreciate you doing that for me."

She hung up after apologizing at least two more times. I disconnected the landline from our custom phone, which seemed to be staring at me woefully, and hooked it up to the fax machine. The machine answered a call moments later and, with a little technospeak, whirred into life and began to spit out paper.

I collected the documents, a large spreadsheet with cells that carried over onto other pages. I'd have to put these together, like a giant jigsaw puzzle, in order to see all the information. So I set up a table and began doing just that. When I had the pieces in place, I rummaged through the drawer, found a glue stick with a little life left in it, and glued it all into one large sheet.

The document was longer than I'd been expecting because Peggy had created a line for each toy donated rather than for each donor. Each line also had pertinent information about the donor, including address and telephone number, which seemed a bit useless considering these particular people were all dead. Presumably their houses were occupied by others and their phone numbers out of service.

I found the cells I was looking for. A small column for an item number followed by an identification, manufacturer, and condition. This was Dad's area of expertise, of course, but if he was still napping, I didn't want to wake him, especially for what was probably going to end up being a wild goose chase. Everything here looked in order. There was nothing sloppy in Peggy Trent's operation, not that I expected there to be. If Sully had any qualms about her management, one glance at this spreadsheet, in all its organizational glory, should have put them to rest. Every toy was chronicled and evaluated and its location tracked. A column even listed the JPEG name of a picture of the item that was evidently also kept on file.

Dead end.

I jumped when someone tapped their fingers on the glass window. Miles, being funny, pushed his face against the glass until he resembled a Dick Tracy villain and held that position until I smiled.

Moments later, he opened the door. "Man, you are jumpy. Is the old man around?"

"He went up to nap earlier. I'm afraid he might be asleep for the night."

"You sure he didn't sneak out again?"

I started to answer, but then I realized I didn't know what that answer was. "The alarms should be on," I said. "Maybe I'd better go check. Mind the store?"

"Sure." He removed his coat.

I found Dad sleeping on the sofa with Othello curled up on the armrest next to him. Dad's snores mingled with the cat's loud purrs. "My two fellows." I petted Othello's head, then grabbed a throw blanket to put on Dad. He didn't budge.

I locked the apartment door on the way down and checked the alarm on the back door leading to the alley before rejoining Miles in the shop.

"All tucked in," I said. "I think this murder business keeps him up at night. I expect his body needs to catch up."

Miles was leaning over the printout from the museum. "These aren't ours."

"Those toys have been donated to the museum."

"Too bad. There's a few things in here I wouldn't mind getting my hands on." He tapped one row. "This old tin rocket ship. Japanese. Some of the old Japanese tin is highly collectible. I'd have to fight buyers off with a stick."

I followed his finger to the line. "That's a lot of zeroes." I scanned the whole entry. This item, in good condition, was currently on display in the museum. No surprises there.

"Too bad about the astronaut. That would have been a wicked set." He pointed to the line below it. The tin astronaut was identified in the "Condition" column as a "Repro."

"Someone is reproducing these?" I continued to scan the line. The value was listed at about twenty dollars, and the location of this one was the archives.

"Yeah, there's quite a market in repros. Old tin toys. Even pull toys. Some antique dealers even buy a few to put in their shops. They rough them up to make them appear older."

My eyebrows jumped up. "Fraud?"

"Not if they don't make false claims. All they have to do is price them low and say that they don't know a lot about toys. Unsuspecting buyers rarely ask a lot of questions. They think they're being all shrewd and getting a steal, but they're the ones getting ripped off. They find that out when they realize they've got nuts where they should have rivets. Or plastic feet when they should be wood. Or the parts don't line up right. They never make these repros perfect."

"Where did you learn all this?"

"Your dad." Miles winced. "I, uh, might have gotten taken a time or two when I first started buying for the shop online. I felt bad about it. Offered to repay the difference. He reminded me that if things are too good to be true, they're usually not."

"One of my first life lessons." I scanned the "Condition" column on the spreadsheet with my finger, stopping several places where the condition was listed as a "Repro."

"Looks like the museum got taken for a ride a few times," Miles said.

I massaged a knot in the back of my neck. "Not really swindled, since these are all donations."

"Why would someone donate repros to the museum?" Miles asked. "You think they didn't know?"

"These donors are all deceased. No way of finding out." Well, at least short of asking Althena if we could set up another séance.

Miles shrugged his coat back on. "If your Dad is pulling a Sleeping Beauty, I guess what I had to tell him can wait until tomorrow."

"Was it about your friends? Did you learn anything new?"

Miles paused. "I'm not going to call them my friends any-more. I did find one of them who was a little less tight-lipped than the others."

"And?"

He shuffled on his feet.

"I am working with Dad on this," I said. "I promise, nothing you tell me goes past the walls of this shop."

"I didn't learn anything much. Just that they were being paid to retrieve something from the house. Only whoever wanted them to do it wouldn't pay enough to make it worth the risk."

"That's not much more than we already knew. No ID on who made them the offer?"

"Well, no name. But I did learn that negotiations are ongoing."

"So someone still wants something from inside the house. And wants it badly enough to try to hire a gang of kids to break in."

"They almost got caught last time. If they were smart, they'd take it as a sign to go straight. Apparently they've taken it as a sign to ask for more cash up front."

"No idea what this item is?"

"Nor am I likely to find out. Asking questions is making me look suspicious. I told them I wasn't working with the cops. Not sure I convinced them."

"Even though it's true?"

"I'm sure they still consider your father a cop, despite his retirement. I have the feeling they have more regard for him, anyway."

"No love for the new chief?"

"They're pretty silent on the subject."

"I wonder why."

Miles snorted. "I struggled through Psych 101 in school, so I'm not sure I can help in that area. But I'll keep poking around." He pushed on the door to leave.

"Miles?" I called after him. "Be careful."

"Always." He waved and was out into the December night.

The wind drifted in from the door, giving me a brief chill that I hoped was temperature related and not some sense of foreboding. Dad would never forgive himself if something happened to Miles, especially if the young man was acting as an informant. I rubbed the goose bumps down on my arms and sneaked off to the back room for a cup of coffee. I changed my mind and went for the hot chocolate. With marshmallows.

By the time I'd carried my steaming mug back into the shop, I was frustrated and a little spooked. The chills remained and reminded me of Kimmie and her ghost hunters. They claimed a sudden chill was a response to spirits in the room. But who would be haunting the shop? We had no claim to Millard Fillmore, at least not that I knew of. But Sullivan O'Grady immediately popped into mind. Not that I thought his spirit lingered in the shop. At the same time, could any of us really be at rest until the killer was caught? At any moment, Ken might decide that the circumstantial evidence he had against my father was enough to hold him. Then my whole life would come tumbling down like the blocks in a poorly played game of Jenga.

I slid back into my chair, cradled the warm cup in my hands, and stared at the spreadsheet. Its precise rows and full accounting of every object was complete and irrefutable. Why had I wanted this so-called evidence? My own dislike for Peggy had made her a target of my investigation, maybe because she was convenient. Like my dad was convenient in Ken's investigation and the Wallaces were convenient in Cathy's estimation. But choosing convenient scapegoats wasn't what police work was supposed to be. It was supposed to be about truth, evidence, and justice.

The evidence I'd collected only proved that Peggy was organized and efficient. Still, all was not lost. I could probably replicate this spreadsheet to keep track of our own inventory at the shop.

I glanced at it again as I sipped my hot chocolate. Peggy was sharp, I had to give her that. Not only for her organization, but she had to really know her toys if she recognized all these repros among this donated lot.

Then I think I inhaled a minimarshmallow, because I started coughing and my eyes teared up. I rubbed them with my sleeve and tried to wash down the tickle with more hot chocolate, even as I stared at the spreadsheet through the teary blur.

Why would someone donate repros?

The question was not as simple as it appeared at first blush.

These donors had all been patients of Sullivan O'Grady. They had all been terminally ill. Sully had presumably found these toys while cleaning their attics or basements. At his request, they donated the toys to the museum, toys that had probably been forgotten and left in storage for years or decades. Treasure in the attic.

But what about the repros?

I found the lines for the expensive Japanese spaceship that was on display in the museum. The reproduction robot had come from the same donor. Had the owner bought the reproduction so that he'd have a set? Possibly.

Then why donate the reproduction to the museum? He would have realized its negligible worth. Unless the owner didn't know he was buying a repro. Perhaps he had bought the other toy at an antique shop and didn't realize he was being taken.

The uneasy feeling grew. The donors weren't collectors. These were elderly people who had toys from their childhood secreted away somewhere. I recalled the dusty cardboard box that Sullivan O'Grady had brought in. Dad had handled all those toys. If a repro was among them, I'm sure he would have noticed, like Peggy had identified the repros from these earlier donations.

But how did those modern repros end up in those old collections?

I immediately thought of Miles's former associates. Had they been hired to break into other places and switch old toys for new reproductions by some sadistic, opportunistic toy collector?

What kind of money were we talking about here? I pulled a few of Dad's price guides from the shelf behind the register and started to spot-check the list. If some of these reproductions had been the real deal, they would have been worth hundreds or even thousands of dollars. The spaceman alone was worth about two thousand. Pretty pricey for a toy, but nothing to kill over.

Only . . .

I retrieved my laptop and fired it up. I rummaged through the toy sales on eBay and Etsy, to discover if any originals had recently sold. Price guides are fine, but sometimes the market is more volatile than that.

I discovered that all of them had recently sold on eBay. All by the same seller: Knitwit6709.

"Very shrewd, Peggy," I said as the final piece snapped into place, tighter than new Legos. Peggy took in donations, which were all scrupulously cataloged, photographed, and evaluated. That process took time. Time that Peggy used to locate reproductions for some of the toys, which she then substituted for the originals. Nobody living had studied those toys enough to notice the difference, and the original owners who knew their history and provenance were all dead. Nobody was around to complain about the switch.

She then was free to sell the originals to collectors. Each payday wasn't exactly a jackpot. One sale netted her a few hundred or perhaps a thousand or two. She played at fraud like she played Monopoly. Not a big haul all at once, but a bunch of regular payoffs, accumulated patiently over a long period. Maybe decades. Why, that could add up to be . . .

Motive for murder?

Sullivan O'Grady had seen a few of these toys before they were donated to the museum. He might even have been the one to discover them in a dusty attic. He wasn't expert enough to know their values, but it would be hard to convince him that the toy he discovered in a box of old ones, in a decayed cardboard box covered with a layer of dust, was made in China a few months earlier.

"Go directly to jail, Peggy Trent. Do not pass go. Do not collect two hundred dollars."

I needed to call Ken. I got up and walked to the glaring telephone and picked up the receiver.

Dead.

Knucklehead, I chided myself. The fax machine was still hooked up. I bent down to unhook the landline from the old piece of office equipment, and the bell over the door rang.

"Be right with you!" I called out.

"No problem."

I froze. The voice was Peggy's.

Chapter 21

My heart rate kicked into overdrive. "Peggy, what are you doing here?" Then I paused to take in what had become a normal picture: Peggy standing in the shop with a plate covered with foil.

"Is your father around?" She glanced around the shop.

"Napping, I'm afraid."

My mind raced, playing various scenarios. Did she know about the information that Jillian had faxed over? I hurried to put myself in front of the table, hopefully looking casual and nonchalant. I didn't know what to do with my hands, so I clenched them to keep my fingers from shaking. I forced a smile. "What brings you over?"

She took two steps toward me. "I baked more cookies."

Was it my imagination, or had she tried to look over my shoulder to see the spreadsheets on the table? I stepped toward her. "We've barely had time to make a dent in the ones you brought over last night."

"You know me. I love baking." This time there was no mistaking it. She was clearly rubbernecking the table. "I . . . hope I didn't disturb your work."

"Oh," I said airily, "just taking a break during the slow time to go over some figures."

She whipped around to face the other direction, her hand on her bowed head as if to stave off a sudden pain. "You don't know how sorry I am to hear that."

"I beg your pardon?" At this point, I wondered where I'd left my cell phone. Probably charging upstairs. Although I'd bet I could outrun her to the shop phone if needed. I inched back in that direction.

She whirled around and withdrew a scary looking kitchen knife from her coat.

"Peggy, what is this all about?"

She gestured toward the spreadsheet. "You know exactly what this is about, don't you? Jillian told me what she sent you."

"Spreadsheets from the museum. Professional curiosity. I must admit, you do a fine job. Everything neat and in order."

She shook her head. "If you were sure everything was neat and in order, you wouldn't have tried so hard to hide it from me when I came in."

Wouldn't you know my plans to avoid a confrontation had led to one. "I . . . was embarrassed you caught me checking up on you. But I didn't find anything." I forced a blank face and tried not to flinch.

She tilted her head, and her eyes bore through me. I hazarded a glance to the telephone, which now seemed so far away. "You're lying." She followed my eyes to the phone. Holding the knife in front of her, she backed over to the phone, yanked out the landline, threw the modular connector on the floor, and crushed it under her boot. She then backed to the door and flipped the sign to "closed" before securing the lock. "I'm sure neither of us wants more people involved in this situation."

She was wrong. I wanted the whole town involved in this situation. I took several steps toward the back of the store. Dad was still upstairs. He could help. And if I couldn't get there, if I made it to the back door, the alarm would sound and help would come.

As if sensing my thoughts, Peggy said, "Don't think about calling for your father. I'd hate to hurt him, too."

"I don't understand hurting anyone. Peggy, there must be some kind of misunderstanding here. I admit, I did see how you profited from the museum."

"Stole from them, you mean."

"I wasn't going to say that."

"But it's what you meant. Look, you have no idea what it takes to live from grant to grant. If the museum is underfunded, I don't get paid. Meanwhile, the gas and electric companies want their share."

"See, that could hardly be called stealing when you're just trying to recover your salary, right?"

"That's what I said. For a lot of years, that's what I said. Then it became a habit. A given. A modus operandi, as the cop shows like to say. I couldn't let that information get out."

"A good lawyer could get you off, maybe with a plan for repayment."

"I'm afraid it's gotten well past that."

"I don't see why . . ." Why it had led to murder. I didn't want to voice it.

"Don't you? Repayment plans, probation, and community service. Even if I'd gotten off with a slap on the wrist, can't you see how that would have ended my life right there? What would *he* have thought?"

"He?"

"Your father, of course." Her forehead pinched with emotion.

"I don't understand. How did Dad get involved in this?"

She shivered. "That disagreeable man."

"Dad?"

"No, whatever his name was. Sullivan O'Grady. I followed him here. Why couldn't he stay out of it?"

"O'Grady had been to the museum in the past. His wife said he took their kids there often."

"I thought he was coming to the museum so often because he liked to show his kids the toys. I had no idea at the time that he was looking for *specific* toys."

"Toys he knew had been donated to the museum."

She nodded, then stopped to dry a tear. "He was so proud. Like he wanted a plaque or something. Said he'd been instrumental in encouraging his employers to donate to us. I was on red alert right away. I had been so careful. Almost all the donors I'd drawn from were ignored by family and had outlived their friends. I didn't think anyone would question what had happened to the donations. No one cared."

"But Sully cared."

"Do-gooder. I explained to him that we only had room for the best of the collections. That seemed to satisfy him.

At least I thought it had. Then that whole business with Sy DuPont came up."

"Sy was going to donate his toys to the museum."

"He didn't even know what he had until Sullivan O'Grady found them while cleaning out the attic. I guess Sully suggested that he donate them. For that I should be grateful." The last part was clearly sarcastic.

"Only Sully got suspicious."

"Right about that time, Sy called me. Said that he'd rather give his toys to the museum while he was still alive. Something about making sure nobody took what wasn't theirs."

"Like his family or Kimmie Kaminski."

"Exactly. I went to the house to pick them up. Only Sy was livid. He told me the toys were missing. That someone who worked for him had absconded with them. He didn't mince words. Sullivan O'Grady was right there in the room. But Sy said he was going to have them back or certain people would be charged with theft in addition to being let go."

"Sy thought the toys were stolen."

"They were missing. He drew his own conclusions."

"That must have been when Sully brought the toys here for Dad to evaluate." I bit my lower lip. "He was testing you. He wanted an independent evaluation of them before they were donated."

"I didn't know where the toys were at the time. I figured O'Grady had a lot of nerve to practically accuse me of theft when he did the same thing. So I stayed parked in front of the house until he left. I started following him."

"He must have made plans to meet with Dad." Secretive plans that didn't include me.

"I couldn't have your father finding out."

"You might have gone to jail."

"Jail?" More tears streamed down her face. "You still don't get it. Jail wasn't what I was afraid of." She slowly shook her head and then looked up. "I couldn't have *him* knowing. Thinking that of me. It's important to me that you understand the reason."

"But to kill a man . . ."

"It wasn't like that!" She stepped toward me with the knife, and I took another step back.

She obviously wanted to explain this to me. Could I talk my way out of this situation by pretending to understand her? "Why don't you tell me what it was like. I want to understand."

She froze in place, nothing moving but her shaking arm. I couldn't tell if it was from emotion or the stress of holding the knife.

"You followed Sully here . . ." I began.

"Your father must have been expecting him. The lights were on, and when Sully knocked on the windowpane, your father answered and waved him to the back alley. Then all the lights went off. I got out of my car and followed on foot. I just wanted to hear what they were saying. I waited for a few minutes after Sully had gone inside, then I tried the back door. It was unlocked."

"What did you hear?"

"Footsteps at the top of the stairs. I looked up just in time to see your father go back into the apartment. Alone. So I sneaked into the shop."

Dad must have gone back to the apartment to gather the box of toys. "What were you planning?"

"I wasn't planning anything!" Her voice betrayed a growing agitation. "If only I had time to think it through, things might have been different. I just wanted to listen. I crept around the back aisle, by the lunchboxes, thinking I could stay out of sight. But it was so dark and I was going mostly by memory. I hit a spot on the floor that creaked and gave me away."

"I know the spot." It was right by the lawn darts.

"I stumbled and my elbow went through some kind of cabinet. I grabbed the first thing I could find, then O'Grady attacked me."

"He attacked you?"

"He grabbed me. Started to shout. To call your father. Instinct took over from that point."

Instinct and a lawn dart.

"I didn't even know where I'd hit him, but he fell to the ground, and I could feel the blood on my hands. When I realized what I had done, I knew I couldn't be found there. Not by Hank. I heard his footsteps coming back down the stairs, so I hid." She pointed to the doll room.

"You hit him on the head." I backed up another step. "You hit my father on the head?"

"Stop!" she said.

I froze.

She gestured with the knife. "Over to the counter. This is going to have to pass for an attempted robbery. Open the cash register."

Only my feet were made of lead. "You stupid woman!" For some reason, the knife was failing to register. "You hit him so hard you gave him a concussion. Don't you know you could have killed him?"

"I wasn't thinking at that point. I grabbed a croquet mallet and just swung. What would you rather I had done? Stab him with another lawn dart? I couldn't do that to a man I loved."

"You have no idea what that word means. And what do you expect to do now? Kill me and then be there to offer him comfort? And a casserole?"

She said nothing.

"You're delusional."

"Over to the counter." She gestured with the knife.

I started walking but took my time. She'd been monologuing like a Scooby-Doo villain, but she wouldn't keep it up forever. I suspected the knife would come into play as soon as she staged her robbery. So I made a grab for the nearest object, whirled around, and hurled it at her.

The monkey with the cymbals went flying right at her face. I don't know if it hit the knife and knocked it out of her hand or if she'd let go of everything she was holding (she still had the plate of cookies in her left hand) to catch the monkey, but the knife and colorfully iced Christmas cookies went flying everywhere.

That gave me a few seconds to play with. When she bent over to pick up the knife, I upended the barrel of marbles and sent them rolling in her direction, then I rushed her. My force, combined with the slippery icing, cookie crumbs, and marbles, was enough to knock her to the floor. I'd like to say I landed on top of her on purpose, but credit for that should go to the marbles, inertia, and gravity. Once down, however, I managed to keep her there with a knee to her back.

The spring on the monkey toy must have slipped, because it sprang to life, lying on the floor surrounded by cookies and still-rolling marbles, and started to beat its cymbals together in an unearthly round of applause.

Now what?

"Dad?" I yelled. "Dad!"

He came rushing down the stairs into the shop, rubbing the sleep from his eyes. "You shouldn't have let me sleep so long. I'm going to have trouble . . ." He stopped and gaped at the sight: Peggy trying to squirm out from underneath me like an earthworm, frosting covering her face and hair. "What in the world?"

"She killed Sullivan O'Grady."

He tiptoed over. "Peggy Trent, you're under arrest." Then he froze, his gaze darting from her to the cookies and the marbles. I guessed his training had never prepared him for this scenario.

"Maybe you should call Chief Young," I said. "For backup?"

"Right." He made a couple of careful steps toward the phone, tiptoeing around the marbles, and picked up the smashed landline connector. "I guess I'll call it in from upstairs."

# # #

Fewer than five minutes passed before the police chief arrived, but it took much longer to fill Ken in on Peggy's confession, especially since she clammed up and stopped talking. He was wide-eyed through the entire process. I couldn't blame him. Both Peggy and I were smeared with icing and sprinkles. As were the knife and the flying monkey. The floor was still a sea of marbles: aggies, cat's eyes, swirlies, and steelies. They started rolling whenever any of the officers inadvertently hit one with their shoe. It probably would prove to be the most memorable arrest of the young chief's career.

Somewhere in the process, I had begun to shake. I wasn't sure if it was all the cold air let in as officers came and went through the front door, or some delayed form of shock. Either way, Ken had noticed and I ended up huddled under a blanket someone had retrieved from my bed upstairs.

After Peggy had been taken away and just Dad, Ken, and I remained, Ken raked a hand through his hair and stopped to stare at me. "You could have been killed. You know that, right?"

I shivered again and tugged the blanket closer. "For a few moments, the thought crossed my mind."

Dad came up behind me and squeezed my shoulder. "Is there anything that can't wait until tomorrow? My daughter has had a long day."

Ken looked around. "I should make sure to get photos and prints from the shop, to process it as a crime scene. Again." He put his hand on his hip. "Mrs. Trent didn't go upstairs?"

"Never," Dad said. I patted his hand.

"My guys should be out of here in an hour, tops. I don't see any reason you can't stay in your own place tonight."

"Sounds good," Dad said.

"Let us know when you're ready to leave so we can lock up and set the alarm," I said.

Dad hovered over me the rest of the evening, propping me up on the sofa with pillows and tempting me with warm drinks and light snacks like I was a sick child. I can't say I didn't find it comforting. "Sit down and rest," I told him.

"I would," he said. "But it seems I've been sleeping all afternoon. I should have been downstairs to help you."

"And put us both in danger?"

"From what you said, I doubt she would have hurt me." He blushed a little.

"She conked you over the head," I reminded him.

"Goes to show your mother was right. She always said I was hard*head*ed." He tapped his head. "I guess that proves it."

The corners of my mouth turned up into a smile, only because it was more work to frown.

He kept pushing on his head. "I can't feel it! I guess it's official. I'm a num*skull*."

I didn't stifle the groan.

"Come on, child. Your turn. I'm getting too far a*head* in this game."

My brain swam, but no puns came to mind. I didn't care. I stood up and hugged him tight, burying my face into his shoulder and taking in his warmth and every scent, every sound.

And I didn't let go.

Chapter 22

I wasn't sure when Ken finished downstairs. Dad had apparently let the officers out and locked the doors. After an early breakfast the next morning, Cathy and Parker met us downstairs to clean up the shop and prepare to open. As the news spread that the killer had been caught—and it wasn't one of us—I expected the regulars to return in droves. I even sent out an e-mail about a special potluck game night for that evening, in hopes of drawing them back. Maybe we could channel some of their guilt about doubting us into profits, to make up for the recent lack of business.

The shop was a disaster: wet, salty footprints from all the cops, frosting, cookie crumbs, and more than a thousand marbles covered the floor. They would all have to be picked up, cleaned off, and safely enclosed in the barrel before we could open the shop.

Parker, Cathy, and I got down on our hands and knees, while Dad was stationed at the table with paper towels and a spray bottle, cleaning and drying any marbles that had gotten dirty.

"I should have stayed last night," Cathy said.

"You would have had to be psychic," I said, dropping another frosting-encrusted marble into a clean plastic tub that still bore the Bison Dip label. "None of us knew what was going to happen."

"Who would have thought Peggy Trent could be a killer?" Parker said. "Remember those little potatoes she sent over that time?"

"With the rosemary?" I asked.

Parker scrunched his nose. "Rosemary is like eating twigs. No, the other ones."

"Basil, oregano, olive oil, and parmesan cheese?"

Parker wiped his mouth. "I think I'm drooling. I don't suppose she'd send us the recipe from prison."

"She might if Dad asked," I said.

"She couldn't have loved him all that much if she hit him over the head," Cathy said.

"I guess in her mind, she was just trying to keep him from discovering the truth about her," I said. "In the process, she escalated from embezzling and theft to murder."

"Which I find as a real turnoff in potential girlfriends," Dad said.

I pushed myself up off the floor and took my full container of marbles to the table, almost tipping it over when I set it down.

Dad grabbed for it. "Careful. Don't want to lose your marbles."

I swooped down and kissed him on the cheek.

"You know, there are several nice older women in my writing group," Cathy said to Dad. "Maybe I could fix you up."

"Can they cook?" Parker asked.

"I think Althena can. You've met her," Cathy said.

Dad held his hand up. "Not interested."

"You think she's a fake?" Parker said.

Dad didn't respond, but I found myself shaking my head. "I'd say she's sincere in what she believes."

Dad pointed at me. "I'll give you that."

Cathy crab-walked to a spot where she could better reach more marbles. "I've married into a family of skeptics. You don't trust what you can't see."

"I don't trust half of what I do see," Dad said. "People aren't always what they seem."

I sat back on my heels. "What about Kimmie Kaminski? And that house?"

Dad got up to dump a container of shiny, clean marbles into the barrel. "Something was going on in that house."

"Half of that was you and those tiddlywinks," I said.

"Now who's a faker?" Parker said, but his voice held admiration, not accusation.

"I did it so we'd have more time to look around, that's all," Dad said. "But I wasn't responsible for *all* the noises. That disembodied voice at the end was weird."

"So it's legitimately haunted," Cathy said.

"That's one possibility." Dad stopped to stretch his neck.

I squinted at him. "You working on another theory there, Chief?"

He smiled and leaned back in his chair. "Maybe, Lizzie, but I might need your help to prove it."

# # #

Potluck game night was a huge success, even if a few of our regulars mistook my meaning. By "potluck," I'd intended to imply that players could pick whatever game they wanted to play. Instead, some brought their favorite casseroles. We gave in, even ordering a few pizzas to augment the offerings. Dad and I set up a special table for the food, as far from the vintage games as we could find space. We piped in Christmas music. Dad banished Othello to the apartment and even ran the electric trains. A light snow fell outside, and holiday spirit filled the place.

Peggy's normal spot remained empty, and I imagined it would for some time.

Jack looked over the pile of available games. He picked up a box. "Want to play Risk?" he asked me. "I could fancy a little game of world domination."

After feeling like so much of my life was spinning out of control, it sounded good to me. "You're on. See if you can find a couple more people to play."

While Jack went in search of players to complete our game board, the bell sounded and Ken walked in. Carrying flowers. At least I think they were flowers. They were wrapped up to protect them from their brief exposure to the weather, but they were in the general shape of a bouquet. As soon as he spotted me, he came right over.

"Peace offering?" He handed the parcel to me. "I've been told there are actually flowers under all that insulation."

"I'm sure they're lovely. But why did you feel the need to bring a peace offering?"

"I can't imagine I'm your favorite person right now. I wanted you to know that nothing I said during the investigation was personal. I had to follow up on every lead. In fact, I like your father." His voice softened. "I like you."

I hugged the flowers closer. "You were doing your job." I had to break away from the intensity of his gaze. "But you're not working now," I added playfully. "Come join the fun. Do you like Risk?"

"One of my favorites."

"Jack!" I called across the room. "Got some fresh meat."

Ken seemed to straighten up. "Aren't you playing?"

"Yes, let me put these in water."

I didn't find a vase, but I found a quart-sized mason jar in the back room. I unwrapped the bouquet, which turned out to be a rather festive bunch of red and white flowers, and put them in water.

Cathy stole in behind me. "Flowers, huh? I said he liked you."

"Just a peace offering." I turned to face her. She had her hands behind her back. "What do you have there?"

"An early Christmas present. A game I thought you'd like to play."

"I already promised Jack and Ken I'd play Risk with them."

"Oh, Jack *and* Ken. You might want to play this one instead." She then revealed a vintage copy of Mystery Date from behind her back. "Will it be the handsome chef or the dashing cop?"

"Very funny. Cathy, Jack is a friend, and Ken just wants to apologize for threatening to send my father to jail."

"Keep telling yourself that." She poked my upper arm. "Have fun."

When I left the back room, Ken and Jack had taken seats opposite each other, leaving me a spot on the end of the table.

"Three okay?" Jack said. "Nobody else wanted to play."

I looked over to my father, who normally loved Risk. He winked at me. This was payback for all that teasing about Peggy Trent.

"Fine," I said. "I'll take the pink armies."

As we got into the game—and I must admit, the pink armies began to multiply on the board—conversation naturally flowed to the investigation.

"There's only so much I can comment on," Ken said. "It's an ongoing investigation."

"Ongoing?" Jack said. "I think Liz did an excellent job of catching your killer for you."

I decided to help Ken out. "Almost getting killed in the process."

Ken glanced up from studying the board. "I don't recommend the public getting involved in these situations. It can be dangerous. If you had brought your evidence to me . . ."

"I was about to do just that." I shook my head. "I had no intention of confronting Peggy. That was her idea."

A furtive smile stole across his face and disappeared just as quickly. "I'm only sorry you lost your marbles in the process."

I was never going to live that one down. "Dad warned me that I would be called to testify."

Ken nodded. "But we have found some corroborating evidence in our search of Peggy's house."

"The toys?" I guessed.

"Don't let my mother know," Jack said.

"What's going to happen to them?" I asked. "It may have been Sy DuPont's intent to leave them to the museum, but Irene and Lenora may have a prior claim, at least to one of them." I pictured them as girls with Fred and Ginger. "We finally got in touch with the expert, and the toy with the two boxers is worth close to ten thousand dollars."

"For now they're evidence," Ken said.

"Will it help much?" I asked. "I mean, now that Peggy has denied her confession." When she recanted, perhaps under advisement of her lawyer, Dad had warned me that her lawyers would try to destroy my testimony.

"It corroborates more than you think." Ken leaned forward and whispered, "Bloody fingerprint. O'Grady's blood, Trent's fingerprint. On an item that more than one person can testify was taken from the crime scene. And found in a hidden cubby in Trent's basement. It's the holy grail of evidence."

I leaned back in my chair, feeling palpable relief. "Good job, Chief!"

He smiled, his face coloring a little. "Let's be happy that she's off the street, and it looks like she's going to stay there."

I smiled back at him and then used my pink armies to drive him out of North America.

Chapter 23

"Are you sure it's okay to be here?" I asked. Dad never liked unanswered questions, and that trait had led us to be sitting in the car in front of Sy DuPont's old house. "Ken specifically asked us to stay away from the murder investigation."

"This has nothing whatsoever to do with the murder investigation." He reached for his car door and climbed out.

Since I'd let him off in the driveway instead of a snow bank, I pulled the car forward and parked. By the time I joined him, Dad was helping to load boxes into Kimmie's trunk.

"Hey," I said. "What's going on?"

"I'm being evicted," she said.

"Now?" I asked.

"Oh, no," she said. "I thought I'd move a few things out I didn't need." Judging by the addresses on the packages, she was "moving" a few more of Sy's things on eBay. "I have sixty days and enough time to fight it. Even if I lose, it's not all bad. That's sixty more days to carry out my investigation."

"Any more paranormal observances?" I asked. I also wondered if she had found Dad's tiddlywinks.

"You know, it's spotty. And unlike any investigation our team has ever done. Sometimes we get disembodied voices, and other times nothing. Some tools aren't working at all."

"Really?" Dad said. "How remarkable."

"We haven't gotten a single EMF spike," she said, "even during some of the more active times. You'd think when that voice came, it would be off the charts. Nothing. All we seem to get are sounds. And not near as many as Sy said he'd experienced. Still, it's better than nothing, I guess."

"I guess so," I said.

Dad looked smug, like he was one step away from winning a game. "Let's go pay a visit to Irene and Lenora while we're here. Shall we, Lizzie?"

I took his arm as we trudged back down the driveway to the sidewalk and then started up the driveway belonging to the two sisters. Two young men were shoveling some of the recent snow from it, but there was one cleared path to the door.

I was eager to get inside where it was warm, but to my surprise, Dad stopped and greeted the two young men by name. "George, Javier." The truly impressive feat was that he managed this identification even though the young men were bundled up with heavy coats, scarves, and hats and facing in the opposite direction.

They slowly spun around. "Chief," one said. Bright, curly red hair peeked out from beneath his cap.

"Liz, I'd like you to meet George and Javier. Our paths crossed, oh, officially a number of years ago, right about the same time I met Miles. Isn't that right?"

They looked at each other, then George answered, "That's about right."

"Nice to see you young men being productive and on the straight and narrow." Dad squinted at them.

The two shared a few nervous glances, giving every appearance that they'd rather be buried in the snow than shoveling it.

"Yes, sir," Javier said. "Straight and narrow, from now on."

Dad patted his upper arm. "Good man." Then he looked to George.

George dipped his chin. "Straight and narrow."

Dad shook gloved hands with him. "When you're done here, could you come to the shop? I have a little errand I hoped you could help me with."

The young men stammered their agreement, then resumed shoveling.

Dad and I mounted the porch. "What kind of errand did you have in mind?" I asked.

"Just a little delivery. I set aside a few nice toys for the O'Grady kids. Only I'd rather it be anonymous."

I kissed his cheek. "My favorite Santa."

He blushed and knocked on the door.

The sisters ushered us in quickly, offering us all manner of hot drinks and sweet treats. Apparently they'd been bitten by the baking bug.

"No thanks," Dad said. "Save them for your workers." He did, however, accept their invitation to sit and visit in the parlor. Once the sisters and I sat, Dad got up to pace the room. One of his first stops was the stereo system, where he pulled out a record: "Ghostly Sound Effects." He held it up for display.

Irene started to say something, but Lenora hushed her. "I'm afraid I don't know what you're getting at, Chief."

"I'm not the chief anymore," Dad said. "You're not in trouble. But I think it's time to come clean." He gestured out toward the two young men shoveling the driveway. "Do you realize they could be sitting in jail right now?"

Irene stood up. "We wouldn't have let them go to jail. If it came to that, we would have told the whole story."

"Irene!" Lenora hissed. "We don't need to say anything."

Irene turned to Dad. "Are you telling us the truth? We won't get in trouble?"

Dad held up his hands. "I'm not going to tell on you."

Irene looked to Lenora. Eventually Lenora nodded. Irene then opened the old console stereo cabinet, picked up the transmitting portion of a baby monitor, and tossed it to Dad.

"You've been using this to haunt Sy DuPont's house?" he asked.

"Only for a few years," Lenora said. "We had a really good monitor before that. Lasted fifteen years. Not everything we've used has lasted that long."

"Exactly how long have you been haunting Sy?" I asked.

The two sisters held a whispered consultation, then Lenora said, "We were just trying to figure that out. As best we can recall, we always played tricks on Sy, like he used to play on us."

"But those disco parties in the seventies really got us worked up," Irene added.

Lenora leaned forward. "One of our nephews was here watching *Scooby-Doo* on the television, and that's how we came up with the idea of haunting his place."

285

I couldn't help the smile. This haunting had reminded me of Scooby from the beginning. Now it turns out the ghost was unmasked as two elderly sisters? Jinkies.

"But it wasn't always baby monitors," Dad said.

"Oh, no," Irene said. "See, our families were always close, and Sy didn't realize we still had a key to his place."

"If only that stubborn old coot had changed the locks," Lenora said.

"We used to sneak in to play our tricks," Irene said, "and then sneak back out. I'm surprised we never got caught, but, oh, those were exhilarating larks. I made us matching black jumpsuits. Well, that was when jumpsuits were in style, you understand."

Dad leaned forward, his forearms on his knees. "Sy called the police. More than once."

"You almost caught us the last time," Irene said. "We barely got home before you knocked on our door, asking us if we'd heard anything. I had to slide my bathrobe on over my jumpsuit. My heart was pounding so hard!"

It was almost fun to hear these elderly women reliving their sprees.

"Only it got to be too much for us," Lenora said. "We were getting slower. Sooner or later, we'd get busted. So we decided to take advantage of technology. Once when Sy was off at a doctor's appointment, we sneaked in and hooked up the first baby monitor. Was that back in the eighties?"

"Late eighties maybe," Irene said.

"We didn't do it all the time," Lenora said. "We'd pick nights when it seemed especially dark and gloomy."

"Storms were fun," Irene said. "He'd get good and creeped out in a thunderstorm."

Lenora put her hand over her mouth, but her eyes were twinkling. "He'd come out of his house the next morning, dark circles under his eyes, asking us if we heard anything. Of course, we'd say we slept like babies. And then . . . oh, I feel so wicked."

Irene finished for her. "We'd make up stories of heinous things that happened in the house. Made them up right on the spot and told him we'd learned it from our parents or the historical society. He drank it right in."

That explained a lot of things. I touched Dad on the arm. "So the ghost hunters and psychics . . ."

"Heard and felt what they wanted to," Dad said.

"We felt bad about that, too," Irene said. "When Sy died, we were all set to stop."

"Which is why you hired the young men who shovel your driveway to break into the DuPont house?" Dad asked.

"They were not breaking in," Lenora said, folding her bony arms across her chest. "We gave them our key. They were only going in to retrieve what belonged to us."

"The baby monitor," I said.

"Only they ran away when that new chief showed up," Irene said. "I don't like him."

"We've always liked you better," Lenora said to Dad.

"Why, thanks," he said. "But you mustn't put those lads in a position where they can get in trouble again."

"Do we just leave it there?" Irene said. "What if she tracks it to us?"

"You can't track baby monitors," Dad said. "Just get rid of the transmitter. And the key."

The two women sent him relieved smiles.

"Besides," I said, "even if Kimmie finds it, I doubt she'll tell anyone. It could tarnish her reputation if people learn she was a victim of a fraudulent haunting."

I almost felt bad for her. Almost.

# # #

Two weeks later, I was back in front of the DuPont house. Kimmie's car wasn't there, which was okay with me. I'd just learned from Jack, while picking up a gorgeous meatball sub for lunch, that his family's attorney had settled with Kimmie's lawyer. She was dropping all claims to the house and moving out.

She'd married the old man and gone after his house only because she thought it was haunted—and her willingness to walk away from the deal was obviously due, in part, to the complete cessation of any paranormal activity. But she'd done so sincerely, only to be caught up in a decades-old feud between Sy DuPont and his neighbors.

My warped mind had decided I should give her an early Christmas gift, something she might appreciate as much as I was happy to be rid of it. So without bothering to ring the bell or leave a note or card, I set the monkey, that possessed monkey that taunted me from the shop, onto the porch, facing out, so that its demonic face would be the first thing Kimmie saw when she returned home. As Dad always says, "There's a perfect toy for every person, if you only take the time to look."

"You're welcome," I said as I patted it on the head and turned to walk back down the sidewalk.

When the cymbals clapped together, I ran the rest of the way to my car.

# # #

"All fixed!" Dad wrestled his toy soldier back to its sentry post by the front door, then stepped back to admire it. "It's enough to make your heart grow three sizes, isn't it?" In honor of the holiday, Dad had switched from his favorite puns to holiday movie references. I hadn't let him answer the phone since this morning, when he greeted a potential customer with, "'Buddy the Elf. What's your favorite color?'"

I joined him by the door. The inflatable soldier had a few clear patches over one leg, but he remained upright this time, his smile undimmed by recent events.

The shop bell rang.

"I know," I said, rolling my eyes. "'Every time a bell rings an angel gets his wings.'" Dad had repeated that line so often, I was considering disconnecting the bell.

Irene and Lenora walked in, primly clearing the salt from their sensible boots.

"We brought cookies," Irene said. "Everything we had in the freezer. I hope it's enough!"

I took the tote bag she offered. "I'm sure these will be great. Come on in. The kids will be here any minute."

Dad looked at his watch. "My cue to go change! Excuse me, ladies."

"I guess we should go, then," Lenora said.

"Oh, no! Stay for the party! It'll be great. We have about a dozen military families coming. Each of the kids will get a gift from Santa, then we'll load them up on cake, cookies, and candy. It's kind of our way of paying tribute to Sullivan O'Grady."

Cathy came up behind me with a cake in her hands and a patently fake smile on her face. "And after we hype them up on sugar, we get to send them home." She carried the cake over to the sweets table, which looked worthy of a spot on the Candy Land game. To give credit where it's due, Cathy sets a lovely table—just as long as she's not responsible for cooking anything on it.

"I think we will stay, then," Irene said, looking at her sister, who nodded.

I herded them to the chairs we'd set up for the adults. "And help yourself to the punch bowl." Then I remembered who I was talking to. "Only no spiking it. Most of the guests today are minors."

I handed their cookies to Cathy, left Parker in charge of greeting our guests, and went to the back room. George and Javier, Dad's elves for the day, were there, still busy wrapping presents. "How's it going, guys?"

"Almost done," George said, attaching a bow to a wrapped present that was clearly a hockey stick.

I helped them carry the last of the presents to the large chair by the tree. By then the bell was ringing like crazy as children piled into the shop. A few were practicing their salutes on the toy soldier. Others perused the aisles, but most had found their spots on the large rug in front of the tree and were eyeing up the presents. Their excited chatter drowned out all but a few stray *rum-pum-pum-pums* of "The Little Drummer Boy" playing over the stereo system.

I was checking the back room one last time for stray presents when Dad walked down the stairs. Or rather, Santa did.

When he got to the bottom, he did a little spin so I could inspect his costume. "'Yes, Virginia,'" he said, "'there is a Santa Claus.'" He had it down, from the rosy cheeks, which remarkably resembled my shade of blush, to the twinkle in his eyes, which was all his.

I put my arms around him and held him tight. "I never doubted it for a minute."

Acknowledgments

If publishing were a board game, it would be a cooperative one, where all the players work together, pooling their strengths to accomplish one complex objective. It hardly seems fair that only one name goes on the cover.

First, I'd like to thank my agent, Kim Lionetti, who was there on this project from square one, when the vintage toyshop was just one idea jostling around with a bunch of others.

Next, I'd like to thank my critique partners and readers, who helped slough off the rough spots and make the story even more fun. Thanks to Lynne Wallace-Lee, Aric Gaughan, Katie Murdock, and Ken Swiatek, who've spent lots of hours with me strategizing around a table. Thanks to Alice Loweecy and Kathy Kaminski for brainstorming with me when I was stuck. (Kathy's ideas gave birth to a whole character. Alert readers will easily figure out which one.) And thanks to Janice Cline and Rob Early for reading for me.

I'd like to thank the village of East Aurora (yes, it's a real place) for their patience while I repopulated their town with people of my own imagination—some of them victims and killers. I plead guilty to wreaking havoc on the geography, but hopefully I kept all the cozy charm.

Of course, I'd like to thank Matthew Martz at Crooked Lane for taking a chance on what was, when he saw it, still a pretty rough draft. And thanks to Sarah Poppe, the copyeditors, cover artist, and the whole team there for helping make all this happen.

And a special thanks to my family and friends, who seem to instinctively know when I need to be left alone to work and when I need to be kidnapped for an evening of pizza and board games. (Set it up; I'll be there in a minute.)

Finally, I'd like to thank you. You picked up my book and got to this point. Nothing makes the writing process more rewarding than meeting a total stranger who says, "I read your book!" I'd like to think the hours we've spent together have made us friends. And as E. B. White said, "That in itself is a tremendous thing."

Early, Barbara.
Death of a toy soldier : a vintage
toyshop mystery /